Fleur de Lis Brides

by

Linda Joyce

A Wild Rose Press Bouquet

This is a work of fiction. Names, characters, places, and incidents are either the product of the author's imagination or are used fictitiously, and any resemblance to actual persons living or dead, business establishments, events, or locales, is entirely coincidental.

Fleur de Lis Brides

Cover Art by *Diana Carlile*

The Wild Rose Press, Inc.
PO Box 708
Adams Basin, NY 14410-0708
Visit us at www.thewildrosepress.com

Publishing History
First Mainstream Women's Fiction Edition, 2017
Print ISBN 978-1-5092-1382-5

A Wild Rose Press Bouquet
Published in the United States of America

Branna

by

Linda Joyce

Dedication

This book is dedicated to all who dare to reach
for what makes their heart sing,
just as Branna does in this story.

Prologue

"Who said hurricanes are romantic because they come with pretty names?" Branna stepped out on the front gallery of Fleur de Lis to join her cousin, Biloxi, and her younger sister, Camilla. Sweat dripped from her temples. She shoved her hair back. What she needed was a break from cleaning up the damage left days ago by Hurricane Katrina.

"Hurricane naming. Had to be a man," Biloxi quipped. "Anyway, I'm *so* tired. But thankful at the same time."

"Damn that man to hell and back," Branna said. "We're all about to drop, nearly sleeping on our feet. All of us."

"I never imagined coming home to this." Camilla swept her arms with a flourish. "The house on the outside isn't too bad. Water damage inside—a catastrophe. The gardens are unrecognizable."

The list of required repairs to the house and grounds grew longer the more they worked. Fixing one problem, like removing damaged plaster from the walls, brought to light the need for additional repairs. The constant barrage numbed Branna's mind. She'd taken to carrying a notebook with her everywhere, just to remember details needing attention.

Reaching into a large cooler, she pulled out bottles of water. "Hydration is important." She handed them out. Taking a big gulp, she lifted her chin and allowed the water to slowly slide down her throat. The coolness of the thirst-quenching beverage tempted her to pour it over her head in hopes of cooling off her growing frustrations.

Humidity clung to her skin like liquid air. She mopped her face with the bottom edge of her t-shirt and heaved a deep sigh. The stress of her secret weighed heavily on her mind. Everything had changed in less than a day once Katrina made landfall. The monstrous storm snatched away her hope of a double wedding with Biloxi, her cousin, and sent life into a whirlwind with no obvious end in sight. The blessing in it all—everyone in the family had survived. Yet each person she encountered, family or friend, wore the same expression of shell shock as they traversed their devastated town picking through pieces of their life. Some days, bad news about losses came in waves. Sadly, some of their friends remained unaccounted for still. Never before had she experienced the depth of grief she carried now.

"I never imagined the likes of Katrina." Camilla plopped onto one of the rocking chairs. Branna had them moved to the front gallery the minute she returned to Fleur de Lis. They provided one tiny bit of familiarity in the midst of chaos. She grieved for the normal that had been her life. However, surviving a catastrophic storm, postponing her wedding, and now being pregnant described her new normal.

It didn't mean she had to like it.

"The shock and awe of the aftermath makes me feel as though I'm living in an alternate reality." Biloxi straddled the railing and drank from her bottle.

"Camilla, you've just recently returned, so you haven't had time for the situation to truly sink in."

"I'm sure you're right," Camilla said. "And I was gone for a long time before that. However, this place is in my DNA. Every detail is etched in my mind. Every scent recorded. Every sound memorized. Despite my absences, I am bound to Fleur de Lis, just like you."

Branna leaned against the railing and fanned herself with pages of papers itemizing all the necessary repairs. "I'm glad you're home," she told Camilla. "I'm going to need a lot of help."

"Excuse me?" Biloxi snapped. "You're still in the pop-in-and-out mode. You haven't moved home yet. I'm the one dealing with all the issues, living in a trailer in the driveway, and stressing about where to find all the craftsmen to restore this antebellum to its historical glory."

"You're right. I'm sorry. I don't mean to be selfish."

"I'm here to help." Camilla raised her hand.

"I am grateful you are," Branna said. "Biloxi and I couldn't do this without you. I admit my focus is on the wedding. I can't stop to think about the magnitude of the property damage for long. It overwhelms me. So I do what I can as I'm able. And to avoid embarrassing this family, I do need to get married. Quick. It's not like I'm growing tomatoes."

Camilla chuckled. "She's always the *good girl*."

"If I don't make this wedding happen," Branna said, "then I'll devastate this family almost as much as Katrina. I do not want to be present if the Old Aunts ever learn of my pregnancy before my wedding day."

"They'll be disappointed, but they'll forgive you.

The storm has put things in a different perspective. I still can't imagine four-hundred miles across. Katrina was a big one." Biloxi opened her tote bag and pulled out a camera. "Driving interstate speeds of seventy miles an hour—if the storm remained stationary—it would take almost six hours to get from one end of the storm to the other." She took a few shots of Branna and Camilla.

"Are you headed out?" Branna stood at the railing, surveying the repairs to the once beautiful front lawn, the formal garden, the three-tiered fountain, and the long, treelined driveway to the main road.

"Yes. I'm going to document everything I'm able," Biloxi said. "Things are bad in NOLA, but the media isn't covering the storm equally. Flooding, the overflowing of the levees, damaged New Orleans. Katrina took out Mississippi."

"It took that bitch only hours to destroy…a way of life. It'll take many times that to rebuild," Camilla said. "I heard on the news that damages are estimated at more than one hundred billion. One hundred billion. I can't wrap my head around that number."

"If we had that much in mulch, I wonder how much that would be," Branna said.

"A gazillion-billion sounds more like it. You haven't seen firsthand what I've witnessed," Biloxi insisted.

"It's devastating," Branna said. "I can't believe the Humphry's house is gone. Beauvoir is standing, but it took on water and sustained a lot of damage. Casinos washed up on the highway. I didn't see that coming. However, we have to look at the positive. We're all safe and alive. Including the Old Aunts, though Momma says they're very unhappy at that assisted-living community. They aren't playing golf anymore."

"You're giving them something to look forward to, Branna. Weddings make them happy." Camilla clasped her hands over her heart.

"Only two more weeks, Branna." Biloxi clicked a few more photos.

"I honestly can't wait. It's not just the pregnancy. I love James so much and want to start the next part of my life. I truly never thought love would feel this way. His kisses still make me swoon." She stifled a giggle and turned to her cousin. "Are you really going to wait until *all* the repairs are made before you have your wedding? Nick wasn't happy with your decision to postpone it for months."

"That's the plan. And it's not like I love Nick less than you love James," Biloxi said defensively.

"I'm going to interrupt before this turns into a who-loves-whom-more contest," Camilla said. "And in case you wanted to know, I think Jared's going to propose."

"When?" Branna and Biloxi asked in unison.

"I don't know…"

"Momma will be so excited. Your wedding has to be here," Branna said. "The Old Aunts can't make a trip to Wyoming. In the cold and snow. It just isn't done. You'll be the *only* girl in the family to ever be married elsewhere. It's just not acceptable."

"She's right," Biloxi said. "You can't break with tradition."

"Really? You think not?" Camilla smiled and batted her lashes. "Branna, you're going against Momma's wishes and getting married in a tent. A tent! And you"—she pointed her finger at Biloxi—"you're going to put Scarlett O'Hara to shame. Your wedding will top *any* of hers. My wedding"—she leaned back and put her hands behind her head—"I'm going to do exactly as I please. I'll not let Momma bully me. After all, it's *my* wedding."

"Wrong!" Biloxi cried. "It's *their* wedding. It's your marriage. Our mommas want their fingers in every aspect of our lives."

"But I've taken the wheel. I'm steering my life in the direction I want to go. And I'm willing to endure the consequences for my decisions. All I will say is that I will wait until after Biloxi marries Nick. That tradition I'll keep. I love you both and respect…my elders—that would be the two of you."

"Oh, hell," Biloxi said. "I feel another storm coming!"

Branna nodded, afraid to voice her further concerns.

Chapter 1

"Soon," Branna whispered her mantra, taking care that her mother wouldn't hear. "I'll be Mrs. Newbern." The thought of her life with James soothed her. Their love knitted them together with enduring strength.

But until the wedding, she needed self-encouragement to maintain a faint sense of reality. Fatigue robbed her energy and chipped away at her hope. Every day since she'd been forced to postpone her Labor Day wedding, she'd repeated the mantra. She continued to breathe through the chaos of life. Only another two weeks. After that, the turmoil would begin to settle. For now, with the growing list of tasks for Fleur de Lis, her hopes of a good night's sleep to battle exhaustion would have to wait until her honeymoon. She sighed deeply.

"At the very least, you're wearing Grandmother's wedding gown. I'm pleased about that, even though you had it redone." Her mother sat across from her at a rented table and folded her hands primly in her lap. They met beneath the shelter of a rented white tent that protected them from the harsh, late-summer sun.

"Momma, you could make a better attempt to cover up your disappointment. And if you recall, you had the same thing done with Great-Grandmother's dress."

"It breaks my heart that neither of my girls will wear my dress."

Branna tried to bite back a retort, but it slipped out after a beat. "That's what grandchildren are for."

Her mother's whining bumped her last nerve. Branna rolled her eyes and chewed her bottom lip. Sometimes it was best to have an unspoken thought. The topic of the dress was closed. With the wedding delayed for another two weeks, her mother had tried to use the time to change a myriad of decisions, but Branna pulled back the reins to keep her mother from taking off like a runaway horse.

"Well, there is that. Don't rush to start a family for my sake."

Ignoring the comment, Branna surveyed the scene around her. White tents dotted the lawn. Blue tarps still covered parts of the roof of the *garçonnière*, matching those covering much of the roof of Fleur de Lis. The driveway and parking area could pass for a used car and RV trailer lot, the likes of which no one in the family had ever witnessed before on the estate.

"The humidity is getting to me." Branna fanned her face with a notepad.

"When you were a child, you played outside all day. Heat and humidity never bothered you."

"Momma, you have me confused with Camilla. I rarely played outdoors. I was always following you or Greta around learning to run Fleur de Lis." Sipping sugar-free tea, ice cubes melting in the plastic cup, she wished for crackers to settle her stomach. She pulled a peppermint candy from her purse and sucked on it. Asking for crackers would open the door to a barrage of questions she didn't want to answer. However, if asked, she couldn't lie. Maybe not telling her mother about the pregnancy was a lie of omission, but she had some right to a private life, or at least, that would be her last line of defense if her secret leaked out. Either way, the news could cause one of the Old Aunts to have a heart attack and maybe die. She couldn't live with that on her conscience. Their fragility had come into sharp focus since the evacuation for the storm. Taking them from their home and changing their usual routine caused them great distress. They were grumpy and often confused about what was going on. She had to move them home as quickly as possible.

"We're almost done." Her mother eyed her.

Under the heavy scrutiny, Branna stared back, refusing to flinch. Her mother had a keen sense for details and a sharp mind for calculating the truth. She'd accurately sized up every bride they'd ever worked with. Branna hoped her mother wouldn't recognize the deeper truth in her push for the wedding date.

Drumming a pen against a notepad, Branna stopped when a cacophony of cranky voices distracted her. A gaggle of workmen shouted at each other as they crossed the front lawn and headed toward them.

"The magnolia tree can't be replaced for another month."

"We can't locate bricks to match the back driveway."

"Paint ain't matching in the upstairs hall."

"The load of windows showed up. Two are not to spec."

Branna considered covering her ears, but that would be impolite. That would send her mother into another scolding lecture, and she'd already suffered enough chaos over the weekend. The wedding couldn't come soon enough. Two weeks had to fly. No more problems. After the honeymoon, she would return to Florida, go back to work teaching communications at the community college, focus on her new husband, and prepare for their baby. Biloxi would manage, with Camilla's help, to complete the repairs at Fleur de Lis. Of course, they would have help. Nick, Biloxi's fiancé, and Jared, Camilla's friend, would do the heavy lifting.

"Momma, my head is pounding. It's too hot." Branna rose, hoping to escape the approaching crowd. "I'm going to the RV. James and I need to leave anyway. If you think of something else for me to veto about the wedding, just call. Biloxi and Camilla are capable of handling the remaining details." If she didn't get out of the heat, she feared she might faint. Branna stopped her retreat when her mother touched her arm.

"Gentlemen." Macy stood. "Please wait over there." Macy pointed to a table in the farthest corner of the tent that served as a meeting room, dining room, and storage space for repair supplies.

The men lowered the volume of their grumbling and did as requested.

"Are we *finally* done, Momma?"

"Sarcasm doesn't become you," Macy said. "I'm still not sure what to do about the Old Aunts. They can't possibly miss your wedding. They're not happy at the assisted-living community without Greta there to wait on them and cook all their favorites. By the way, did we add the Director of Senior Services to the guest list?"

Branna shoved her fingers into her hair and massaged her tight scalp. It was either that or pull out her hair. "We've been over this time and again. I can't take this anymore. Camilla and Jared will deliver the

Old Aunts to the wedding. And you promised family and only *close* friends. No political acquaintances. No networking buddies. I'm not adding anyone else to the list."

"What's got you in such a mood?" Macy frowned. "There's still two weeks to the wedding. People will understand about the late invite given the circumstances."

"Momma! You're challenging me at every turn. Trying to control *my* wedding—which was supposed to take place two weeks ago." Exasperated, she let loose a groan that filled the tent. "But that bit—"

"Don't say it. I hate vulgarity," Macy said. "Well-raised young women can find other words to articulate their thoughts other than cussing."

"Fine. Diva Katrina wrecked my original wedding day."

"So why not wait a little bit longer? I'll make it a perfect event."

"No. I'm determined. Momma, I love you, but I've waited two weeks too long. The only thing that will change my mind is if my groom doesn't show up on October first."

Rumblings from a diesel engine in the distance distracted her.

Beep. Beep.

"That's James' subtle way of reminding me we need to leave. Tomorrow is Monday and back to work."

"He could say good-bye to his future mother-in-law." Pursed lips punctuated her mother's annoyance.

"He will. Walk me to the RV?" Branna picked up the wedding notebook. "All the details are accounted for. We were ready two weeks ago."

"Gentlemen, I'll be back in a moment," Macy told the group of complaining men.

Nick Trahan had conscripted most of his farmworkers from upstate, along with other men who had worked on his farm at one time or another, to help restore Fleur de Lis. Jared, with his construction background and his grandfather's expertise with antebellum homes, helped guide the repairs to ensure the home remained historically accurate.

"They're worse than old women." She hooked her arm through her mother's. Together, they followed the path toward the *garçonnière* where outside the motorhome General Beauregard lay at James' feet while he chatted with Biloxi.

"I can't understand your insistence to get married in this mess." Macy unlinked her arm and flailed hers in circles as if to emphasize the amount of repairs taking place. "Why not wait until Fleur de Lis is fully repaired and ready? Another month or so and the public spaces will be usable. I never liked your idea of a double wedding with Biloxi—a wedding should have a single bride. You deserve the spotlight—but at the very least, I always dreamed of you walking down the aisle at church with a reception *inside* the house, not in a circus tent. And how are Greta and Camilla going to cater? Camilla's in the wedding. The kitchen won't be ready."

"Rent a food truck? I don't know, Momma. They say they'll manage. I trust my sister to keep her word."

In the sunlight, burning rays attacked her skin, and humidity added unwanted glistening. Her irritation shot upward. "Thank God for A/C."

"I'm not sure those portable air-conditioning units will keep everyone comfortable during your wedding.

Thankfully, Nick managed to locate enough diesel generators since the tent company couldn't. Just another reason to wait."

"Yes, thank goodness for Nick," she said. Without him, all her wedding plans would've been just another casualty of Hurricane Katrina. The florist, photographer, and caterer had lost their businesses to the storm.

"Ready to go?" James called out as she and her mother approached.

"Yes, sweetie, I'm ready." Branna turned to her mother. "It will all be fine."

"But it's two weeks away," Macy wailed.

Biloxi cut her eyes to Macy and quickly shook her head, almost a shudder. Branna contained a laugh. Her cousin's subtle rebuke had gone undetected by her mother.

"Back to work, Aunt Macy. Let's go," Biloxi encouraged. "I'll talk with you later, Branna," she said, escaping before Macy could offer further argument.

Branna squeezed James' hand. "Let's go, darlin'."

He pecked the air beside Macy's cheek. "We'll see you soon, Mother," he said, putting his arm around Branna's waist.

Her mother puffed with pride whenever James used a familial term rather than her proper name.

"Momma, we've been planning my wedding my whole life. There's nothing to it. And by the way, you promised no media. I expect you to keep that promise."

"I turned away a reporter from *Southern Nuptials* magazine," Macy said.

"Thank you." Branna sighed, some of her anxiety shuffling away.

James opened the door to the motorhome. Beauregard bounded upward. Branna climbed the first step and then turned back to her mother. "I love you. The only other thing that matters is that I will be Mrs. James Newbern."

Branna waved good-bye as the hulking vehicle pulled away and threw kisses to Biloxi. "I'll call you!" Then she settled into the seat and buckled the seatbelt. The motorhome rolled on Loblolly Lane toward the main road leading to Bayou Petite, and beyond there, to the interstate.

"I couldn't get away," Branna said, sighing. "She means well, but…"

"The wedding drama will soon end."

"I don't know…that's Momma you're talking about. There's only one way to end it all. I have an idea. What if we elope?"

"What?"

"Elope, Professor."

"After all you've put me through? No, I want a proper wedding. You're not serious. This is your exhaustion talking."

"No. It's perfect. I want to elope. Tomorrow. Vegas would work."

From its perch in a cup holder on the console between them, James' cell phone rang.

"Would you look at that?" James asked. "I'm waiting for news of my brother."

"*He* might be coming to the wedding? Oh Lordy, we're definitely going to elope." She reached for the phone. His family had been trying to locate their eldest son since she first met them. Each lead proved to be a dead end.

"No. But my mom is frantic to find him now since I'm leaving Lakeview. If it's her, don't answer it."

"We *agreed* about leaving Florida," Branna said. "We'll get positions near here after the spring semester. To help Biloxi run Fleur de Lis, I must be closer." She picked up the phone. "Yes, it's your mother."

The ringing stopped.

"But Branna, that doesn't mean I can make my parents like our decision."

"Vegas is looking better and better to me."

James chuckled. "You can't possibly mean that. Wedding in Vegas. Not in this lifetime."

She shook her head. She meant exactly what she'd said. A wedding tomorrow in Vegas would end all the torture. "I'm telling you. It's what I want. I can't take a moment more of craziness. The wedding has morphed into dinner theater for family. It isn't the wedding of my dreams." Glaring at James, she said, "Voicemail from your mother."

"Would you please play it?"

Branna pushed a button, and the recording started.

"James, it's very important for you to call me when you get this message. We must talk about Caroline. This is quite serious." Mrs. Newbern's voice warbled as though she were frightened.

"You're talking to your ex?" Branna demanded.

James frowned.

"What's going on?" she insisted. He'd never kept secrets—that she was aware of—about things impacting their life together.

"Not right now. I need to focus on navigating this road. The storm took out all the street signs. I'm not used to driving this big rig on narrow two-lane roads.

I'm grateful my grandparents let us borrow it for the trip, but I need more behind-the-wheel time to be familiar with its nuances."

Branna fumed. "When you get to I-10, I want to know what's going on with your family and...*that* woman." The last thing she wanted was James' busybody ex-fiancée wrangling an invitation with James' parents to attend the wedding. Caroline had no boundaries, no sense of grace or manners, and she'd harassed James since he'd proposed. That woman wouldn't dare cause a scene on her wedding day—but, in fact, she would, given the chance. Just another reason to elope. Branna had to face facts. Emmeline, James' mother, hadn't warmed to her as she'd hoped. Instead she saw Caroline as pitiful, and those two had actually grown closer since James announced their engagement.

"Calm down. Don't get upset. It isn't good for you or the baby."

"I've asked you a dozen times. Stop telling me to calm down!"

Grabbing a package of crackers from the pocket beside her, she nibbled. Unloading her temper never helped anything. James had grown so protective since she'd shared the news of the pregnancy with him. After losing his first child, the man lived in terror of something happening to their baby. He never mentioned it specifically, but his actions shouted his concerns. He exuded kindness and patience. His love wrapped her in a safety net. She'd become a pampered princess. But occasionally his protectiveness bordered on smothering.

Trying for calm, Branna leaned the seat back and closed her eyes. James was right. She needed to relax. Come hell or more high water, storm or no storm, in two weeks they were getting married. If not at Fleur de Lis, if not in Vegas, then at the nearest Justice of the Peace. Even if they had to pay witnesses to stand up for them.

She dozed in and out for a little while. Smooth jazz playing from the radio woke her. Chris Botti on the trumpet belted out *The Look of Love*.

Completely caught up in the notes, swept away by the seductive music, Branna reached for James and traced a finger from his shoulder to his elbow. "We could take a *break* at the rest stop." She winked. Hormonal shifts caused by her pregnancy made her daring.

He threw several quick glances her way. "We could."

His response was more of a placating reply, but she caught the slight twitch of his mouth as he tried not to smile.

She kissed her finger. With a slow motion, she drew a line from her chin, down her throat, between her breasts, ending below her waist. She caught his wide-eyed surprise and wiggled her eyebrows. "That could be you touching me," she said softly, her tone purposely throaty and sexy.

"Woman, you're killing me. We'll park at the rest stop. I'm not turning down *that* invitation."

"Oooo," she cooed. "I love it when we get sexy in the middle of the day."

"This," James chuckled, "from the prim and proper tease I met a year ago."

"I. Was. Not."

"Branna, in the beginning, you were wound so tight, I would've bet money your panties were starched."

She cast a coy glance at him. "And you were delighted to discover how soft and luxurious my panties really were."

"You're driving me crazy, woman!" James shifted in his seat.

The configuration and the distance between the motorhome's seats made it impossible for her to reach for the bulge in his pants.

James' phone rang again. She picked it up. "It's your mother again."

"Answer, please. Talk with her for a moment." He stopped to make a left turn onto the ramp leading to I-10 eastbound. "Let her know we're headed there."

Branna pushed the green button on his phone.

"Thank goodness I reached you," Mrs. Newbern wailed before Branna had a chance to let her know she wasn't talking to James. "Caroline has gone completely mad," Mrs. Newbern whispered, the sound muffled as though she was trying not be heard.

"Mrs. Newbern. It's Branna. James is driving. What can I do to help?"

"Put James on."

Panicked, Branna thrust the phone at James. "She sounds scared."

"Speakerphone," James instructed.

"Son, Caroline is talking crazy. Your father and Papa aren't here. She arrived when Granny and I were sitting down to lunch. She claimed she had to show your granny the newest addition to her daddy's collection. A gun. Some sort of antique wooden-handled revolver. Now she's talking about shooting it."

"Did you call the police?" James demanded.

"Last time, I promised her father I'd call him first, but I can't reach him."

"Last time?" Branna said, clutching her hands to her chest. "She wants to shoot you?"

"Could you ask her to let you take a closer look? Hold the gun? Then take it away from her?" James coached his mother.

"She's at the dining room table talking to Granny. I excused myself to go to the bathroom, but really to call you. I don't think she's a danger to us, but I'm worried just the same."

"Mother, she's a loose cannon. I doubt the gun is loaded. Her father keeps his ammo in a special safe. If you can't take the gun away from her, and since you don't know if it's loaded or not, hang up and call the police. Now!"

"She's up from the table and on the move. Got to go."

James mopped his face with his hand and groaned.

The anxiety Branna had released during her nap rushed back like a boulder rolling downhill.

"What's going on?" She feared looking at James and discovering some life-shattering truth.

"Crazy has cycled again. Crazy Caroline."

James took exit 34 off the interstate and pulled into a half-full shopping center parking lot. Unbuckling his seat belt, he stood and motioned for Branna to do the same. He waved at her. "Come on."

"You *can't* seriously be thinking of sex after what just happened," Branna said.

"I'll explain what's going on, but over here. Let's sit over here together." James took a seat at the far end of the couch.

Wavering, she finally gave in and joined him. The fight-or-flight anxiety she'd been drowning in since the hurricane skipped up several notches. The knot in her gut tightened. Everyone recognized Caroline's imbalance, but rather than encouraging her to seek help, people treated her like she was a petulant child in need of protection.

"You've been keeping secrets." She wrinkled her brow and crossed her arms over her chest.

"Damn straight. I will do anything to keep my woman safe."

He wrapped his arm around her, pulling her close to his side. The strength of his embrace comforted her some. Relenting, she draped her legs across his lap.

"I love you." He kissed her forehead.

Resting her head on his shoulder, Branna whispered. "What's going on with Caroline that you feel the need to keep me safe? I thought she and your mother had grown much closer."

"Sometimes, darlin', what we think we see isn't necessarily the truth. I think Caroline will be better after our wedding. The delay of the date has brought out the crazier side of her. My mother's been running interference to keep Caroline away from you. I didn't want to tell you any of this before, but she's made crazy threats, and they're getting crazier."

"She wants to shoot *me*?"

"That's why we haven't spent much time since Mother's Day with my family. At first, I thought her threats were just talk. But when she started going on about deeper violence, that changed things. I don't understand it, but she hit a high-anxiety wall and took a big bounce into crazy just before our original wedding date. It's escalating since the date was postponed."

"So your mother doesn't like Caroline more than me?"

"Of course not."

"Does she or Caroline know I'm pregnant? Has that made things worse?"

James squeezed her shoulder, tilted her chin, and placed a warm kiss on her lips. "I haven't told *anyone* about the baby yet. We agreed to keep that secret until after the honeymoon. The idea of a shotgun wedding isn't appealing to me."

James' phone rang again. Branna jumped up to get it. "It's Caroline! You had better talk to her."

James sighed. "I don't know if that's the best thing to do."

She shoved the phone at him. "Answer it. I have to know your mother and grandmother are unharmed."

"I could call the sheriff's department to send someone out."

"Answer!" She thrust the phone into his hand, and then she sank into the couch next to him.

"Hell-o," James said flatly.

"James Newbern, are you listening to me?" Caroline shouted. "I will not allow you to leave me. It's illegal to marry that woman when you're still married to me. I won't have it. You understand me. I. Won't. Have. It."

"Yes, Caroline. I understand."

"Good. Otherwise, I'll have to make sure she gets the message. Just like the other slut, Nelda Lynn, you took up with. Come home now, James. I'll be waiting at your parents' house for you to pick me up. We've waited way too long to make another baby. That's what we've needed. A child to seal our marriage."

Another voice came through the speaker on the phone. "Now Caroline, you agreed to lie down once you talked with James," Mrs. Newbern said.

"I will kill that bitch if she tries to take James from me!" Caroline said.

"James, we've got it under control. Granny managed to convince Caroline to give her the gun. It isn't loaded. I slipped the girl a sleeping pill. I think it's taking effect. Granny's talking to Caroline's mother on the other phone now. I think it's best if you don't deliver the motorhome back tonight. Just go straight home. I'll call you later."

Branna stared at the phone after Mrs. Newbern ended the call.

"I don't know what to say." Branna's entire body trembled. "No one has ever hated me like that."

"Caroline seems fine most of the time. It's just me. Anything to do with me sets her off. Her parents hired someone to watch over her whenever they're not home. Caroline thinks the person is an exchange student. Her therapist recommended inpatient care, but so far, her mother has resisted that option."

"Do you think she'd really hurt me?" Her hands went to her belly. The depth and breadth of the reality of her pregnancy hit like a dart squarely in her heart. Was there a chance she could reason with Caroline? After all, the woman had been a mother...even if only for a very short while.

James rubbed her back. "I'm unwilling to chance it. I won't let anyone harm you or our baby." His deep melodic tone resonated in her heart, sending a bit of comfort to her raw nerves.

"Who is Nelda Lynn, and what happened to her?" Nestling close to James, she clung to him, her knight in shining armor. No big family wedding, a string quartet, a designer dress, or a honeymoon in Maine meant anything if she didn't have him.

"Well," he began. "Someone ran her off the road, but she was fine. We'd only dated a few times before I met you."

"Caroline did it?"

"No one but Caroline knows for sure. And given her current state, who knows what she remembers to be the truth."

"Caroline is crazy. I don't want to do this," she said quietly.

"Do what?" James' voice was laced with apprehension.

"The wedding. It's too much."

He drew back. "That's nerves talking. You want to marry me. You love me. We're wonderful together." He shifted and knelt down in front of her. "I promise you're safe." He took her hands. His, warm and larger than hers, grasped hers protectively.

She would always love him, but the level of crazy brought about by the wedding and now Caroline, well, she couldn't take anymore. "You're jumping to conclusions. Giving my words meaning they don't have. I *want* to marry you. I just don't *want* this wedding."

"You said that you and your mother have been planning it all your life."

"And a girl can change her mind. Let's elope. Honestly. Let's fly to Vegas and make it our private event."

He blinked. "Why?" Confusion settled on his face.

"It's perfect. We want to be married. Let's do it. We won't tell anyone. We'll go through with the circus my mother wants, but we'll already be married. The show is all for her, for the family. I've done a hundred weddings at Fleur de Lis. Vegas makes perfect sense. Let's do this. You said Caroline would settle down once we're married. Let's do it tomorrow."

James frowned. He rose and paced in the aisle of the motorhome. "Who are you? We can't go to Vegas."

"Then I guess you don't want to marry me. Let's go home. I will have this child out of wedlock. I don't care who it shocks. It's my life and for once in my frickin' life, I'm doing what *I* want."

She marched to the passenger seat and buckled herself in. "Let's go. Drive."

Chapter 2

James remained rooted in the aisle of the motorhome. If they went ahead with Branna's wild-ass scheme, she'd regret it. He would hear about it for years to come. Nothing worse than a hormonal bride. Mood swings and tears. Besides, their schedules didn't have room for a penciled-in *What happens in Vegas stays in Vegas* trip. He had to make her see reason.

"Branna, I want to marry you once. Not twice. I want family present. I'm tolerating the circus your mother's concocted for our wedding," he said, talking to the back of her head. The stubborn shift of her shoulders was a move he recognized. "Tents, candles, and a strolling quartet."

"You think I'm joking? It's Vegas or nothing." She folded her arms over her chest.

James furrowed his brow. He expected there to be bumps in the road, but he'd hoped for a happy bride, not a reluctant one. The next two weeks would be interesting. What new things would he learn about his bride-to-be? His biggest concern now was keeping her safe. Once they got past the wedding, Caroline was sure to settle down. He hadn't previously shared anything—about her meltdown, irrational behavior, or death threats—no reason to cause undue worry for his lovely, pregnant bride-to-be.

He huffed out a deep breath and climbed into the

driver's seat. Putting the motorhome in gear, he proceeded to the interstate. A long silent ride home suited him fine. He had plenty to think on, like about how he had to be clear with Caroline's family about the unwanted intrusion into his life. If they didn't watch her every minute, the next time she showed up uninvited or made a threat to harm Branna, he'd call the police. He smacked his palm against the steering wheel.

There were other things on his mental to-do list beyond the wedding and a weeklong honeymoon. Decisions loomed. Rent or sell his house before the move to Bayou Petite? In the meantime, they'd decided they would live at his place and rent hers after the wedding. But what about next year? Was he ready to take up residence at Fleur de Lis forever?

He groaned inwardly. Getting accustomed to the grand place would take more than a minute. Living there with the Old Aunts, Greta, and other family rotating in and out would be like living in a hotel. Would he ever have any privacy with his wife? How spoiled would his child become? He never thought he'd be raising children in a commune-like environment. Where would they put the nursery? They hadn't discussed that. Besides, the house didn't have even one spare room. Male or female, his kid damn sure wasn't sleeping in the *garçonnière*. No one spoke of expanding the house, *and,* lest he not forget, etiquette and family tradition ruled Fleur de Lis. He reached for the back of his neck. Tension was growing knots there the size of grapes.

Each trip he'd made with Branna to Bayou Petite, he was relegated to the *garçonnière*, roommates of her brother and Cousin Linc, and any other single man who happened to be in residence. Who did that anymore? The Old Aunts, Branna had insisted. They maintained their notion of required decorum—or *gasp,* the neighbors might gossip.

One saving grace, the fact that his child would be raised with grandmothers, great-grandmothers and great-great-grandmothers counted a lot. That knowledge anchored a deep commitment in his heart. He would find a way to make her wild-ass family situation work.

"Well?" Branna demanded, intruding on his thoughts. She turned in her seat to face him.

"Deep subject."

"James!"

"Branna?"

"I want us to go to Vegas. A sweet wedding chapel, nothing big or fancy like the Bellagio hotel."

"I'm not fighting. I'm not taking you to Vegas. As sentimental as it sounds, I want my parents and my grandparents at my wedding. I want them to see you, my beautiful bride, walk down the aisle. My grandparents are important to me. I want them to share in our special day. My parents would understand Vegas, though it wouldn't make them happy." He chuckled at the irony of him arguing in favor of a big wedding with accoutrements he'd never imagined, rather than eloping from the insanity of their current circumstance. But he did understand her reasons.

Branna folded her hands, fingers biting into her skin, on the verge of hitting him, he feared. He'd worked hard to stay even-tempered over the last weeks, but his intentions were tested almost daily. The hurricane brought out a tempestuousness in his fiancée he'd never experienced before.

"You make me sound very selfish. All my life, I've done what was expected—"

"Wait. Don't play that card with me. From the moment we met, you've been dancing to your own tune, literally. We even made love on our first date—"

"Our second date. *For shame*, James Newbern. Don't spread false information. I've never slept with anyone on a first date. Ever!"

James let loose a guttural groan. "The data speaks for itself," he muttered.

"I want to get married in Vegas. We'll do the reception at Fleur de Lis. Otherwise, I'll call Momma and tell her the whole thing is off."

"You do that. In fact, let me call her right now. You want to tell her or shall I? You won't marry me? No problem. Just as long as our child has my last name on the birth certificate."

"Is that all you care about?" Her voice cracked as though a floodgate of tears was about to break. "Fine!"

Branna leaned her seat back, closed her eyes, and sniffed. And sniffed. And fell asleep.

He hadn't intended to be so harsh with her.

Ring. Ring.

He grabbed for the phone. "James here."

"It's Biloxi."

"The perfect woman at this moment. What's up?"

"Perfect? Why thank you, James. That's the nicest thing you've ever said to me. Branna didn't answer her phone."

James glanced at his sleeping fiancée. The long weekend had taken its toll. "She's asleep. Had a meltdown. She's demanding to go to Vegas to get married." He kept his voice purposefully low so as not to wake Branna.

Biloxi chuckled. "Bless her heart. She's trying to be anything other than a good girl."

"What's that mean?"

"She would no more run off to Vegas to get married than I would become a shrimp boat captain. Idle threat."

"I'm telling you. We just had a fight because of it. She says she *won't* marry me any other way."

Biloxi's belly-shaking laughter rang through the phone's speaker and plucked his nerves. He snorted in response.

"You're kidding, right?" She chuckled.

James fumed. "Me, kid? I think not. The woman stole my heart and is now having my child, but doesn't want to marry me. Not a joking matter." Sometimes dealing with Branna's look-alike cousin was like listening to dueling pianos. Crazy women!

"Stay calm, and stay the course. She'll show up at the altar if I have to drag her by the roots of her hair. She's getting cold feet. Tired. Hormonal. Branna would never shame the family by not showing up, especially after what happened last time."

"Last time?"

"The Lind-Sterling nonevent wedding."

"Got it. Well, I trust you, Biloxi. You'd better be right. However, things are a bit more complicated than that. It seems my ex-fiancée has lost her mind and is threatening Branna. I'm trying to handle it all, but as we talk, I wonder if it might not be wiser to turn around and bring Branna back to Fleur de Lis until the wedding."

"I'm vetoing that idea. Not to add to your troubles, but we have a problem on this end. I called to give Branna a heads-up. I overheard Aunt Macy on the phone. It seems the Sterlings responded with *four* as in Mr. and Mrs. Sterlings, Steven, *and* his new fiancée. Apparently, they've invited themselves."

"Shit. I'm getting whiplash from all the shocks today. First, the crap with Caroline, then the out-of-nowhere Vegas idea, and now her ex-fiancé's family wants to crash the wedding?" He needed a run on a country road, a long one, to exercise the stress away. Otherwise, he was about to blow the same way his neighbor, Mr. Granger, did when his tractor hit an underground natural gas pipeline.

"Mrs. Sterling, the pillar of the community that she is, assumed their invitation was lost in the mail. After all, mail isn't being handled right now with so many lost homes. And since it's not truly a formal wedding, i.e., not after five p.m., not in a church, and her son isn't the groom, she sees it as a local gathering. One in which she must be present. Oh, and of course, they want to send a gift. They couldn't be so *gauche* as to bring it to the wedding. She wanted to know where the two of you were registered. She'd checked the registry at Maisons, but you and Branna aren't listed."

"That's some eavesdropping you did. Branna might have the right idea. Maybe we should elope to Vegas and call this circus off."

"No! Buck up! I'll hogtie you and drag y'all here. This wedding is taking place. What you and Branna do reflects on this family. This is our home. You're moving here. You don't want your arrival next May met with ugly gossip and whispers. It would—"

"—kill the Old Aunts." James finished her sentence.

"Yes. You understand this family very well." Her smug tone made him want to punch something. Hard.

"So my ex-fiancée wants to kill my current fiancée, whose ex-fiancé's family thinks we're having a flea-market party, instead of a wedding, open to the public. Great."

"James? Who wants to kill whom?" Branna yawned.

"It's all under control. Thanks for the info. I'll figure out a way to tell Branna the news. Vegas is looking better." He ended the call with Biloxi.

Branna yawned again and reached for a tote bag, pulling a blanket from it. "I changed my mind."

James glanced her way. "You played opossum the whole time?"

"I fell asleep for a moment but woke up while you were chatting with my cousin."

"I've changed my mind, too," he told her. "Let's go to Vegas. Just you and me. I'll have my parents host a reception party for us when we get back. We'll have a photographer and take pictures, like it was our wedding."

"That's good, but it would crush my family if your family didn't show up. It is meant to be a full family affair."

James hit the brakes, taking the exit off the interstate, heading into the Florida Welcome Center. He navigated the motorhome to the large open lot for trucks and RVs. Pulling into a slot, he brought the vehicle to a stop. "I need a break. I thought I could handle you and your family. You're all crazy. Decisions by committee. Pecking orders that make no sense... I'm taking Beau for a walk. Do you want anything from the vending machines?"

"No, thank you." The sweetness of her reply set his suspicions on alert.

With Beau in tow, James walked quickly across warm asphalt to a grassy patch designated as a dog walk. In search of shade, he found meager shadows from tall, arching palm trees. Noise of big rigs speeding along the interstate distracted his attention from his mental whiplash.

He watched the rushing traffic as Beauregard sniffed the bushes. James stretched his arms over his head and then bent at the waist. Anything to relieve the tension cramping his shoulders.

From the first time he laid eyes on Fleur de Lis, he pictured himself standing before the three-tiered water fountain in the front of the house watching Branna descend the stairs from the front gallery, the train of her wedding gown flowing behind her as she walked to him and the minister about to marry them. That had to be how they'd begin their married life together, not in a chapel on the strip in Vegas. Cheap neon and noisy casinos.

His bride-to-be had a stubborn streak, and just to prove him wrong, she just might dig in her heels. Might not marry him...for a while. Tightness cinched his chest. His patience thinned. He needed a plan.

He halted his walk with Beau when an idea popped into his mind. There might be a way to pull off the wedding without all the public fanfare and still have the nuptials at Fleur de Lis. All he had to do was recruit Nick Trahan's flying expertise and Biloxi's help to convince Macy his idea was the only way to achieve a successful wedding.

Opening the door to the motorhome, he put Beau inside, turned away without a word, and headed to the welcome center. His coins clanked in the vending machine. The purchase of chips, and then soda, slid down the chute. He walked toward the picnic tables and pulled out his phone to call the one man who understood all his frustrations.

"Nick here."

"I'm between a rock and a hard place, and I need your help."

"Anything. Just name it."

"This is confidential. I need you to fly to Lakeview and pick us up on Saturday morning. I'm moving the wedding date up. I'm recruiting you and Biloxi to help me make it happen. Just family. Only family. I'll need a second pilot, maybe Linc, to pick up my parents and grandparents. The wedding will take place at 7 p.m., this Saturday night. Not a word about this to anyone other than your fiancée and her brother. I'll handle everything else."

"You got it."

James entered the motorhome, his spirits buoyed. The challenge he faced required attention to every last detail. He had to ensure Branna's safety. The one thing he hadn't counted on was Sterling. If he did indeed meet up with Branna's ex, he had to rein in his anger, but if the man gave him the least provocation…it wouldn't be pretty.

But he had to be careful.

Branna would never forgive him if he landed in jail on their wedding night.

Chapter 3

Branna yawned and stretched her arms over her head. Her exhaustion proved more than she realized. The sway of the RV with its rumbling engine had lulled her to sleep as they traveled down the highway. She'd slept soundly, not even waking when James pulled off the interstate in Lakeview, Florida. Now the motorhome was parked.

Peering through the window, she recognized James' house. Why here? The original evening plans included dinner with his parents…then she remembered about Caroline.

Rubbing her temples, she hoped to halt a dull ache from worsening. Thoughts flooded in. The mental hamster wheel her brain circled on made the idea of eloping especially appealing. Who knew her groom would insist on all the pageantry of a large formal wedding?

She inhaled deeply and let the breath escape slowly. Beyond the window, the brightness of the stars illuminated an inky sky. Soon a full moon would bring magic to her garden. She needed to go there. The sanctuary helped her think. She wanted the best plan to end the madness surrounding the wedding. The hardest part—convincing James to agree.

Stretching, she prepared to go in search of him to have him take her home. She leaned forward when the door to the motorhome opened and a light popped on.

"Hello, sleepyhead. Are you feeling better?" James offered a bottle of water. "Hydration always helps."

"No dinner with your parents?" She opened the bottle and drank.

"Not tonight. Right now we need to get over to your house." He held out a hand to assist her.

Branna frowned. "What's wrong?"

"The police just called. Your neighbor across the street alerted them to something funny."

"I guess that's not funny ha-ha, but funny serious." A break-in? She didn't have anything worth stealing. Her laptop traveled with her wherever she went. The only thing of any real value was the TV. She scanned a mental list.

"Oh, no! Great-Grandmother's pearls," she gasped. "That's my *something old* for the wedding."

"Please stay calm," James urged. "Stressed out isn't good for you or the baby." He backed out the door and held her hand as she descended the stairs. "Let's not jump to any conclusions."

"If they're gone…I don't know what I'll do." She cringed at the pitch of her whine. On the verge of tears, she fought to contain them.

James led her to the car and whistled for Beau. The dog came running and jumped into the backseat. He rested his head on the console between them. She petted the sweet dog for something to do—anything to keep calm.

While traveling between their homes, Branna practiced deep breathing. She feared the worst. Anxiety inched up. Knowing had to be better, right?

James turned off the main road to her treelined

street. It was lit up like a carnival midway. Three patrol cars with blazing red and blue lights greeted them. She reached for James' hand, and squeezed. He squeezed back. But it didn't stanch the flow of panic.

He slowed the car. Once he stopped, Branna popped the seatbelt and hopped out.

"Hello?" she called from the front door.

An officer approached. "You're Miss Lind?

"Yes, this is my house."

"There are clear signs of breaking and entering." He pointed to the drilled lock on her front door.

A knot in her stomach tightened. She tried to swallow past her closing throat. Lacing her fingers together tightly, she placed her hands over her stomach. "Who would do this and why?"

Stepping forward, James offered his hand. "Hello, Officer. I'm Miss Lind's fiancé. May we enter? She wants to check her valuables."

"If you'd wait a few more minutes and let us finish up, then I'll take a list from you of missing items. The living room is torn up, but the bedroom is worse."

Branna gasped. "Worse than this?" The room had been tossed. Her brain turned to noisy static like the snow on a television station after a station signed off. Weak-kneed, she leaned on James. "This can't be happening." He helped her sink to the front step.

"You're moving in with me until the wedding," James insisted. He pushed a strand of hair behind her ear. "I want to look after you."

She peered up at him. "How do we know I'm any safer there?"

"Do you think Caroline is responsible for this?" she whispered hoarsely.

"God, I hope not." He tightened his grip on her hand.

"Then who? A disgruntled student? This can't be a random crime."

"Let's not jump to conclusions. We'll get this handled. I'll call Bobby and ask him to secure the place, board up the front door. As soon as we finish here, you need to eat."

Her gut roiled at the thought of food.

His warm hand rubbed her lower back, soothing some of the tightness, but anxiety still raced like cars at Daytona.

"Miss Lind? Are you okay?" the first police officer who'd greeted her asked.

"I'll be better when you allow me inside." She turned to look up at the man. "It's been a very hard day, and now this."

"We're clear in here. You may enter. I'll walk around with you and make notes of your observations, beyond the obvious, that is."

James offered his hand. "Come on. I'm with you. We'll get through this."

As she stepped inside her home, her hand flew to her chest. She sucked in a breath. Couch pillows ripped open. Stuffing exploded from gaping holes and was scattered around the room. The television screen gouged with an X. As she stood in the middle of the living room, it looked as though Edward Scissorhands had practiced his craft.

"Oh, God!" She began to shake. Forcing her feet to move, she hobbled to the kitchen. Pots and pans pulled from the cabinets and scattered on the floor. In the sink, a collection of broken china in pieces so small they could only be used in making an intricate mosaic.

She raced to the bedroom. James and the policeman followed.

"No!" she screamed. Folding her arms over her chest, she rocked forward and back. "No." Her words mixed with sobs. James wrapped his arms around her. She noted his nearness, his warmth, the kiss on the top of her head, but shock overwhelmed her mind.

"Who would do this?" she wailed.

Bed linens, scooped from the bed, were piled in a heap on the floor. The mattress, ruined by a large X from corner to corner, looked naked and raw. A bedside lamp had been smashed against the wall. A gaping hole in the drywall sprouted pink insulation.

"Miss Lind, do you have any enemies? This appears to be a threat or a message rather than a burglary. Can you identify anything taken?"

"My pearls?"

James stepped away. She ran to her dresser, her heart thudding faster than racecar pistons. She yanked on the top dresser drawer. A moment of hope shot through her as she reached for the dark blue velvet box.

The string of perfectly matched, white pearls was gone. Her wedding would be incomplete without that special *something old*. The thief had robbed her unborn child of a precious family heirloom. "Oh, God."

A wave of nausea chugged up her chest to her throat. She ran to the bathroom to rid herself of the rising bile. After a moment, she sank to the floor and rested her back against the tub, her head pounding. Hot fuzzy sensations covered her cheeks.

James handed her a cool, damp washcloth. "Are you okay?"

She waved him away.

"Ma'am, I'm sorry you came home to this. Take an inventory when you feel up to it. Maybe tomorrow," the policeman said. "I know it's tough, but the sooner we know, the sooner we can contact pawnshops and further the investigation. Do you have someplace to stay tonight? We'll have a patrol keep an eye on your house, but whoever did this, I believe, was sending you a message."

"She'll stay with me, Officer," James said. "Branna, sweetheart, how about you sit in the chair?" He helped her up and then led her to her bedroom.

He grabbed a blanket from the floor, draped it over her shoulders, and gently helped her to the wooden rocker, the only undamaged chair in the house. Entombed in numbness, she sat.

"Officer, may I have a word with you in the hall? Branna, I'll be right back. Then we'll go through and see if anything else was stolen."

When the men were in the hall, she overheard James.

"She's pregnant. Our wedding was postponed due to Hurricane Katrina. We're getting married in two weeks. This is all very hard on her, but I have a bigger fear."

The voices of James and the officer began to fade. She blinked and tried to focus to keep from passing out.

"Do you think she needs to be hospitalized for shock?"

The voices faded more.

"I'll see how she feels about it, but in the meantime, I have a bigger concern. I have shared with her the threats…"

She covered her face with her hands. "This can't be happening."

"It will all be okay." The voice of Grandmother Elise whispered to her. Was it a hallucination?

Searching her reserves for strength, Branna went to her dresser to gather some clothes. When she opened the first drawer, she found her panties, bras, and other lingerie had been shredded. Some ripped. Every single item damaged. Turning, she checked the closet. All of her best clothes and shoes were missing.

On the back wall of the mostly empty closet, words were scribbled there.

You take what's mine, I'll take what's yours.

"James!" Branna cried. "Look!" Anger steadied her. Adrenaline shot through her body, clearing some lingering mental fog.

Her fiancé and the officer scrambled to get into the room at the same time. Under other circumstances, it might have been comical. But nothing about the trashing of her home held any humor.

"Just how demented is Caroline?" she shouted. "Look at what she wrote!"

Another officer appeared in the doorway. "Excuse me, ma'am, there's a woman demanding to see you. Says she's a friend."

Branna glared at the men in her bedroom. Whoever did this deserved to be strung up by their fingernails. She'd never experienced a deep urge to maim a person, not even after she caught Steven with another woman. But Caroline had gone too far.

"Miss Lind?" the officer asked, as though he thought she might want to speak with the person requesting her presence.

"Not now," James said. His mouth turned down into a deep frown. His fingers curled into fists at his side. She paused to see if he would punch the wall.

"We'll give you a moment." The police officers left the room.

James radiated with anger she'd never experienced before. He reached for her, pulling her into a tight bear hug. "Nothing. Nothing will hurt you. I won't allow it. Do you understand?"

She nodded.

"How about you sit? Whoever is here can wait a minute more."

She nodded again and did as he suggested.

James pulled out his cell phone.

"Please don't call anyone in my family," she said. "I can't deal with any more today."

"I talked to Bobby. He's on his way. I'm calling Dr. Greene. You need rest. I need to deal with this situation, and I can't drag you all over the county to do what I'm going to do. I'll explain to Dr. Green what's going on, and then you're going back to Fleur de Lis."

"No! I can't. I have to stay here until the wedding. I want to be with you."

"Branna, think of your health. Think of the baby."

"What's best for me is best for the baby. I'll stay with the Walkers while you deal with whatever you've got to do tonight." Branna stood toe-to-toe with James. She thumped his chest. "I know Caroline did this, and I want her locked up."

The first investigating officer appeared in the doorway. "Miss Lind, your car was just reported in a police chase. Did you lend it to someone?"

Branna pushed past James and the officer, running

for the garage. Flipping on the light, she stared at an empty room. Anger bubbled up again, shoving fear and anxiety aside. "My car was parked in my garage. Right there"—she pointed—"when I left. I lent it to no one. I want that witch caught!" she shouted. "I'm going to—"

"No," the officer interrupted. "You leave the investigation to us. The driver of your car got away."

"Branna! Branna!" Mrs. Walker called out.

"Branna," Ida cried. "Where are you?"

Branna turned in the direction of the voices.

"Oh my God!" Ida stormed into the house, stopping at the sight of the room. Her eyes grew wide. Her mouth gaped open. She ran back to her mother.

"Ma'am, I asked you to wait outside," an officer said, clearly annoyed by the sudden burst of company.

Mrs. Walker ignored him. She and her daughter hurried to Branna, hugging her. Ida began to cry. "I was scared when I saw all the cop cars here. I made Momma stop. Are you okay?" She grasped Branna tighter around the waist.

"This is the perfect solution." James joined the group of women. "Would you mind if Branna stayed with you this evening until I get back? I'll come by and pick her up later. Food would be good for her now, along with some calm and quiet."

"I'll need to know how to reach you," the officer said.

"You have my number," James replied. "These are friends of Miss Lind. Ida, here, is her garden guru. The Walkers live a couple blocks over."

Ida nodded, confirming his words. Her eyes remained big and round.

Mrs. Walker handed the police officer a card. "You

can reach her here."

"Thank you," Branna said softly. She kissed James. His lips offered love and strength she couldn't do without. "I...I...I don't know what to feel after all of this." She hung her head. Her shoulders slumped. Mrs. Walker wrapped her arm around Branna, leading her from the house. Ida held her hand.

Just as Branna reached the threshold, she turned back. "James, I love you. But after all of this, I'm calling off the wedding. Not a good idea."

Chapter 4

James paced the room, punching his fist into his hand. Fear and rage stirred inside like a boiling concoction. How had their wedding turned into a sinkhole, gobbling up their happiness? His greatest concern was Branna's health. The stress of the hurricane, the delay of the wedding, the secrecy of her pregnancy, and now this. The whole ordeal could make even the strongest person crack.

He stopped and perched on the arm of the couch. He was certain she would listen to reason, and they would get married. But when? After the baby was born? That wouldn't work. Not a satisfactory answer. If she submitted that idea to him in writing, he'd grade it with a big, fat, red F.

Lost in agitation, he looked up when a hand squeezed his shoulder. "Remember, I'll need a list of the stolen items," the first officer said. "Miss Lind will need to come down to the station to fill out an inventory report. We'll continue to hunt for her car." The officer offered his card. "Why don't you tell me more about Caroline?"

"As I was explaining before, our families have been friends for years. We attended the same church. She and I were engaged once. A lifetime ago."

"You said she's been threatening Miss Lind."

"Yes, but she's...not quite right. I didn't take it

seriously. She's very single-minded. Been in therapy since we ended our engagement. I never took her threats seriously. She talks smack but never backs it up."

"Until today."

James sighed. "Until today."

"What started things off wrong today?"

"I'm not sure. She showed up at my parents' home waving a gun. No bullets, though. A scare tactic to gain sympathy from my mother. I thought her parents had picked her up from my parents' house and the situation was being handled. But I guess not." Emptiness filled the space in his heart that once held a glimmer of hope for Caroline's recovery. He'd done all he could for her, but it wasn't enough. Now his concerns focused on Branna, their baby, and their future together. Moving would be a big change, but maybe the best thing for all of them, including Caroline.

"Is there anyone else who might want to harm Miss Lind?"

"No one."

"Any other ex-fiancée retaliating like your Caroline?

"She's not *my* anything. Branna has an ex. He's an ass, but respected lawyer-ass in Mississippi." James shook his head. "I can't believe Caroline caused all of this damage." He walked to one of the couch cushions. "Look at this cut. Deep. Straight, not ragged. Whoever did this has to be strong. I'm not sure Caroline could do this."

"Maybe she had help. Or adrenaline. It gives people superhero strength."

"Maybe."

"Might have agreed with you before we found the message written inside the closet, but now she's our prime suspect. I need your address, too. We'll have some extra patrols on Miss Lind there. Wouldn't want your house to end up like this one."

"I appreciate that."

"If Caroline did steal the car…I advise you to stay inside tonight," the officer said.

"Will do."

"Hey!" A shout came from outside. James walked to the door as Bobby Parker, his best friend, emerged from the darkness. "What the hell happened here?"

"Mr. Newbern—" the officer said.

"Actually, it's Professor Newbern. I teach at the college," James explained. "But James will do."

"I'll be in touch as soon as I have more information." The officer passed Bobby as he came farther into the living room.

"Sure thing," James called back.

"I repeat," Bobby said. "What the hell happened here?" He smacked James on the arm. "Man, hurricanes follow you. First, Katrina destroys your wedding plans. Now this. Shit. What a mess."

"Did you bring the supplies to board up the front door?" James asked. "I need to leave you with this. Don't worry about the mess. Just secure the house. I'm going to call my parents to find out what they know about Caroline."

Bobby whistled low. "Wow. She did this?"

"I'm not sure. But someone also stole Branna's car, too."

"Is this your bad karma or hers?" Bobby glanced around the room.

"I don't think karma is involved. I think it's craziness of a woman who's lost her mind. And because of all of this, I'm making a big change of plans. I need you at Fleur de Lis Saturday for the weekend. I want you to drive Papa's motorhome over there."

"Sure. I'll bring my tools, too. Want me to round up a few hands to work?"

"No, just you and your bride. I'll explain more later."

James left the house at a fast trot and climbed into his car. "She only *thinks* she wants a Vegas wedding. And there's *no way* I'll allow the wedding to be called off again," he grumbled to Beau. The best thing he and Branna could do was to get married. Once the two of them were legally man and wife, he hoped the largeness of that fact would trigger something in Caroline's warped mind. He hadn't been able to save her when they were engaged, nor after their baby died. He couldn't save her now, but he could head off any further harm to Branna.

He hit speed dial for his mother.

"James?"

"Mom, is Dad there with you?"

"Yes."

"I need to speak with both of you. What happened to Caroline today?"

"Her mother picked her up. Said they were going to Paris for a few weeks. I got the distinct impression she meant until after your wedding."

"Someone burglarized Branna's house and trashed it. Her pearls, a gift from her great-grandmother, were stolen, along with most of her clothes and shoes. What was left was sliced, diced, and julienned. I believe the police are going to question Caroline."

"You are not responsible for what happens to her, son," his father said. "That one has been damaged goods for many years. You did what you could."

"I need you to trust me and not ask any questions," James said. "Next Saturday, be at the Lakeview airport at ten a.m. A private plane will be there to pick y'all up, along with Granny and Papa. Bring your Sunday clothes for an event Saturday night."

"What's going on?" his mother asked.

"I can't tell you. You'll just have to trust me."

"But—"

"No buts," James interrupted. "I'm asking you to do this for me. Blind faith."

James refused to divulge his plans no matter their wrangling.

After starting his car, he turned the radio low. Music calmed his racing heart to only a double beat. His next call was to Dr. Greene as he headed home to drop off Beau.

"Sir, I need to make an adjustment in the schedule. I hate that we keep moving dates around, but I need the next two weeks off. Branna, too."

"James, I'm not sure I can accommodate your request."

"I don't want to be melodramatic, but it could be a matter of life or death. We must be at Fleur de Lis on Saturday and then out for the next two weeks."

"What about the wedding? This isn't like you." His heavy sigh reached James through the phone.

"Exactly the reason I need to do this. I would hate for Branna and me to have to resign. We'd like to work through the end of the semester."

"Let me see what I can do. How's the restoration coming at her family's old house?"

"Slow, but steady. Her extended family is jumping in to help, a big bonus. Talk with you more tomorrow."

James raked his finger through his hair. He could make his plan work. He could surprise Branna, but he needed a bit more help. His final call—Biloxi.

"What's up, James? Nick said you need his flying services."

"I need you to swear on Nick's life that you won't breathe a word of this to Branna."

"Okay. You're scaring me." Her trepidation let him know he had her full attention. "You want me to swear on Nick's life? Or else what?"

"I need your help. Only you can help me help Branna."

"Is she okay?"

James sighed. "She's still threatening to *not* marry me."

She chuckled. "The only way she'd cancel is if you'd slept with Camilla, which I know has never happened."

He had to make her understand the seriousness of the situation without raising alarms that would bring her family racing to her. "Not funny."

"Aw, come on. You have to admit it's a tad humorous."

He ignored her and pushed on. "We both know Branna's under the influence of extreme hormonal fluctuation—"

"I love when you get all professorial on me," she cooed.

"Stop that!"

"And, as I said, you're scaring me," she said.

"Biloxi, buck up. Branna's house was broken into today. It's trashed."

"Her pearls?"

"Gone," James said.

"Oh, crap. How is she? Why didn't she call me?"

"It's a long story, and I'll share it with you later, but for now, I need your help."

"Anything. I swear, but I just can't swear on Nick's life."

"This is the plan for Saturday…"

When he finished filling her in on the details, he waited for her reply.

"I got to hand it to you. You're one brave SOB. Aunt Macy is going to have a meltdown when I share what's going on."

"Appeal to her sense of vanity, but don't tell her until Saturday morning. She's the master at making events grand in a moment's notice. And, if that doesn't work, then sit her down and tell her the stress is killing Branna—and quite possibly her unborn child. Your aunt won't want *that* news leaked, let alone reach the ears of the Old Aunts."

"You're very devious, Professor. Remind me to stay on your good side."

"Well, let's just say, where Branna's concerned, I'll murder to protect her."

"I don't doubt it for one minute."

James ended the call. "Beau, sorry guy, you need to stay home."

Putting the dog in the house, James took off westbound. His heart thudded like a bass drum. Every ounce of energy he had would be devoted to protecting

Branna. Caroline had to understand, even if he had to step into her fantasy world to keep his fiancée safe. He wasn't void of compassion. Helping Caroline find the best place for treatment might save her life. Could he reach her before the police? Could he convincingly lie, telling her that he and Branna had already married, to rein in her outrageous behavior? Jail time could make things worse for Caroline.

Then it hit him. Caroline loved the river. She would go there to hide. Maybe even to his grandparents' cabin.

Could he find her in time?

Chapter 5

Branna sat with her feet elevated on the couch. Mrs. Walker had insisted. Taking a cup of tea from Ida, Branna held it in her lap to cool. "Thank you."

Ida smiled big. "I can't wait to be your flower girl."

"Oh, Ida. Life is rather complicated. I'm not sure there's going to be a wedding. I'm so frustrated I could spit."

She wondered what Mrs. Walker would think if she knew about her pregnancy, and therefore, the push to marry sooner rather than later. If the truth were known, would she object to Ida participating in the wedding? Hopefully, that notion would never have to be explored. Only five people shared her secret. She trusted them implicitly, especially Camilla.

Ida scowled. "You promised me. I can't be a flower girl unless you marry James."

"I know I promised."

"But I have the most beautiful dress. I want to walk down the aisle."

"I know you do. Let's just wait and see."

Ida's protests were not lost on her. She hated disappointing the girl. Branna swallowed hard. Her silly emotions had gotten the best of her, but the surging emotions overwhelmed her the way the storm had overwhelmed the Gulf Coast.

Trying not to glance at the clock, Branna itched to call James. Had he heard anything from the police about her car? Maybe her pearls would be found if they searched the vehicle. It took all her self-control not to pick up the phone and call Biloxi with the details of the latest setback. Her misery needed company with someone who knew her well. Her home might be in shambles, but the pearls meant everything. She rubbed her hand over her flat stomach. The police left her with little hope of ever finding the heirloom, and the loss of it would be felt for generations.

"He knows you love him," Ida said matter-of-factly, speaking older and wiser than her years. She perched on the coffee table and stared her down. Leave it to a girl about to hit her teen years to try psychological manipulation. Branna chuckled.

Ida was right. She did love James. Wanted to marry him. But she was melting down like a nuclear reactor on full alarm.

Mrs. Walker entered the living room, balancing a plate of cookies on her fingertips. "Bottom off the table, Missy, and leave Branna be," Mrs. Walker chided her daughter. "She'll make the best decision for herself. She knows what's in her heart."

"You make me feel guilty," Branna said. She sipped cooling tea.

"Now Branna, you know I don't have the power to make you *feel* anything. It's all your choice." Mrs. Walker sank into a chair near the fireplace with her own cup of tea.

"Ohhh," Branna groaned. "You're right. I'm just overwhelmed."

"Do you want to marry James?"

"Of course, she does!" Ida piped up. "He's smart. Hot. And he's going to be her baby daddy." Ida nodded as if that settled all the mysteries of the universe.

"What?" A jolt shot through Branna. How could Ida have guessed about her pregnancy?

Mrs. Walker frowned, her brows furrowed, and she closed her eyes. "Out of the mouth of babes...comes unsettling slang."

"You certainly make me see things clearer, Ida," Branna joked with fear rolling in her stomach. "Where did you come up with all that?"

Ida shrugged her shoulders and cast her gaze to the floor. A blush pinked her cheeks. "I read about making babies."

"Reading magazines at Katie's house again?" Mrs. Walker asked. "Am I going to have to stop you from visiting over there? I've spoken to her mother twice about letting you read *Cosmo*."

Ida jerked her attention to her mother. Horror flashed on her face. "No. Don't embarrass me like that."

"Well, it's your choice. You know you're not supposed to read that stuff. You need to redirect Katie into doing something else. Like video games."

Branna smiled at the exchange between Ida and her mother. The conversation was reminiscent of those she had growing up with her own mother. Maybe one of the reasons she and Ida connected so well was because she saw herself in the young girl.

Branna's thoughts bounced back to James. She couldn't run off to Vegas to marry him. She needed to follow her plan to share her special day with family and friends, like the Walkers. Who was she to deprive Ida of her first ankle-length party dress?

Moving her feet to the floor, Branna patted the cushion on the couch next to her. "Come sit with me."

Ida twisted her mouth to one side but rose slowly and parked beside her. She took Ida's hand. "I know how fond you are of James."

"He's so much fun. I like going fishing with him," the girl said eagerly. "He taught me to bowl."

"He enjoys your company, too. And I *am* going to marry him. Only, I think we need to keep this between the three of us—he's right, but don't tell him I said so—we do need our family and friends surrounding us when we marry. I want your support on my special day. Running off to Vegas probably isn't such a great idea."

"May I still be in the wedding?"

"Yes. I promise. In two weeks. At Fleur de Lis. You'll be a beautiful flower girl."

"We'll be there," Mrs. Walker said.

The ringing phone interrupted their conversation. Mrs. Walker disappeared into the kitchen to answer it. She returned a moment later.

"Branna, do you have your phone turned off? The police are trying to reach you." Mrs. Walker handed over her home phone. "It's the investigating officer."

"Hello?" Branna said. She paced in front of the fireplace.

"Ms. Lind, we have some additional news. We believe we've found the driver of your car. She is being transported to the hospital."

"Will she be okay?" She gripped the phone, wishing James was there for support.

"I'm not able to share that information with you, but I want you to know we're maintaining our security check on you until we have identified that this person is the one, and the only one, who damaged your home. For all we know, she had help and that person is still at large. Your car was towed from the scene to our impound yard. You'll want to check it out tomorrow— retrieve your personal belongings."

"I hope she'll recover. And my pearls?" Hopeful anticipation clotted in her chest.

"No sign of them yet."

Branna noted the address and hung up. Deflated, she sank to the hearth and handed the phone back to Mrs. Walker. Closing her eyes, she offered a short silent prayer for the injured woman. Caroline or not, clearly someone was hurt.

"Branna, are you all right?" Ida sat beside her.

"I don't know. They think they found the person who stole my car. She's in the hospital."

"Is it bad?"

"I wonder if the car thief is also the same person who vandalized your home," Mrs. Walker said.

"The furniture, my car—just stuff—replaceable. But my pearls—priceless." In the back of her mind, her mother's voice whispered that the damage and missing jewelry wouldn't have happened if she'd stayed at Fleur de Lis.

"The necklace is really old?" Ida whispered.

"Very old. But more than that, it carries the history of women in my family. Every woman who's owned them has a portrait hanging in the ballroom. Mine was to be painted after my wedding with the unveiling on my first anniversary. It's tradition."

"Your family has a long checklist." Ida wrinkled her nose. "So many rules to remember."

"Yes," Branna replied, "my life is plotted by events of the past."

"Well, I think you could buy a new string of pearls. Your *something new* for the wedding." Again, Ida sounded wiser than her years. She crossed the room and sat next to Branna on the hearth, wrapping her arms around her neck. "Don't you worry. I'll go shopping with James. We'll surprise you with a new necklace. They have lots of them in the window at Lovelies Jewelers."

"Ida!" Mrs. Walker cried. "You don't interfere in other people's business."

Branna hugged Ida back. "Thank you for being my special ray of sunshine. Even though I don't have the pearls any longer, they do still exist in the paintings. My family will always have that memory…and the sad story of how I lost them. If you don't mind, I'm going to rest some more." She lay back on the couch. Ida draped a light throw over her.

Closing her eyes, Branna brought forth in her mind's eye the family portraits. Sadness settled over her just as the throw covered her body. She had failed her family by leaving Fleur de Lis. Broken tradition by sharing the Keeper duties with Biloxi. Now she'd lost the most precious gift entrusted to her, an heirloom she would have one day passed on to her daughter or daughter-in-law.

Restless, Branna turned onto her side. Was the loss of the pearls the price for breaking tradition? What other punishments waited?

Chapter 6

James turned onto the limestone road after leaving his grandparents' cabin. He took the only other road leading to the main hard road. At the intersection, he spotted Branna's car—the front end rammed into a concrete telephone pole with the passenger side facing him.

Someone opened the driver's door.

He hit the gas and shot across the two-lane road.

In the distance, sirens whirred.

He jumped from his car. A person dressed in black, wearing a hoodie, collapsed to the ground in a heap beside the car. The angle and the low light made it impossible to determine if the person was a man or a woman.

Wading through knee-high brush, he approached the car. Ambient light from his headlights offered a bit of visibility.

"Ohhh."

"Caroline?" He rushed to her. "Where are you hurt?" He scanned for evidence of an injury. No signs of blood, but in the dimness and with black clothing, it could be impossible to see.

"J-James," she whispered hoarsely. "I…"

"Shh, where are you hurt?"

"Messed…up."

He knelt beside her, hesitant to touch her, fearing

he might cause her further pain or injury. She gingerly rolled halfway onto her side. Her hand inched out from beneath her.

Blood.

Adrenaline shot through him.

"Can you turn over onto your back?" he asked. "Where do you hurt?" Pulling out his cell phone, he checked for a signal. Nothing. "Damn it!" The sound of sirens still floated on the air, but with flat, open farmland, they could carry for miles. Were they even coming this way?

When she let out a strangled cough, James moved between her and the car. He crouched. "I'm going to turn you over, very slowly," he told her. He cradled the back of her head with one hand, while with the other, he pulled gently on her shoulder to roll her prone.

"Ohhh," she wailed. Her cry was drowned out by the approaching siren.

James gently rested her head on the ground. Her face dripped with blood. He moved to roll her hips and legs, resting her entire backside on the ground.

A police car halted. The siren stopped. Blue lights flashed like a strobe in the dark making it harder for him to see. A second siren wailed in the distance.

"Over here," James shouted. "Ambulance. Call an ambulance."

"What's going on?" an officer shouted.

"She needs help," James cried. "I don't have cell service. Couldn't call 911."

The officer rushed to him and knelt. Pushing back the hood of Caroline's jacket, he exposed a gash in her forehead oozing blood. "Head injury," he said. "Someone called in this crash. The ambulance is already on its way."

"Did you hear that?" James told Caroline. "Help is coming."

"Ma'am," he said. "What's your name? Where do you hurt?" Bending close to Caroline, the officer listened for her words.

"Hurt," Caroline moaned. She lifted a shaking hand upward. It flopped to her chest.

"You know her?" the officer asked.

"Yes. An old friend," he told the officer. "Caroline. Caroline. Look at me," James pleaded when her eyes closed.

The second police car arrived. The first officer jumped up and moved out of sight.

James pulled off his shirt and wiped blood from Caroline's face. He balled up the shirt and placed it like a pillow beneath her head. It was minimal comfort, but all he could do. He held her hand. "Caroline, hang on."

"Looks like no seatbelt. Windshield is cracked. She might have a punctured lung, or worse," the second officer said.

Panic hit James. The closest town was nearly twenty miles away. Mostly two-lane roads between here and there. Not much traffic. "Can't we put her in one of your cars?" Urgency punched his gut.

"We can't move her," the first officer said. He turned to the second officer. "Check for a purse. ID."

The officers walked out of James' field of vision. Behind him, the two discussed the accident scene. The trajectory of their conversation intimated they were concerned the accident might turn to homicide. Then state troopers would need to be called.

"Caroline," James cried. "Stay awake." He moved

from a crouch to sitting cross-legged beside her. He squeezed her hand. Her eyes remained closed, but she moved her hand in his. A sliver of hope surged.

"Now, don't laugh, but I'm going to sing to you." Helpless, he didn't know what else to do.

"*Aa-ma-zing grace.*" He began the first lines of the song.

Images of their past together—when they first met, their first date, their engagement party—flashed through his mind. She'd been so carefree...almost ethereal in the way she moved and carried herself. He didn't know then, it was the result of her mental illness. Never grounding her in real life.

"Hey, you!" the first officer shouted as he approached, then stopped three feet away. "Get away from her."

James continued to hold her hand and sing, shutting out all other sounds. Something beyond his understanding conveyed to him that Caroline was slipping away. "Stay with me, Caro."

"I said to back away, man. I want to see your ID."

"She's dying. I can't let go," James pleaded.

The second officer approached from James' right. "Mister, stand," he ordered. "There's a note. We found it on the front seat of her car. Says someone is trying to kill her. She lists a name. Slowly take out your wallet and give us some ID."

Angry, James popped to his feet. Caroline had done some bad things, but it didn't mean she needed to suffer when he was there to offer support.

"No fast moves!"

The first officer drew his gun.

James froze. Slowly, he lifted his hands in the air

in surrender. "Wallet is in my back pocket." He turned slightly to give the officer access. The second one grabbed the wallet.

"James Newbern," the officer said.

"Professor Newbern," James added. "I teach at the community college." He shifted his weight from one foot to the other. Admittedly, the scrutinizing stares made him wary. If they knew he had some standing in the community, they might show a bit more understanding.

Sirens screamed closer. The ambulance slammed to a stop in the road. Two EMS workers came running.

"Come with me." The second officer motioned to James. The first one holstered his weapon and waved the EMS workers over to Caroline.

James followed, but glanced back. There was nothing he could do for her now. Sadness filled him the way water fills a balloon until it threatens to burst.

"Do you have any weapons or contraband on your person?" the officer asked.

"No."

"I'm going to pat you down."

With his hands in the air, his legs spread, James stood as the officer checked him thoroughly. He'd never suffered these indignities before. Tired from the drive, shocked over the condition of Branna's house, and now witnessing Caroline covered in blood, he couldn't remember a worse day…except the day his baby daughter had died.

When the officer finished, he stepped back, waving a piece of paper in his hand. "This says you're trying to kill her. What's your side of the story?"

James started to speak but stopped when the EMS

workers finished loading the gurney carrying Caroline. "I'd like to go to the hospital with her."

"No. Answer the question."

"Look. If she dies, I…"

"Could be a murder suspect."

"What? No! I didn't cause her to have an accident. I came upon her after she already had the wreck."

"Prove it."

"How? I was looking for her. She trashed my fiancée's home. Caroline isn't stable. As in she needs mental care."

"Where is the home?"

"In the next county. My grandparents have a place"—James pointed—"down that road, on the river. I came here thinking Caroline would come here to hide—"

"How do you know her?"

"Our families are friends." He paused. That wasn't exactly true anymore. Not for a number of years. "We were engaged once. She needs help." He pointed toward her car. "Not just with the injuries from the accident, which could have been a suicide attempt." How did he impress upon this officer Caroline's true nature?

The office nodded. "I see." His frown didn't offer James much hope that he truly did.

The ambulance pulled away. Sirens split the night. Blue lights fanned across the fields. A part of James' heart went with Caroline. He never wanted their relationship to be reduced to this.

"Could you call the police in Lakeview?" he asked the officer. "They have an open case. And better still. Let's check Caroline's car—she may have some of the items stolen from Branna Lind, who also teaches at the college. She owns the car. It's been reported stolen." He started toward the car.

"Hold it. Tow truck will pick up the car. It will be examined at impound. I don't have any evidence to arrest you, except this note lists you as a threat, so Professor, I expect you to follow me to the station. We'll do Q and A there."

The officer handed James his driver's license and insurance card. "I'll return the wallet back at the station."

Thirty minutes later, James sat in an interrogation room at the River County Sheriff's office near the Suwannee River. How did an innocent person prove lack of guilt?

The interrogation began, escalating to accusations.

"I have nothing to hide. Find her shrink. Talk to her parents. Talk to my grandparents and parents."

"You're pretty nonplused about the whole thing," the interrogating officer said, leaning back in his chair. "A woman accuses you of trying to kill her."

James shrugged. "I've not done anything to Caroline, so I have nothing to hide. If you'd take a moment and check her out, you'll understand all that's going on is due to her mental condition."

Hours later, after midnight, James collected his wallet.

"Professor Newbern, don't go far. We may have more questions for you."

With his energy reserves bumping against empty, James walked to his car. His feet moved like they were bricks shuffling across the ground. Exhaustion weighed him down.

The only saving grace of the night—Caroline's injuries weren't too serious. He'd been told her parents called in a plastic surgeon for the laceration on her forehead. The officers had shared that tidbit with him.

"Who would've thunk it? Me questioned for attempted murder. Branna's gonna laugh when she hears that." Weary, he hung his head and headed home. Alone.

Earlier, on his way to the station, he'd chatted with Branna and explained what he knew about the situation. Her decision to stay with Ida and her mother rather than face an empty house gave him some comfort. She would have support. The last thing she needed was to worry about any little bump in the night. When he explained about being questioned, she started to cry. A lump formed in his throat. Not being able to hold her, to protect her, was worse than being castrated. If he didn't understand the ramifications of Caroline's mental condition, he'd be raging over the situation rendering him impotent when Branna needed him.

Arriving home, he opened the door. Beauregard scooted past him. In the moonlight, he kept an eye on the dog, lest he go charging after rabbits.

"Beau," he called, then whistled. The dog came immediately. "Let's go. It's time for bed."

James trudged up the stairs in Beau's wake. He prayed that Branna slept peacefully and tomorrow would bring reason and right to the screwed-up mess Caroline had wrapped them in.

"Branna, I love you," he whispered into the darkness after turning out the lamp. "Woman, I can't wait for Saturday. It'll be a great day for a wedding. Or at least, I hope you'll think so."

Chapter 7

With the first rays of dawn lighting the sky, Branna turned the key in the lock at James' house. Beau greeted her with a body-shaking wiggle. Together they climbed the wooden stairs one by one. She hoped the squeak in the third one from the top wouldn't spoil her surprise.

Standing in the doorway to the bedroom, she smiled at the sleeping form, hidden head-to-toe, beneath the covers. Love surged in her heart. Tingles washed over her. He was the love of her life. Their worlds orbited each other with a special gravitational pull.

Of course, she wanted to marry him.

She shook her head, remembering her irrational rants. Chalking it up to lack of food, exhaustion from hurricane cleanup—everyone's emotions were stretched thin due to Katrina storm stress—and her mother's constant pecking about wedding details, she'd lashed out at James unfairly.

Never did she imagine the turns life would bring. Her house in shambles. Her prized pearls—missing. James questioned by the police. Caroline in the hospital.

Branna tried to shake off the sadness. She'd left Fleur de Lis to escape drama, and it followed her to Lakeview. Yet, she wouldn't allow it to consume her the way her breakup with Steven had.

She and James had a greater concern—the welfare of their unborn child.

After kicking off her shoes, she gently sank down on the bed and stretched out. Curling up to James, she spooned her body close to his. Just as she reached to pull the comforter away from his head, Beauregard bounded onto the bed.

"What!" James shot up to sitting.

Branna moved quickly aside to avoid an elbow to the face. She curled into a ball, her back to James. "It's just me and Beau."

Beau jumped off the bed. He settled on the floor, resting his head innocently on his front paws.

"Oh, shit. I could've hurt you." James rolled her over to face him. Cupping her cheeks, he pressed his lips to hers. So warm. So relaxing. She kissed him back.

James reached for the buttons on her blouse.

She gently slapped his hands. "We have to get ready for work." She puckered and kissed his lips.

"I need to hold you," James said.

The intensity of his stare focused her attention. Want, need, desire, and love swirled there. When he again began to unbutton her blouse, she didn't stop him. The anticipation of skin touching skin excited her. After what they'd been through, their need for intimate connection had to come first.

He removed her top. She shed her pants. James lifted the covers. She climbed into the bed and stretched out, lying on her side, facing him. Frenetic energy vibrated between them.

"I missed you last night. I was so worried. A thousand questions are looping through my brain. Most of all, are you okay?"

"Shush." His hand ran from her shoulder to her hip, pulling her closer. His hand rested on her butt. The warmth of his body was soothing, and that melted some of the tension she'd been carrying like a weight about to crush her.

"Please, tell me what happened." She searched his face for answers.

"I fell more in love with you," James whispered, his lips only a breath away from hers. He kissed her tenderly.

"What?" She blinked when he broke the kiss.

His tongue traced the outline of her lips and then flicked over them. It started butterflies dancing in her stomach. Maybe they did have a few minutes to spare before getting ready for work.

"You are my woman. There's nothing I won't do to keep you safe, to make you happy. I am the man that you will spend the rest of your life with."

She nuzzled closer to him.

"I love you, Branna Lind."

"I love you, too, James Newbern." She lifted her chin to kiss him again. The tenderness in his kisses radiated through her. Need for him shot a new tension through her body.

Ring. Ring.

"Don't answer it," Branna whispered, her hand traveling down his chest.

"Sorry, darlin'. It could be the cops. There are a few details still dangling loose."

He rolled to his back, reaching for his cell phone.

"Newbern here."

Branna waited, straining to hear the voice on the

other end of the phone.

"Sure. We'll be down in a bit," James said, then dropped the phone on the bed beside him.

"Branna"—he pulled her to his side—"I want to make love to you right this minute."

Her heart pounded. The butterflies in her stomach fluttered more. An ache bloomed. She wanted him, too.

He kissed her nose. "But we're being summoned to the police station. They have news."

****

"The cleaning company will haul away all the damaged furniture," Branna told James as she climbed out of her car parked next to his.

"We'll move the rest of your things into my house after they're done," James said.

Climbing the stone steps to the police station, Branna let go of a sigh. Life had been one storm after another, but she wouldn't let any of them, Katrina or Caroline, bring her down.

Once inside, an officer led the way to a conference room. Branna followed with James behind her. When they entered, an older couple sat next to each other on the opposite side of the table. The woman immediately reached for the man's hand.

"I think you know each other," the officer said.

Branna looked at him, then back to the couple. "No," she said. "I don't know who these people are."

"We're Caroline's parents." The seated man offered his hand, reaching across the table. "Bill and Margaret Conway."

Out of politeness, she shook his hand and then threw a glance at James. He nodded.

"It's been a while, James," Caroline's father said.

"Yes, sir. I'm happy she'll recover from her physical injuries. Are you going to get her the help she needs?"

Mrs. Conway teared up. She batted her eyes as though trying to keep from crying. "I'm asking you not to press charges." She reached for Branna's hand. "Please, Miss Lind?"

"Why don't you have a seat?" the officer invited. He pulled out a chair for Branna.

Her neck tensed. She shook her head. Lacing her fingers together, she asked, "Have my pearls been recovered?"

"We've not completed processing the car, so I can't say," the officer explained. "Caroline claims to know nothing about any pearls."

"Then I have nothing to say," Branna stated. "Maybe the Newberns will overlook the disruption she's caused. I would've been willing to discuss this, but your daughter has threatened me. Trashed my house—would you like to see it? But when she stole my pearls, a family heirloom, she ripped away the last ounce of generosity I had."

They hung their heads but made no comment.

"Take it easy," James cautioned. She glared at him.

"My home is destroyed—"

"We'll replace everything with new," Mrs. Conway begged.

"—and the pearls? They're irreplaceable." She turned to the officer. "Is there anything else you need of me? Otherwise, I need to go to work." Branna stormed out of the room.

"Branna," James called as he caught up to her in the lobby.

"Don't you dare tell me to turn the other cheek," she snapped. "Just because you used to be engaged to a lunatic." James held up his hands as though surrendering. "I'm not here to tell you anything."

"And don't mention Katie as a backup plan to get me to drop the charges." She rapped him in the chest.

He reached out, grasped her wrist, and pulled her to his chest, hugging her. "That's not why I stopped you. Darlin', I'm sorry this baggage is mine and that my past has made such a mess of things. I just want your forgiveness."

She lowered her guard. Half her anger drained away. He wasn't responsible for Caroline's actions, just as she wasn't responsible for Steven's. "I don't think I can bear to go back to my house." She sagged against him. "I'm heartsick about the pearls. It's also going to crush my mother and grandmother…the pearls are priceless to us."

"I know." He stroked her hair. "Let's maintain some hope. If you don't let Caroline off the hook, then her family will have to deal with the issues. Maybe it's the way to get her the help she needs. In the meantime, I'll get with Bobby. We'll get the place cleaned up. Then you can take a better look around. There's still a chance we'll find them. But if not, I'm very sorry about the necklace."

"Thank you." She hugged him. "And I'll thank Bobby for his help, too." She released James and took a step back. "I'll see you at work." She snorted a laugh. "Who would've thought dealing with students could be the least stressful place in my life?"

She left the building and drove toward the college. As she passed the spot where the plane had run off the runway and struck her car during her first teaching semester at Lakeview, she recalled how James had rushed to help her, though he barely knew her. How he'd generously spent his time taking care of her. He never tried to control or force his will. He offered solid support, standing by her side like a guard, and helped her rise when she fell, but never interfering. He understood mistakes were part of learning. He possessed a quiet wisdom.

Her hand went to her belly. Her baby would be healthy and loved. The wedding would be perfect no matter what, and she'd leave her mother to stress over all the details. James was safe. She would be fine, pearls or none. After the honeymoon, she and James would announce her pregnancy. They'd make a good team, good parents. The ugliness of the last twenty-four hours was only a blip on the radar. The rest of life would reveal itself, one moment at a time. All would be just fine, as long as she had James to share her life.

Chapter 8

When Saturday morning rolled around, James waited for Branna to descend the stairs at his house. He held a cup in one hand and a bandana in the other when she appeared.

"Ahh, more coffee. I can smell it from here," she said. "You spoil me. Breakfast in bed *and* you for dessert. No better way to start this day. I'm so glad the weekend is here."

"We have a full agenda today," he explained. When she reached the last step, he handed her the cup.

She sipped. "Just the right amount of stevia and cream. But what's that for?" She pointed to the dark blue printed fabric in his other hand.

"After your coffee, I'll blindfold you," James said. He'd already packed a suitcase for each of them and hidden them in the trunk of the car.

"Absolutely *not!*"

"Be a sport, Branna. Let go. Don't be a stick-in-the-mud type," he cajoled. "I've planned a big surprise."

"I'm sick of them," she moaned. "Let's face it. My days in Lakeview have been full of shocking news, beginning from the moment we officially met, running the timeline until now. Learning about my pregnancy ranks up there at the top."

"But not unwanted." He smiled and reached his

hand to her belly. "Not everything in life can be perfectly plotted." Their approaching wedding and the birth of their child filled him with contentment that weaved them closer and had made their bond stronger.

She swatted his hand away. "Maybe not, but as much as I can have within my control, I prefer a plan and a schedule."

"Then, baby, I'm gonna rock your world. Today will be filled with the unexpected. I know when you curl up beside me tonight, you'll be singing my praises and thanking me." He dangled the bandana and gave it a couple of shakes to keep her attention.

"Wow. Not modest are we. You're trying to bait me. You know I can't resist a good challenge."

"That's what I'm counting on, Miss Branna." He put one arm across his waist, his other behind his back, and bowed low. Lifting his eyebrows, he wiggled them "So what do you say?"

"I hate surprises, but I trust you." She planted a light kiss on his lips. He deepened the kiss, tasting her lips, her mouth. Her warm, soft body melded against his. She stroked her fingertips down his back. Her touch heightened his senses. The current between them energized him. His urge to carry her back to bed raised his adrenaline, but he had a plan, and a schedule to follow. If she only knew the level of detail he'd put into the plan, she'd be proud of him.

"You think to distract me from my mission, Madame. Is that your game?" he asked, disengaging from her grasp. "Your plan," he chuckled, "on another day would be a great success. But not today."

"Fine." She pouted. "Let's get this charade underway. Blindfold, please. But if I so much as break a nail, you're dead meat."

"Fair enough." He turned her around and covered her eyes with the cloth, then turned her to face him again. "If you'd prefer, I could carry you to the car."

"I am able to walk. Just lead me with instructions." She held out her arms in front of her and began to fondle his arms.

"But wait. Where's Beau?"

"Bobby borrowed him to help train another hunting dog." He hoped he didn't have to come up with anymore white lies.

"That will be fun for Beau."

Once he had her seated inside the car, he reached around and buckled her seatbelt. Before withdrawing from the vehicle, he paused, their faces almost nose to nose. Her lips parted slightly as though she anticipated a kiss. Never wanting to deny her anything, he flicked her lips with the tip of his tongue until they glistened. Then he closed the door.

"I'll bet I can figure out where you're taking me," Branna challenged him. "What do I get if I figure it out? And I'm not talking about guessing."

"You only get one prize. It will come at the end of the day. Be patient. I know that's like asking the wind not to blow during a hurricane, but give it the old college try."

He pulled out from the driveway onto the street. If he traveled the most direct route to the airport, it would be a total of four turns, but driving around the lake and making several extra turns would adequately confuse her sense of direction. Once they hit Highway 90, she'd recognize that stretch of road. Plus there was only one place in the whole town with the constant *buzz* of airplane engines, but maybe she'd think they were headed to the college rather than the airport.

When he passed the spot where months ago a plane skidded off the runway and collided with her car, a shudder passed through him. That day, sealed in his mind forever, he feared he might lose her. The memory burned bright in his mind and had turned a spotlight on his feelings. He loved her and couldn't deny it.

"I know we're near the airport," Branna said. "I hear engines. Are we going to school?"

"You only get one guess about the surprise. This is the question you want answered? You won't get another one."

Branna folded her hands over her chest. "No. I'll wait. I do know where we are. I just don't know why, but I'll figure it out. I'm prepared to win this bet."

James pulled into a parking spot on the side of the building. "This is just the first part of the journey to your surprise. Wait here. I'll be right back. Give me your word of honor on your mother's life that you won't peek."

Branna slashed an X in the air with her hand and then held up two fingers. "I swear I won't peek. It will make my win that much sweeter. I hope you're prepared to lose. I'm considering my reward."

James laughed. "You keep thinking on that. I'll be right back."

He pulled the suitcases from the trunk but left the top up so as not to give Branna any clues. He checked the front zipped pocket of his bag. A special surprise was tucked there, compliments of thorough police efforts. Jogging inside the small airport, he found Nick checking out aerial maps on the wall. "Hey, you're right on time."

"Worried?" Nick grinned.

"Yeah, a little." He set the suitcases at his feet. "You're not the type to be late for an important date," he joked. "But I've been watching the news about Hurricane Rita all week. Got up very early this morning, before she made landfall, just in case she made a hard cut eastward. I thought the storm might delay you."

"What's a little turbulence and some rain? My 182 runs like a cruiser. Cessna makes a fine plane."

"Here's the deal. Don't say a word in Branna's company. Once I get her on the plane, I'll give her noise-cancelling headphones. I don't want her to hear your voice. So far, so good. She's clueless about what I've got planned."

"You have no room for error. Every moment is orchestrated. One hiccup could cause a chain reaction."

"Yeah," James agreed. "And I've got a backup plan in case this blows up in my face."

Nick adjusted his cowboy hat on his head. "Let's fly. Linc will be here to pick up your parents in an hour or so. Macy had Camilla hire a limo out of Mobile to deliver the Old Aunts to my house. I don't know how you wrangled silence out of her, but man, you're good. Biloxi turned her trailer into a dressing room. The entire female Fleur de Lis clan will be dressed and ready to help Branna." Nick leaned in close. "I know you think Macy is a control freak, and I'm not disagreeing with you, but man, between the two of us, you got the calmer mother-in-law. Deidre, she's a hurricane all unto herself. She doesn't want the Old Aunts, or anyone else for that matter, to know that Biloxi stays at my place sometimes."

James slapped Nick on the back. "Thanks. You're taking some of the pressure off me. And you'll have to give me your take on Jared. He really seems to know his stuff."

"Construction is his middle name. He pulled the crews together, sure enough. Running a tight rein, but his biggest problem is sourcing products. There's no hardware or supply store for miles."

"Appreciate the update. Your fiancée called me earlier. She said the cake arrived, and air conditioning is working in the tent. That's all we need. Maybe next year for our first anniversary, we'll have a big party, but all that matters to me right now is that Branna and I marry."

"I'll take your bags. You get your bride-to-be. I'll be at the plane." Nick turned and walked in the opposite direction. James headed back the way he came.

He led Branna through a terminal not much bigger than the average gas station convenience store. When the automatic doors *whooshed* open, the heat from the asphalt tarmac hit as a blast of hot air.

"A plane. Interesting," Branna said, her hands patting the fuselage within reach.

"Is that your question?" James guided her into Nick's plane.

"It's not a question. I know for a fact where I am. The question—the flight plan. But I'll figure it out."

"Raise your foot up on the step and duck your head." James assisted her in boarding. "No peeking. You can't win if you cheat."

"I can't see a thing."

"Someone inside will assist," he told her. "Don't

be alarmed when he touches your arm."

He took her hand and slid it into Nick's grasp.

"Ah…" Branna felt with both hands. Nick raised an eyebrow.

James motioned for him to remain calm.

"Clearly a man's hands. Could be my brother. Or my cousin. Either way, I'm safe. I trust them."

"And if it's not either of them, do you trust me?" James asked while helping her settle into a seat. He clicked the seatbelt and tugged on the end of the strap, cinching it close to her waist.

She giggled. "Well, it depends. I don't trust you with a bag of potato chips. Especially those with the ridges. Yet, I trust you with my life."

He kissed her cheek. "That's good to know. Now I'm going to put headphones over your ears. We'll be taking off immediately. No peeking. Promise?"

"And ruin my surprise? Wouldn't think of it."

Once in the air, James handed her a neck pillow, and she relaxed. Moments after liftoff, her breathing evened out into soft puffs of air. Peacefulness illuminated her lovely face, and he wanted to experience that same serenity for himself. But pings of frenetic energy ricocheted through him. Small planes made his nerves stand at alert, especially after Branna's accident with a plane. Shaking off the image in his mind of her covered in blood, he searched the green horizon for something to shift his focus. Closing his eyes, he hoped for a few minutes of sleep.

James was startled awake when the plane hit turbulence.

Branna sat up. "James?"

He patted her hand. "Are you all right?"

"Just hold my hand."

Nick motioned him close.

"Give me a moment, Branna. I need to talk to the pilot."

"We're getting some of the residual from Hurricane Rita," Nick whispered. "Nothing to worry about."

"I'm not worried."

"No? Then why the white face and white knuckles?"

He slapped Nick on the shoulder. "Just fly. I'll take care of myself." Sitting back, he grabbed for the ends of his seatbelt, wishing he had a parachute. Locking himself in place, he turned and grasped Branna's hand between his.

"How long?" she asked, reaching for his hand. The softness and warmth of hers always gave him comfort.

"A little while longer. Few hours total."

"If we were heading south, to the islands, it would take more than a few hours. I guess we could be seeking refuge in the mountains. Maybe Asheville, North Carolina. But I'm thinking you're deliberately trying to trick me. I think you're taking me to Vegas for a quick and very private wedding."

"Would that make you really happy?" Uncertainty added more apprehension to his fraying nerves.

"It would." She squeezed his hand and grinned.

He kissed the palm of her hand. Was his course of action leading them down a path to disappointment? Could Branna truly buck tradition, knowing how much the wedding meant to her family, his family, and him? Would she refuse to marry him?

"A bet is still a bet. Want to take a final guess?"

"Nope. I'm kind of liking the surprise factor. Building anticipation. This is fun. And Lord knows we haven't had any of that since the storm."

Another bout of gusts followed. The plane jostled and dropped. His stomach chased him down. He grabbed the armrests for support.

"Are you okay?" Branna asked. "You don't seem to be taking this well."

"I'm good." He swallowed hard. Of all the ways he ever considered he might die—like getting caught in gun crossfire at a truck stop—going down in a small plane on his wedding day wasn't one of them.

Chapter 9

Branna stepped from the car, free from her blindfold and headphones. She breathed in calmness. The rain had come and gone, leaving behind unusually low humidity and a slight breeze. The familiar scents of Fleur de Lis surrounded her, and even with eyes and ears shrouded, she would recognize the hallowed ground of her home beneath her feet. Releasing a deep sigh, she shed tension like trickling water, but her knees still wanted to buckle after the seesaw plane ride. Nick's artful piloting was a honed skill. Not many men would willingly fly through the turbulence produced by hurricane feeder bands. Especially something like Rita.

She took in the wonder of the moment. Anticipation tickled the outer edges of her mind. What did James have planned? Surely he didn't bring them here to work the weekend before their wedding? Her mother would have called and clued her in if things weren't going well.

"I lost," she said.

"What?" James asked, leaning in close.

She brightened. "It's so good to be home. I had no clue this is where you were bringing me. You win. What's next?"

Biloxi swung open the screen door with a flourish, stepped onto the front gallery, and cried, "*Magnifique!*"

Branna bit back a chuckle at her cousin's French

accent, though Biloxi's black-rimmed glasses and red scarf around her neck, along with a red and white polka-dot dress, intrigued her. The click of her stilettos echoed against the newly boarded gallery as she descended the stairs. "*La future mariée. Suivez-moi.*"

Nodding, she gestured for Biloxi to lead the way.

"What did she say?" James set down two suitcases he'd pulled from the trunk of the car.

"She said, 'The bride. Follow me.' And so I shall."

"Shit, I'm going to have to learn French to live here, aren't I?" James asked when Biloxi joined them on the driveway.

"*Ce serait bien.*" Nick came from around the car, leaned in, and kissed his fiancée.

"Not you, too?" James frowned.

"Nick is a Trahan, very Cajun." Biloxi pinched James' cheek.

"That's right, *chèr.*" Nick chuckled.

"*Où m'emmenez-vous?*" Branna asked.

Biloxi linked arms. "I'm officially hijacking you. We're going to my trailer. I have *food* for you and nonalcoholic champagne."

"I'm taking James with me." Nick reached out and clamped a hand on James' shoulder. As he did, he slid a small box into Biloxi's hand.

After a dozen steps, Branna turned around as James and Nick were about to enter the house. "Wait. What's going on? What's for dinner? What are *you* going to do?" she called out.

James waved without looking back.

"Branna, don't worry." Biloxi tugged on her arm. "*Suivez-moi.*"

"But why?" A prickling awareness inched up

Branna's back. Her nerves flipped to high alert. Taking in the surroundings, she scanned the area. All was quiet. No construction noise. None of her other family members greeted her. Nearby, a generator hummed—clearly someone had hooked up the air conditioning to the large tent. Its flaps sequestered whatever was inside.

What the heck was going on? Had something happened to one of the Old Aunts and Biloxi was protecting her until the last minute from the bad news? No. That couldn't be it. But what? And where was her mother? She chewed lip gloss off her bottom lip.

After another tug from her cousin, Branna willed herself to remain calm and followed along. "A sheep to slaughter, am I," she mumbled.

When they reached the trailer, Biloxi opened the door to a dark room. "You first."

Branna climbed three steps. As she stepped inside, a soft light lit the living room.

"Surprise!" her mother and sister shouted. They were dressed in their wedding attire.

Stunned, Branna drew in a sharp breath. The once boxy space had been transformed into an elegant dressing room. White lace panels hung over the windows and were tied with lavender silk sashes. White chiffon hung in draped swags. Bouquets of flowers, similar in size, yet with different colored blossoms, added a feminine touch and scented the room. Flickering candles rested on every surface. The dining table had been converted to dressing table, complete with her favorite perfume.

"Today is your wedding day," Macy whispered.

Her mother's soft voice barely registered in Branna's brain. Her attention focused on a silver mannequin showing off her gown near the back of the room. Beside it, her lace-trimmed veil hung from a special hook. Silver rhinestone shoes perched nearby, her only nod to modern bling.

She blinked when her sister wrapped an arm around her waist and gently led her toward the dress— her beautiful wedding gown. She fingered the lace of one sleeve. Her heart danced a waltz, like she was at Cinderella's ball.

"James planned it all." Camilla beamed. "In three hours, you're getting married. Just family and a few close friends. A photographer, a string quartet, and a sit-down dinner. Intimate. Private. Oh, and the priest."

"No. Really? You lie," Branna said. "Is this all true?"

"Every bit," Biloxi said, taking a seat on the white couch.

"No." Branna shook her head. "We're supposed to get married next week. But I had told James I wouldn't marry him." Her hand went to her belly. Her baby would have his last name and a father's love. It wouldn't matter if she and he wed. They would still be parents.

"Branna." Biloxi's tone chastised.

She looked to her cousin.

"It's time to do the right thing." Her cousin raised one eyebrow. "By James."

"Or what? Don't threaten me," she warned Biloxi and crossed her arms over her chest.

"I'm *going* to have him as a brother-in-law," Camilla insisted. "You've been doing this Miss Independent thing, and now it's time to realize that you're part of a team. The Branna and James team. And you've got a huge cheering section. Family."

She loved him. Hated to spend a day without him. Was it stubbornness or plain old foolishness driving her decisions? *If* she were to agree to a wedding in a few hours, a few details had to be determined.

"Did you get James a groom's cake in the shape of an alligator?" she asked. The reality of the situation started her brain spinning like a tornado. "Is Ida going to be my flower girl? What about the menu?" A surge of panic hit her. "Do the Newberns know? Are the Old Aunts here?"

Macy hugged her. "Sweetheart, everything is handled. Yes, the Old Aunts are here. They're at Nick's house resting comfortably. Linc is flying in the Newberns now."

"Nick has power and air conditioning? I don't want the Old Aunts to be uncomfortable. They've endured so much with the storm."

"Generators," Biloxi said. "Been around a long time. The Old Aunts are just fine. Nick's grandmother is seeing to them. They're probably playing rummy and sipping champagne."

"Here's the rundown, Branna," Camilla explained. "Our family, including Greta and Nick's grandmother. All Daddy's clan from Louisiana. James' family—minus his brother, I'm told. Ida and her parents. That's it for the guest list. Cakes—check. Caterer is from Baton Rouge—check. Flowers you can see"—she lifted one of the bouquets—"these are for your bride's entourage: Biloxi, me, Melody, Elvie, and Nola." She picked up a small white wicker basket with rose petals. "This is what Ida will carry."

"Lucky for us, I was able to get the string quartet,

the one you had your heart set on, to move up their date," Macy said.

Sinking onto the tufted ottoman, Branna said, "I can't believe all of this."

Camilla opened a bottle of sparkling cider and began pouring it into four glasses. Foam rose to the top. Branna held her breath, waiting for the foam to roll over the top, but it didn't. A sign, she believed, that all would be fine.

"To Branna," Camilla said, passing out the glasses. Biloxi and Macy gathered around.

"To Branna," her family said in unison.

"Cheers!" Branna clinked her glass with the others. After a sip, she whispered, "I'm really getting married today."

"The tent is set up in two parts, the chapel side and the reception side"—Macy used her fingers to count— "Tables are set. Candles and Stargazer lilies for centerpieces. We made all the changes after James' call last Sunday."

"The menu was tasted by Greta and passed with her approval. We rejected two other caterers. They didn't light up her palate with flavor," Biloxi said.

"Well, imagine that," Branna whispered. "I'm getting married."

"Yes!" Macy walked behind where Branna sat. "Honey, put the glass down."

"Why?"

"Branna," her mother said sternly.

She rolled her eyes. "Yes, ma'am."

Her mother reached around from behind. "It seems that in all the brouhaha that you and James went through last weekend, you failed to mention to me that your pearls were stolen. They were found and turned over to James. You'll walk down the aisle with them." Her mother took the small box Biloxi offered. She pulled a pearl necklace from the box and hooked it around Branna's neck, then leaned in and kissed Branna's cheek.

"That man's a keeper." Biloxi raised her glass. "He planned every detail."

As they toasted her groom, Branna's nerves settled to a low hum. James never ceased to amaze her. She'd question him later about the details of the recovery of the pearls. She'd bet Caroline had them all the time. But their return meant some of the unbalance of her world had righted, and she would forgive Caroline. That poor woman had enough problems.

Branna stroked the smoothness of the pearls. Someday she'd pass them down, upholding the Fleur de Lis tradition. If she and James had a girl, their daughter would be the next Keeper. The baby would represent a whole new chapter in her life and a new generation at Fleur de Lis.

What would her family think once they learned the grand house would soon welcome a new bundle of love?

Chapter 10

Branna waited with her father outside the white tent, her hand securely snuggled in the crook of his arm. Gripping her bouquet tightly, she smiled at her father. He patted her hand. She wiggled her toes inside her shoes. Then she tilted her head to catch a glimpse of her glittery shoes.

"This is really it," she said. Every nerve in her body tingled. She shifted her weight from one foot to the other. Breathing in and out quickly, she prayed she wouldn't trip.

"It's five o'clock on the dot," Greta said. She kissed Branna's cheek. "Showtime."

When the string quartet began playing Pachelbel's *Canon in D*, Greta opened the flap to reveal family members rising from their seats. Branna stepped in cadence with her father—step, pause, step—to the strains of lyrical strings singing out the music she loved.

Ahead, James came into view. Her vision blurred, then refocused. The sexiness of his smile. The glint in his eyes. The broadness of his shoulders. The confidence of his stance. He looked handsome in his black tuxedo. Her heart thundered like the pounding hooves of a band of horses racing across the plains. Her father kept up the pace as they continued, each step bringing her closer to the man she loved. How could she ever have considered not marrying him?

When she reached the altar, the priest motioned for everyone to sit. Had he spoken? She heard nothing but the racing of blood in her ears. She lifted her eyes and caught James' expression of love. All other thoughts fled, except one.

He was hers forever.

****

After the wedding and the reception, James stood at the door of the motorhome, surrounded by a band of men. His father, brother-in-law, Branna's uncles, and his best man, Bobby Parker, shook hands with him. Each slapped him on the back, cited a piece of parting wisdom, and then joined the family lining the driveway.

"Take care of my girl," Branna's father said.

"I will, sir," James promised, shaking the man's hand. His heart swelled at the memory of her walking toward him at the altar, face aglow, smile so sweet and soft. She was refined elegance in her lace wedding gown. She was his wife. Forever. "I will cherish her always."

As Charles left him, James boarded the motorhome where Branna already waited. He cupped her face and pressed his lips to hers. Hers would be the lips he sought first thing in the morning and the ones he'd kiss before falling asleep at night. He kissed her nose, and then with his finger, trailed a line from her nose down to the 'v' of her cleavage. She'd changed into a pink and white sundress.

"Alabama bound," James said, climbing into the driver's seat and turning the key. The diesel engine rumbled. The start of the engine was the start of their honeymoon. He couldn't wait to get underway.

With dusk settling around them, James pointed the RV down the long front driveway of Fleur de Lis. As the motorhome passed family members lining the road, they shouted good wishes and waved sparklers in the air.

"I love you," Branna said, leaning over to blow the horn. "I'm so glad you know me so well. I would've been miserable with a Vegas wedding."

"And I would've been miserable until you agreed to marry me." James chuckled. "Why don't you nap? Get ready for our honeymoon." Her face radiated with joy, yet faint shadows beneath her eyes hinted that she needed rest.

The trip from Fleur de Lis to their destination near the beach in Alabama would put their arrival in just over two hours. Branna slept as he drove. He imagined them together on a blanket at the beach listening to the sound of the waves with her cradled in his arms.

As he drove, tiredness seeped in. Too much had happened within a week. As he crossed the state line into Alabama, he decided to take a short break at the welcome center.

"I'll be back in a minute," he whispered to Branna, but doubted she heard a word as he lumbered down the RV's steps to the parking lot.

After stretching, he jogged to the building, ran a quick lap around, and made his way back to his bride. A week at an RV resort with a spa, golf course, and marina might not be the dream honeymoon he'd hoped to give Branna—he dreamed of Paris or the Swiss Alps—but with a baby on the way…maybe at Christmas break, he'd pack her up and take her to Yellowstone for the holidays. It wouldn't be

Switzerland, but they wouldn't need passports to visit Old Faithful. They had a lifetime of travel opportunities ahead of them.

Arriving at the RV, he opened the door and climbed aboard. The passenger seat was empty. Where had Branna gone?

"I'm back here," she called out. "I need *your* help, please."

He paused at the sweetness in her voice, a tone he hadn't heard since before they postponed the Labor Day weekend wedding. Her plea ignited his hero instincts. Anything for his woman.

Checking the lock on the door, he then made his way to the rear of the motorhome where blackout shades shrouded the room in darkness. His eyes took a moment to adjust.

"Hey there, handsome," Branna cooed.

A spotlight over the bed suddenly illuminated her. He sucked in a breath. Stretched out on white satin sheets, Branna leaned against several pillows with one knee raised. The pearls glistened around her neck. A sheer, short pink top covered her torso. The garment appeared to float over her body and accentuate her mounds and curves. It ended just above her sweet spot, which was covered by a small triangle of fabric and hid nothing from view.

She motioned him closer.

Ravage popped into his mind. He swallowed hard. He wanted to send her body into frantic need that only he could satisfy. He let go of a ragged breath. All other thoughts faded away. Only she existed in that moment.

"I have something for you." Branna ran her hand from her knee, up her leg, up her torso, and over her breast, bringing her hand to rest over her head. "Like what you see, Professor? It's all for you." She licked her lips with the tip of her tongue. "Do you like my new lingerie?" She fanned the bottom hem. It provided him with a peek of her soft, silky skin.

His gut clenched. His always-professional college instructor was a wanton woman in bed. Their bed. He changed his stance, adjusting for comfort. Hard to believe he could get any harder, but when she moved her legs apart, revealing her softest spot, he clenched his fists and stood even straighter to keep from diving on top of her. She might be ever so traditional to the outside world, but in bed, she offered wild passion.

"Professor, if you do as instructed, you'll receive a very good grade. First, remove your socks and shoes, then your pants."

He wasn't about to argue with a pregnant woman, especially one wanting to give him a reward. So what if they arrived late to the resort?

"I know how to get an A-plus," he challenged.

"Do you now? We shall see. Right now, you need to slowly unbutton that shirt and let me look at your body, so muscle-toned after working outdoors all summer." Her voice was thick with passion. Her eyes widened when he revealed his erection constrained only by his briefs. She fixed her eyes on him until his shirt dropped to the floor. When she licked her lips slowly, he removed his underwear. His manhood stood at full salute. But his pleasure would have to wait a few minutes more.

Climbing onto the bed, James paused when Branna held up her hand. "Stop. No one gave you permission to approach me."

James grasped her hand. Kissed her palm. "You're right. However, woman, you need to relax. I'm going to show you how well I know what you like. I intend to get an A-plus-plus."

He kissed her tenderly, teasing her lips. She tasted of sweet tea and chocolate from his groom's cake.

He moved closer until he kneeled over her. Gently fondling her breast, he tweaked until each bud puckered beneath the soft thin fabric. Then he traced a line down her stomach to the apex of her legs. Slipping a finger beneath the tiniest scrap of fabric anyone might call panties, he found the other sensitive nub he sought. He rubbed with a slow and steady pace.

Branna moaned, opening her legs wider. Her mouth formed a small 'o' as her body responded to his touch. She stroked his erection, keeping pace with his massaging tempo.

"Feel good, Miss Branna? I expect to receive an A-plus," he whispered teasingly.

She nodded. "Oh, yes. Just don't stop." Another groan of delight escaped from her lips. She grabbed the bedcovers on either side of her and arched her hips a bit higher and began to rock. He slowed his pace. This was more than college level lovemaking, and he was the perfect professor for her.

"I'm going to slip off your panties."

"Ah-ha." Her eyes closed.

While slipping the lacy garment from her body, he moved his hands down the outside of her legs. Smooth. Sleek. Sun-kissed.

She undulated her hips faster. "More, please. That is, if you want an A-plus," she urged.

He settled his torso between her legs. Through the

fabric of her top, he tweaked both of her breasts again, then arched over her, and sucked.

"Let me show you what I want," Branna said, guiding the tip of his hardness to her opening. His teasing ended. He slid a finger inside her wetness. Moistened her hardened nub. Her body revealed how much she wanted him. With a gentle thrust, he entered her halfway. When he started to pull out, she grabbed his hips and rocked hard against him.

"My turn," she said hoarsely.

With quick thrusts, her body took him inside. Her muscles squeezed tightly around him. "Now, James, now!"

Always one to do as instructed, he held her hips firmly and pumped against her, never breaking their connection as he moved against her.

"Yes. Yes!" she shouted.

The warm wetness of her body, combined with her firm grasp on his hips, sent him spiraling upward, floating into a world of glorious rapture. Her lips parted. Deep moans escaped.

He thrust faster until stars flashed behind his closed eyes, the pinnacle of their shared experience.

"Branna, I love you," he murmured, collapsing on the bed beside her.

When their breaths evened, she curled next to him, draping a leg across his body.

"You're wonderful, Mrs. Newbern," he whispered.

She snuggled closer. "I *am* Mrs. Newbern," she said, sounding pleased with herself. "You definitely earned an A-plus-plus, Professor."

He kissed her temple. They shared a bond that would see them through the years. For better. For worse. When they first met, he'd been wrong—she wasn't the high maintenance type as he'd thought. While she was intense, demanding, and captivating, life with her would be a high of which he would never tire.

Theirs was a love to last a lifetime.

Biloxi

by

Linda Joyce

Dedication

This book is dedicated to those
who seek to do the right thing,
sometimes against all odds,
just like Biloxi Dutrey.

Prologue

Biloxi Dutrey pushed the kitchen screen door open with her foot while steadying a tray in her hands. The late afternoon April sun warmed her. She breathed in the rich aroma of coffee as she placed the tray on a side table. On the back gallery at Fleur de Lis, she relaxed after the monthly family meeting.

"I brought cream, sugar, and those green packets you like, Branna."

Biloxi sank into an empty rocker and gazed at her family. Her cousin, Branna, rocked Anaëlle in her arms. The sleeping baby had been the constant topic of conversation. It was amusing to watch grown men, her father, uncles, and cousins, reduced to soppy messes over a one month-old's tiny fingers, toes, and cupid-bow mouth.

Camilla, her other cousin, nodded to Branna. "Do you want a blanket or anything? Is there something I can get for you?"

"Coffee and all y'all is what I need."

"May I join in?" Nola, Biloxi's sister, stepped closer to the group.

"Of course." Biloxi motioned her over to the last empty chair. Her younger sister's interest in family affairs had grown since she experienced all the work it took to repair their home and gardens after Hurricane Katrina for the last eight months.

Biloxi relaxed more. Home and family meant everything. Safety, creativity, love, and food. All were intertwined into the fabric of Fleur de Lis. She especially enjoyed the chats with her female relatives and looked forward to catching up with them each month.

"We've been fortunate," Camilla said. "We have each other. Not everyone in our community has been so lucky. But I think we're doing our best to reach out to those in need."

With the conversation going on around her, Biloxi's thoughts drifted. The family had managed Christmas and New Year's Eve with a subdued spirit four months after the storm. Instead of buying gifts for each other, they bought gifts for others in need. They hosted a holiday open house in the same tent that served as a marriage chapel for Branna and James last October. Aunt Macy insisted they host the annual Valentine's Ball, not the formal affair of years gone by, but a bonfire, music, and community potluck to bring everyone together. Dancing had allowed everyone party and laugh.

Yet, the first Mardi Gras after the storm had been dismal. A half-dozen pickup trucks pulled small, barely decorated trailers. Only one marching band participated. There was no second line. However, it gave everyone a reason to celebrate and look forward to good things to come. Sticking to tradition provided a normalcy everyone craved.

The big family news—the early arrival of Anaëlle in March. Branna and James were ecstatic, but exhausted parents. They'd also decided to stay longer in Lakeview since the economy in Bayou Petite was nowhere near what it was before the storm. Jobs remained scarce.

"Biloxi?"

"Oh. Sorry for drifting off." Biloxi took the offered cup of steaming coffee from Nola. "We've had some uplifting moments to keep us moving forward. We need to find something to celebrate in April and May."

"In June, we have your wedding," Nola said. "I'm so excited to be a bride's maid."

"Your wedding will be the crowning jewel for the year." Branna smiled.

"I know brides are supposed to be the star of the show, but for me, all the work we've done at Fleur de Lis—it's the show-stopper. Just to have everyone home, including the Old Aunts and all their sweet doting, will make it my dream wedding. I feel a bit sad for my Nick—he's never located his mother. It would be amazing to have her, along with Edward and his grandmother, in attendance."

"It is curious thing that she's never been found," Camilla sipped from her cup. "But the women of Fleur de Lis love him lots. Maybe that will give him some comfort."

Biloxi looked at the faces of her loved ones. They grounded her and sustained her, and marrying Nick would make her world complete. Her family had buried the past, but Nick's past wasn't so easily remedied. Where the heck was his mother? If she was dead, how would he ever find her?

As clouds drifted in front of the sun, a cool breeze blew. Biloxi shivered. When the sun emerged, she tried to shake of a lingering unease. Things were going well. After surviving Hurricane Katrina, whatever might happen couldn't be worse.

As the conversation turned to babies and other things, Biloxi shivered again. The gnawing unease wouldn't let go.

Chapter 1

The month of May would never be the same. Biloxi sucked her bottom lip as Nick opened the front door to his house. Her eyes misted. Funerals were depressing. Surely after hundreds of years, someone could conceive a better way to send off the dead. She found comfort in her conviction that the souls of the Old Aunts would not evanesce. Otherwise, losing both of them would be too much to bear.

She tugged on the neckline of her dress. The funeral garb had to be stripped—now. Black A-line dress with sheer sleeves, zipped in the back, and above-knee hem imitated a straitjacket. Not that she'd ever worn one, but she'd gamble on Fleur de Lis that her imagination got it right. Restrained was no different than suffocating.

Too bad the cloud of sadness surrounding her couldn't be removed as quickly as clothes from her body.

When the front door finally opened, Nick stepped aside. "Ladies first, *chèr*."

She caressed his cheek and brushed his lips lightly as she passed, never tiring his sweet term of endearment. Nick was her anchor. Always supportive. Always understanding. It didn't hurt that he rocked jeans and a Stetson. He was her man. She'd do anything for him.

Removing her heels, she clutched them and ran barefoot up the stairs. "Come help me with the zipper, please," she called over her shoulder, not wanting to wait a full sixty seconds more for freedom from the constricting clothes.

"Be there in a second."

"Hurry, Nick."

A thrum of anxiety pulsed through her. She had imagined after the wakes and funerals, sadness would lift and the strength the Old Aunts carried through life would vibrate in her. As annoying and demanding as the old women were until the end, no matter their initial hatred of Nick, the Old Aunts exuded a quiet fortitude she hoped to inherit. What character they had shown when putting aside their longstanding prejudice of Trahans, even embracing Nick as her fiancé.

Opening the closet door in Nick's bedroom, she placed black shoes on a rack. Tugging at the waistband, she stripped off black panty hose like peeling away a cellophane wrapper.

"Finally!" Freedom from nylon allowed her to breathe. Air-conditioned coolness against her newly exposed skin lifted her waning energy slightly. But a steady beat of grief and something more—the unsettling realization of the fragility of life—hung heavy in her heart.

"No one else can die," she whispered, fighting for a moment of peace. She didn't expect heaven to heed her command, but speaking the words added a bit of steel to her fading fortitude.

She backed until her bare legs met the bed, then she fell backward spread eagle. Had she been foolish to put the wedding on hold? Nick had been irritated, but not outright angry when she decided to postpone their wedding until she could walk down the staircase at Fleur de Lis in a bridal gown. Her decision wasn't just to please the Old Aunts or to maintain a sense of propriety in the community. The planned delay gave her a sense of accomplishment—delaying gratification for something she wanted so much, as though she'd truly graduated to adulthood and deserved to be the true Keeper of Fleur de Lis. But now the notion seemed just as ridiculous as her insisting they live separately—she at Fleur de Lis and he at his home—until they married.

"Nick, you have the patience of a saint." She hugged herself. In less than a month, they'd be married at church and have the reception in the grand ballroom at home. Looking up, she expected to see the Old Aunts smiling down, a sign of their blessing.

And Nick was a blessing. She wanted him, his love, his kisses, his body, and someday his babies. What they shared intimately always left her pulse pounding and heart soaring. With him, she could conquer even the worst of situations, as evidenced by all the repairs and improvements at Fleur de Lis after the destruction brought by the storm. No hurricane would stop her with Nick in her life.

The sound of her fiancé climbing the stairs floated to her, along with the sound of ice cubes bumping against glass. Nick must have poured himself a drink.

"Selfish man, he didn't offer to bring me one." Four Roses. Her favorite whiskey. Neat. She rarely ever drank, but today she needed a double. Twice in only ten days, she'd donned the black dress. First for Great-Grandmother Marie's funeral, then today for Great Grandaunt Grace's, who passed a few days ago. Two funerals in less than two weeks…Funeral directors, Biloxi decided, possessed no sense of humor. The man had rolled his eyes and practically pouted when she jokingly asked for a discount since they bought two coffins, funeral services, and headstones in a single month.

Rising, she paused at the opening to the closet. "I've never been the little-black-dress sort. Even when I shot fashion." She fingered a sheer sleeve. "A sea of black today. I will never wear black again. Life is too short, and everything looks better in living color, including me."

"Let me help you." Nick set two glasses on the nightstand—his with ice and hers without. He had thought of her—then crossed the bedroom, standing behind her. His kindness warmed her heart.

"I can't wait until you've moved all of your clothes in here. Not long now. Barely a month." He unzipped the dress. Cool air kissed her skin. He caressed her shoulders, brushing the dress away. His touch sent tingles zipping through her veins. Fabric pooled at her ankles. She stepped out of the circle made by the dress and tossed it on a nearby chair. She wanted to feel Nick—all of him.

Wrapping his arms around her waist, he pulled her close, her back resting against his strong chest. He kissed the side of her neck. "I like it when you wear nothing at all."

Twinges of want popped to life like sparklers flashing at night. She lifted her chin. Nick's lips claimed hers. Tender kisses, firm and insistent. The heat of his lips warmed her to her core. She turned in his arms, wrapping hers around his neck and pressing herself against the full length of him. Excitement ignited a burn only he could satisfy. The playful tease of his tongue seduced. Making love only a few hours after the funeral caused her a second of contemplation, but the need to feel loved and alive overrode any sense of propriety.

He scooped her up and carried her to the king-size sleigh bed they'd recently purchased together. Soon she'd be Mrs. Nicholas Trahan. No better time than now to christen the bed.

"Make love to me, Nick," she whispered as he hovered over her, his arms preventing their bodies from melding together. "I need to feel all of you." She pulled at the buttons on his crisp, white dress shirt with the same urgency that pressed inside her, hurrying as though a stopwatch marked wasted minutes until her naked body intertwined with his.

Ding dong.

"What the hell?" Nick said.

"Ignore it." She captured his cheeks and squeezed gently until his lips puckered, then she kissed him. Licking his bottom lip, she drew his full attention. "Take off your pants."

Ding dong.

"Nick? Biloxi?" Pounding on the front door followed.

"We know you're home!"

She recognized the lilting voices. The first one, Grandmother Elise Dutrey. The second one, Suzette Trahan, Nick's grandmother. The two women had formed an unlikely alliance after Nick had proposed to her.

"They won't go away until we answer," Nick said,

rising from the bed.

"Don't go," she pleaded, then lifted and removed her black silk slip. In a playful pose—arms braced, back arched, legs crossed at her ankles, she motioned for him to return to the bed.

"Stay where you are, *chèr*. Don't move. I'm going to ravish you as soon as I get them gone." Nick left the room in a rush. His bare feet smacked out a quick tempo as he descended the stairs.

"I should've spread my legs. Bet he wouldn't have ignored *that* invitation," she grumbled, flopping backward on the bed

Ding dong.

"Nick? Biloxi?"

Biloxi groaned. Sometimes she envied Branna living miles away in Florida, especially when family became a pain in the butt. Yet she loved them all and the minor inconveniences were the price she paid, and in the end, she couldn't abandon Fleur de Lis the way Branna had.

Downstairs, Nick opened the door.

"Hello, ladies." Nick's voice traveled up to her.

The pair of interlopers entered the house, their heels tapping against the wooden floor.

"Well?" Elise raised her voice. "Where's my granddaughter? Not in the kitchen, I'll bet."

"Why don't you take a seat in the living room. Biloxi is changing clothes." Nick's volume increased as though he thought she might not hear his booming octave. "And she'll be *down* in a minute."

Biloxi sighed. Nick's clues weren't subtle. Their late afternoon *tête—à—tête* complete with sexual satisfaction had been chucked in order to entertain the new generation of *granddames*. When she had a moment alone, she'd have a little chat with her grandmother. Recently, she'd taught her how to text, and Grandmother needed to utilize her newest skill *before* invading Nick's house ever again.

"Biloxi?" Suzette called out. "We're going to make tea."

"Save me, Lord," Biloxi prayed. "They know not what they do." If Suzette wanted tea, then the topic she had come to discuss must be serious.

Biloxi slipped on jeans and a t-shirt before joining Nick and their unwanted guests downstairs. She greeted her grandmother with a peck on the cheek, then headed to the kitchen.

"Grandmother Suzette, how about I finish making tea? You take a seat in the living room. Tell us why we're graced with your company."

"If you're sure, dear," Suzette said.

Biloxi smiled warmly. The older woman still didn't trust her in the kitchen, and not without good reason. Since Greta commanded Fleur de Lis' kitchen, she had only learned to make a few dishes, like red beans and rice and gumbo. Learning to cook took a back seat to everything else.

A bud of grief blossomed. She winced at a stab of pain. Greta's life without the Old Aunts would change more than anyone's in the family. She served as their companion for so many years. Her schedule ran based on the needs and wants of the matriarchs of the family. If Branna and James returned, Greta would dote more on baby Anaëlle and feel needed. Something more than cooking for all the family gatherings. Besides, they had to get the Fleur de Lis Café open soon. That would also provide both Greta and Camilla a purpose in life. Her cousin acted restless of late.

After pouring hot water into the teapot, Biloxi pulled out a tray, then gathered cups and saucers. She and Nick would take their tea in mugs, but Suzette would judge that informality an insult for herself and Grandmother Elise. Setting the sugar bowl and the creamer on the tray, she reached for napkins—cloth ones—and spoons.

"Tea is ready." She picked up the tray and carried it to the living room where Nick perched on a chair flanking the couch and the two older women waited.

Biloxi sat on the open spot on the couch closest to Nick. Handing a cup to her grandmother, then to Suzette, she asked, "So I assume you have news?" She couldn't imagine any other reason for their unannounced arrival.

"The wills," Grandmother Elise said, clearly annoyed. "The attorney scheduled the reading of the wills for day after tomorrow. He didn't bother to ask if that was convenient for me." Biloxi guessed the lawyer had discussed dates and times with Aunt Macy, and she approved the plan. Grandmother Elise had never been involved in running the estate, but now she wanted to assert her place in the absence of the Old Aunts. Branna's grandmother, Margarite, had too much sense to get involved in the day-to-day running of things.

"That's an important detail, Elise, but Nick, we have big news. Brace yourself."

Nick reached for a mug and took a sip. His expression remained bland. He shrugged. "*Mais*, Grandmère, you know I don't like guessing games. How about you just tell me this news?"

Clutching her cup and saucer in her lap, Suzette leaned forward and quickly glanced side to side as though the FBI or CIA might be listening. Biloxi coughed to smother a laugh.

"Your mother," Suzette whispered.

Nick straightened. "What?"

"We"—she gestured to Elise and herself—"*saw* your mother."

Nick scowled. "Not mine."

"Yes," Elise insisted. "Suzette showed me a photograph of her on her wedding day. She's nearly the same, as though she's not aged a bit. And there's no mistaking her eyes or her smile. Both are lovely."

Biloxi blinked and cast a quick glance at Nick, then back to the two other women. It had to be a mistake. Nick had hired a PI to find his mother several times and nothing turned up ever. "More tea?" She held up the pot for a distraction as a bad feeling washed over her— hesitation and a growing spot of gloom. This little interlude, something she'd assumed was brought on by the fanciful interaction of two bored old women, had turned entirely too personal, a potentially disastrous encounter.

Nick set his mug on the coffee table. His demeanor radiated calm and unconcern. He folded his fingers together and leaned forward, his forearms resting on his knees. "Ladies, I'm sure you think you know who you saw, but they say everyone has a twin. Did you actually speak to this woman? Ask her name? Get her address or phone number?"

"Well…" Elise began.

"Nicholas, we were just too shocked." Suzette grabbed Elise's arm like the old woman was her lifeline and she might be yanked away at any second.

"That isn't quite true," Elise countered. "You're hurting me, Suzette." She unclamped her friend's death grip. Biloxi patted her grandmother's other arm.

"Nick, I knew you'd want proof," Elise continued. "But the woman, Cat?—is that right, Suzette?—she ducked into a church."

Nick snorted. "*Mais,* that settles it. It couldn't be my mother. Cat in a church…no way." He leaned back in the chair, stretching his legs out long, as though he had not a care in the world. Clearly, he believed the imaginations of their grandmothers had run amuck. "But I can understand how seeing my mother would cause you shock."

"We did see her," Suzette stated emphatically.

Biloxi observed the back and forth like a spectator in the stands at Wimbledon. Nick, always a gentleman raised on values by his deceased Cajun grandfather, Claude, would not do or say anything to intentionally hurt anyone, but…if there was one subject that could make Nick lose his composure, it would be his mother. The last thing Biloxi wanted so close to their wedding was upsetting news. Or someone marching in and dredging up old pain. Postponing the wedding to make Fleur de Lis shine had put a strain on her, and Nick was none too happy about waiting either, it delayed their life together living under one roof and delayed their plans for starting a family—Nick's greatest desire.

"But before she did…" Elise beamed and reached for her purse. "I'm not as untrainable an old dog as you might think. I recently purchased a new digital camera—not sure how all those pictures are in that little box with no film, but—"

"Grandmother Elise," Biloxi interrupted. "Please, get to the point."

"I took a photograph of the woman that almost caused Suzette to have a heart attack."

Chapter 2

Nick pushed to standing. "You have a picture of *her*?"

Excitement and a sliver of fear slammed his chest—excitement over finding her, having her attend the wedding, and fear a ten-year-old boy carried for years because he'd lived without his mother, always worrying she might be dead. Though marrying Biloxi gave him a large extended family, one he valued and loved, he could have a completeness to life if his mother was found.

He swallowed hard. The memory of his mother's voice rang strong in his mind. Images of her flitted in a blurry haze. He wasn't sure he'd recognize her today. The only photo remaining of Cat was the one Elise had seen on his mantel—his parents on their wedding day, over thirty-five years ago.

"I swear"—Suzette pushed to standing—"on my husband's grave." She made the sign of the cross.

"Grandmère, no," Nick cautioned. Her eyesight wasn't all that great, and her memory flickered a bit now and again. She had to be mistaken. It couldn't be his mother, and the last thing he wanted was to crush his grandmother's confidence by proving her wrong.

"Mary Catherine Weston, well, who knows if she goes by Weston or Trahan, *is* the woman in this picture." She took the camera from Elise and handed it to him.

Nick pressed the button to turn it on. His heart bounced in an erratic staccato. What *if* it was his mother?

Biloxi stood next to him, wrapped an arm around his waist, and stared at the camera's small screen.

His palms began to sweat. Could it be his mother? He glanced at Biloxi. Surely she heard the rapid thumping of his heart.

Peering at the camera, he blinked to see beyond the blurriness of the photo, a moving image captured in a stationary moment. It could be anyone in a navy blue blouse and skirt. A colorful scarf draped the woman's head and circled her neck. Part of the blur of the image came from her removing dark sunglasses. Her age was undeterminable from the angle. But her smile… "How can you tell it's her? Between the scarf and the shades, she could be anyone."

"Yes, but she only put on the sunglasses when I gasped. We made eye contact for a brief second. I know without a doubt that woman is your mother." Suzette settled back on the couch and crossed her arms over her chest.

"I don't know…" Nick squinted at the picture, hoping for a revelation. "You hated her. Why would you bring this up now?"

Suzette sighed. She unfolded hear arms. "It was something Biloxi said."

"Me?" Biloxi asked.

"Earlier at your great-grandmother's funeral, you talked about how family had to rally around each member, not just when things were good, but in the difficult times, too. Family needs to respect one another, even when you're not necessarily liking them. You said *love* is a verb."

His darling fiancée *had* said those words. She'd spoken them in relation to her cousin Camilla's return to the fold and Branna's delayed return to Fleur de Lis, and because everyone had Katrina PTSD, had lived in trailers for months—putting everyone on edge. Love required patience, which at times was in short supply.

"I'm not connecting the dots." Confusion spread across Biloxi's face.

"Claude did what he thought was best for Nick at the time—taking him from his father after his mother left, but that doesn't mean it was best. Life changes all of us, for the good, if we allow it. Nicholas, you deserve to know your mother. It's better now than never. And someday, I hope, you're going to make her a grandmother. She might want to know her grandchildren. Lord knows, you were the light of my life. And all that I've said I believe, but I'll wager she wants money...or at least some sort of financial support."

Nick shoved his hands in his pocket and set the camera on the coffee table. "Grandmère, three times in the past—before I graduated vet school, once before and once after Katrina—I hired a private investigator to find her, but always the result was nothing." He made his way to the chest in the foyer. Opening the bottom drawer, he pulled out an envelope. "I have a report from the last time I hired a PI. They say there's no trace of Catherine Trahan. Have you mentioned this to my father?" He offered the papers inside the envelope as evidence.

"Nicholas, I know what I saw. And no, I've not

told your daddy. It might give him apoplexy. Couldn't have that now, could we?"

"I'm happy you've had a change of heart about my mother. However, a chance meeting with a woman in a scarf going into a church?" He still held out hope of locating his mother before the wedding. It could be a pipe dream. Yet, the only reason he hadn't pushed Biloxi hard to have a double wedding with Branna and James last October was due to a lingering glimmer of hope that he might find his mother. He had imagined the storm would somehow bring her home, and they would be reunited. If nothing more than to meet the Dutrey family's sense of tradition. He wanted to give his bride the wedding of her dreams. They would have photos of both sets of parents. Two complete pairs.

"As long as you won't consider it an invasion to your privacy, I'd like to pay a new investigation agency to try to locate Catherine," Suzette said. "This"—she pointed to the camera—"is proof."

He sensed her eagerness. A new project might give her something to focus on besides the misery left behind by the storm. Baton Rouge had been flooded with folks from New Orleans escaping the aftermath of the breeched levees and sadly, crime increased with the swell of population. His grandmother's charmed quiet life had changed due to Katrina.

Nick nodded. "*Mais*, maybe I gave up too soon. Maybe that woman *is* my mother. I'd be grateful if you find her."

Biloxi reached over and squeezed his arm. "This time could be *the* time."

****

Biloxi waved at the two elderly women driving

away before closing the front door. "I certainly wasn't expecting *that* when they barged in and interrupted our afternoon." Turning, she discovered Nick making himself comfortable on the couch.

"Odd that this should come up now," he said.

"How so?" she asked, crossing back into the living room.

"You know the old saying, when one door closes, another door opens." Nick stretched his arms and settled them behind his head. "It's strange that we just came from a burial—closing of a door—and now someone I lost might walk back into our life."

"I don't believe in coincidence. You know that. But we don't know *if* someone is walking back into your life. From the photo, the woman was in a hurry to get away."

"I don't have a good feeling about this." His brow creased. His jaw tightened. He frowned.

She could argue the merits of his mother tomorrow. Spending time together, connecting intimately, was what she needed most in the moment. Her sadness began spiraling down. Teetering on the edge of an emotional cliff, Biloxi fought grief. The Old Aunts might not see her walk down the aisle on the arm of her father, but they had to be there in spirit. How grand it would be if Nick's mother were there, too?

"What do you want to do with the rest of today?" She tried to sound upbeat, seeking to find a positive shift and not give into despair. They had a few hours free of responsibility, and she wanted to make the most of it. "It feels like Sunday after attending church for the funeral, but it's only Thursday. I'm already set up for the wedding I'm shooting on Saturday, so I've got time to kill."

Nick shrugged.

Biloxi crossed the room and picked up the tray of dirty teacups and mugs, taking them to the kitchen. "Nick, it's been months since we had an afternoon in the middle of the week to ourselves. I know something I'd like to do."

"Come over here and let's talk about it. I need to tell you something."

Gnawing began in her gut. Her fingers tingled. Based on his tone, whatever he had to say had to be something she wouldn't like.

As she entered the living room, Nick turned on his side, pointed to the cushion, and motioned for her to join him.

"If you have any bad news, I'm not in a place to hear it right now. I'm too…I feel raw and exposed over the loss of the Old Aunts. That coming on the heels of month and months of work and repairs on the estate since the storm, living in a trailer, all sense of normal life is gone." Her eyes began to water. "At least they got to see the home they both loved mostly restored to its former grandeur before they…"

"You have their tenacity," Nick said.

She stretched out on the couch, the full length of their bodies touching, and rested her head on his bent arm. He was her life. Her family might always see her as number two, but Nick never let her forget she was number one with him. "You mean I inherited something good? Something other than work, debts, and trying to maintain family peace?"

He draped his arm over her waist. She laced her fingers with his, needing the security he offered.

Drawing in a deep breath, she let it go. "Okay. I'm ready. Let's talk."

When he chuckled, the echoing vibration drowned out all other sound. "*Chèr*, always so businesslike."

"Nick," she warned.

"My mind's been whirling ever since our grandmothers barged through the door. Since seeing that photo, I think it could be my mother—"

"But you said—"

"I didn't want to tell you *or* them. It could be her. Not wanting to give up, I recently tried yet another agency to locate my mother. They've collected some data that points to her, including a Social Security number. One of their employees, an ex-NOLA detective, has set up a meeting with the woman next week."

"Oh?"

"I'm not sure how I feel about all of this now. I wanted to find her for years. I had to know what happened. I prepared myself to hear she was dead. I thought in continuing the hunt, I'd receive information leading me to her gravesite. And I want you to have the perfect wedding. Having both of my parents present…well, it checked the traditional box."

"So if it's really her…I'm confused. You do or you don't want her at the wedding?"

"I definitely want Cat there." He pushed her hair back and kissed her forehead. "But this is what I do know—and I'm not trying to cause you any pain."

"Darlin', just say it. I'm a big girl. I can handle it."

"I had asked Linc to be my best man before you agreed to the engagement, but I'm thinking—"

"You want to ask your father instead?"

Nick moved. Biloxi scooted over and sat upright.

"How did you know?"

"A woman's intuition. Oh, Nick," she groaned. "Really? Now? *Another* change in the wedding? You're going to hurt my brother's feelings. And someone will have to tell my mother before the wedding—or it will be a disaster during the ceremony. Anyway you spin it, it will only be a hurricane of trouble." How could he do this to her? To them? Hadn't they just buried the past completely when burying the Old Aunts? He wanted to create a new family feud by snubbing her brother?

"We wouldn't be having this conversation, if you'd married me last October, had a double wedding like we'd planned." Nick moved her to sit up.

"So this is *my* fault?"

"The storm changed all of us. It brought Camilla home and Jared followed. We wouldn't have made it through all the repairs and Historical Society issues, but for Jared and his grandfather. Camilla wouldn't be staying on to run the café with Greta if the expansion hadn't happened—all thanks to Jared *and* my dad, and the crew he rounded up. The storm ripped away the veneer of our life, yet it brought our families closer. Particularly, my father and me."

"Oh, Nicholas, I can't handle more conflict. Camilla is grumbling about going back to Wyoming for the summer. She and Jared are arguing about it. My parents are thinking of selling their home—I love visiting it in the Garden District—and buying an RV, like the one James' grandparents own. Aunt Macy constantly bickers with Momma, they're like pecking hens…I'm tired with a capitol T."

"Which is why, I want my mother to come to the

wedding. If my father is my best man—maybe there's a chance of reconciliation. He's been sober for a long time…but she could be the catalyst for even more change. It's a risk I want to take to bring my family together again. You, of all people, understand that."

Biloxi rose and paced. "Do you understand the explosion that could take place? Your mother materializes out of nowhere, just in time for the wedding. Then you want to change who represents you as best man? All so close to the wedding. It's a slap in the face for my brother. My mother will be so insulted. Grandmother Elise will be so disappointed."

"I'll tell them. I'll shoulder the responsibility for this."

Throwing up her hands, Biloxi shouted, "You don't understand. The minute after you tell my mother, Hurricane Deidre will be on the phone calling me to demand to know why I didn't warn her. I'm damned if I do and damned if I don't. Damn it to hell! Is all of this worth it? I just don't know anymore." She stormed upstairs. She didn't want to be a widow before she had the chance to be a bride.

Chapter 3

"Stop it," Biloxi groaned the next day. Her hands went to her thudding head. Nausea pooled in her stomach. Her elbows hit the dining table at Fleur de Lis. But her mother and aunt kept on as though she'd not spoken. "I've had enough," she said, but they weren't listening, and she was drowning in their continuing conflict.

Yesterday after the fight with Nick, she'd gone alone at dusk to the cemetery to have a few quiet words with the Old Aunts, hoping for a sign, hoping for a moment of divine guidance. But after leaving the sanctuary of that peaceful place, her grief burgeoned greater than before. She cried most of the night. Sleep eluded her, playing hide-and-seek with shadows of the night.

Nick chose the couch until early that morning. He'd said he heard her crying and came to hold her, but nothing more. Curling up to him, she finally drifted into a deep, but fitful sleep, too short with a blaring alarm at six thirty a.m. Then they barely said a word to each other before leaving to start their workday. And they still hadn't resolved the issue of who would be his best man. Damn if she'd bring it up to Momma and Aunt Macy now.

"As mother of the bride, I think I should have a say in the final seating arrangement," Deidre argued.

"As wedding coordinator with years of experience," Macy fired back, "handling many successful wedding *and* other events—"

Reluctantly, Biloxi had agreed to, and now regretted, one last review of every detail of the wedding. She'd made most of the wedding decisions on her own, which irritated Momma and insulted Aunt Macy, a noted expert on nuptial events.

Biloxi shook her head. Not even squawking from two of the most important older women in her life would change her mind about what she wanted for the wedding and reception. She had waited an extra nine months for the privilege of marrying Nick at Fleur de Lis. But that didn't make refereeing the two women any easier. Stepping between them to broker peace ranked up there with stepping into a boxing match between two contending prizefighters. She loved them but wanted to shoot them.

"I've had it. It's *my* wedding. I want silver candelabra and bouquets of spring flowers on every table. I already arranged it with the Rent-It-All place and the florist. I don't care about the seating arrangement as long as Nick and I sit together. Work it out between the two of you."

The well-meaning pair responded to her outburst with wide eyes, mouths gaped in the form of an 'o'.

Too bad. Enough was enough.

She grabbed her empty glass and started out the door.

"What's wrong?" Deidre and Macy's voices joined together sounding innocent of their crime.

Biloxi turned back to them and scowled. She refused to dignify their question with an answer. As if they didn't know! Any response she'd offer would be met with gang-style unity. It was their *modus operandi* to wrestle for control.

"I can't take the bickering. Any. More."

Maybe Branna's idea of a wedding in Vegas needed more consideration.

Biloxi headed for the kitchen. A snack and a glass of sweet tea before tackling the stack of bills would help her frayed nerves, that and the comforting silence of the office.

"Greta, I need relief." She walked into the fragrant scent of shrimp and grits. Her mouth watered.

"The only reason they pick at you is because they can't get their way," Great said, stirring a pot on the stove. "Are they ready for lunch?"

"I'm not sure if handing them utensils is wise. Who knows what bloodletting may occur. Smells yummy in here. I'm not eating with them." She thumbed in the direction of the dining room. "Now they're arguing over my *something old* and *something new*. It's *my* wedding day." Biloxi filled her glass with sweet tea and sipped.

"I'll bring you something to eat in your office."

"Thanks. Something bland. Maybe just grits. Nice to know you'll leave your new kitchen for me."

"Honey, you know, I'll always take care of my girl, but I do love my kitchen."

The heart of their home, the kitchen, the place where Greta created magic that offered comfort when they had no other amenities after the storm, was the first remodeled room once the exterior of the house had been secured. Repainted cabinets, new subway tile backsplash, refurbished wood flooring, and new

27

appliances. Prying Greta from her new kingdom required energy most of them didn't want to invest, especially when she put out the finest food for miles around. Nick was often the first one in line when Greta served.

"I love you. You're the only sane woman in this house." Biloxi blew a kiss.

"Oh. I almost forgot," Greta said. She went to the new bookshelf displaying her cookbook collection. Plucking an envelope from between two tomes, she handed it over. "It's addressed to Mrs. Biloxi Trahan. Odd. No return address. It has a wax seal, letter T. Rather mysterious."

"Did it come by messenger of some sort? There's no stamp."

"No, Camilla brought it in when she came over for coffee. She found it tacked to the back door."

Biloxi paused and ran her finger over the raised spot on the paper where the tack must have been. "Strange. Expensive stationery, though. It's probably a reminder from the landscaper. He's into posh and refined kind of things. So froufrou and dramatic"

"I was up at five a.m. I didn't see anyone. No workmen around at that hour. If there's a problem, let me know." Greta opened the refrigerator and pulled out a bottle of hot sauce.

With the envelope in one hand and a glass in the other, Biloxi made her way to the office in search of quiet. The once small space with built-in shelving, original to the house, doubled in size when workmen removed the wall separating it from the sewing room. The sewing machine, dress forms, and other supplies had been stored on the second floor in a large closet. As soon as she married Nick and moved out, she agreed to turn her old bedroom into a sewing space for Greta. After all, Branna had a new baby, and with any luck in the future, she would, too. Greta sewed as well as she cooked and enjoyed making her own creations. Baby clothes now topped her list.

The larger office allowed Biloxi to handle operations for Fleur de Lis, her photography business, and the launch of Fleur de Lis Café. No one dared bother her when she sequestered herself there—anyone in the family feared her putting them to work.

She glanced at the list on the desk, and just looking at it triggered weariness. Months and months of restoration. Months and months of people around all the time. When would her life return to normal?

The list of minor repairs to complete before the wedding hadn't shortened. With each item checked off, some other little detail came to light. If her luck held, the list would be completed before she walked down the aisle, but she held little hope of that level of perfection.

The important items: a dress that fit, no tripping down the stairs, and Nick at the altar with the minister. That was as perfect as the day needed to be.

Closing the office door, she soaked in the quiet and placed the envelope on the desk—a flat door stretched across two short filing cabinets, useable space until the antique mahogany one returned from the refinisher. The handwriting on the note was unfamiliar. Neat. Scrolled. Feminine. Unease pricked the outer edges of her mind.

"Focus, Biloxi," she said aloud.

Plopping into the rolling chair, she scooted to the bookcase and pulled out a white binder trimmed with pink ribbon. *The Book.* She dropped it on the desk. It bumped. The sound started her headache back into gear. With her elbows on the desk, she massaged her temples. A getaway might solve everything. Nick could fly them anywhere. Maybe somewhere old-fashioned like Niagara Falls. Or the wilds of Alaska. Any place far away to escape the torment of family—maybe Jared's family ranch? Camilla raved about it all the time, she was even threatening to return there for the summer since the café wasn't yet ready to open.

Biloxi's gaze landed on the envelope on the desk. It stared at her. A disquieting unease from unanswered questions about Nick's missing mother bubbled up. Her poor fiancé needed resolution. He'd waited years to find her. A very sad testament about family.

After deeply exhaling, she opened *The Book.* The first page folded out displaying a checklist and timeline. Behind that, pictures of bridal bouquets, table centerpieces, bridesmaid dresses, tuxes, everything for her wedding she'd been collecting since Nick proposed more than a year ago. Her June third wedding day was less than a month away. Only two things remained on the to-do list—gifts for her attendants and a wedding gift for Nick.

Stumped, she again considered a present. What to give him? She racked her brain. He needed nothing. Wanted nothing. He was a man content with his life. Extravagance wasn't his thing. She couldn't afford a Rolex watch, and good thing, because he'd never wear it. She could hear him now, "Not practical when delivering a calf or puppies. Not practical when fishing or working on the house." Maybe a new Stetson or a new pair of boots? No. It had to be something unique, just like him.

He'd left early that morning for his clinic to gather supplies, and then hit the road, making house calls on some of his larger clients. They joked and called those days 'big days'—appointments with horses, cows, and a few goats. She pictured him in his truck, windows down, belting out songs and singing along with the radio. He was the most calm, content, and sexy man she'd ever encountered. And he photographed well. An added plus.

She missed him whenever he didn't make it home for lunch. An ache from missing him welled in her chest. A need to hear his voice urged her to call him. Her fingers reached for the cell phone in the drawer, but she stopped short. The next time they talked, she had to make him understand he couldn't change his choice of best man at this late date. All the changes to their life since the storm overwhelmed her. She just couldn't handle one more. Especially one that threatened to produce major ripples within the family. Besides, it's not the groom's prerogative to change anything. That right belonged solely to the bride.

"No. That argument can wait. I need to hear him call me *chèr*." It would help wash away some of her weariness.

Picking up the phone, she noticed the screen showed a missed call. She played the message. Happiness sprouted inside her just hearing his voice.

"Hello, *chèr*. What say I take you for dinner at our favorite spot? Call me." The man had her wrapped in the most delicious knots. His husky voice turned her insides liquid. She smiled. Tonight she'd surprise him when he arrived home with a picnic in bed. Po'boy.

Abita beer. Zapp's chips. And of course kisses…and more for dessert.

"Hey handsome," she whispered in her sexiest voice while recording a message for him. "You pick up oyster po'boys, and I'll take you to *my* favorite picnic spot. Guess what's for dessert?"

Placing the phone back in the drawer, she eyed the envelope. Curiosity had a magnetic pull. Who had delivered the envelope? Someone skulked around Fleur de Lis unseen? Couldn't be the mailman. Mail service remained spotty since the storm. She had personally taken an updated wedding invitation to the Madisonville cousins when it came back marked as *Undeliverable*.

"Knock. Knock," Greta called out. "Please open the door."

Biloxi moved, giving access to the bearer of lunch. Greta moved past her and placed the tray on the desk.

"You haven't opened it yet?" Greta asked, unloading the bowl, spoon, and napkin.

"Something about it makes me…I don't know, scared. I've been carrying around this uneasy feeling."

Greta scoffed. "Of what?" She planted her fists on her hips. "What's going on?"

Biloxi sighed and plopped into the chair. "If you've got a minute, I'll tell you everything. Maybe it will help me put it all into perspective."

"I've got time."

She began with arrival of the grandmothers—Grandmother Elise and Suzette—finishing with Nick's offer at mending fences with dinner that night.

"Do you really think his mother's been found?

"More like she's found him. The photo was taken

32

in New Orleans."

"But this letter is addressed to you. I'll bet it's from her. The T must be for Trahan." Greta pulled a chair close and sat. "I'm here for moral support. Open it."

"I don't know…"

"Open it!"

Slicing through the paper with a letter opener, Biloxi shuddered at the sound. She paused and glanced at Greta. Once opened and the contents read, she couldn't go back. Pulling the paper from the envelope, she stopped. "No," she said, "you read it."

"It's not addressed to me. Go on," Greta urged.

Apprehension rippled. The tempo increased inside her. "I don't know…Maybe I should wait for Nick. Wait and read this with him. He's the Trahan in the equation."

"Quit stalling." Greta stared down her nose. "Go on."

After taking a deep breath and letting it go, she began to read:

Dear Miss Biloxi,

Please pardon my familiarity, however, based upon the engagement announcement I read in the Times-Picayune last August, I believe you're now married to my son. I've waited as long as my patience would permit. Allow me to introduce myself. I am Catherine Trahan. I am still legally married to Nicholas's father.

I am reaching out to you, asking with desperation for your help. I throw myself on your mercy, one woman to another. I want to see my son. I'm sick. Cancer. Please don't misunderstand, I'm not imminently at death's door, but the illness has made me face my failings and past sins.

My greatest regret in life is allowing someone to take Nicholas from me. I have made amends as best as I've been able for my past, except to my son. I do not seek to intrude, but if you would help me reconnect with him, it would bring me great peace if the eventuality comes.

After living for years abroad, and assuming a different name, I have returned to New Orleans. I now reside on Royal Street. I would be ever so grateful if you'd consider meeting me for coffee and allowing me a chance to explain, with the hopes that you will aid me in setting up a meeting to once again see my son face to face. You may contact me through Chantel Gilbeau.

Your humble servant,
Aurélie Dubois
aka Cat Trahan

"What!" Biloxi's hands shook. "Is the woman crazy? Nick doesn't need anyone's help to meet his mother. But of all people, Chantel. No!"

"What are you going to do?" Greta shook her head.

"Cat's been gone from Nick's life since he was ten. He suffered so much as a kid because of his parents. Yet before reaching out to him, she's in touch with Chantel—and that witch hasn't told Nick? How dare she!"

"Don't jump to conclusions."

"How can you say that? She wants *me* to speak to Chantel to make an appointment to meet her? Absolutely not. Never!" Jerking out of her seat, she paced the room. "Of all the nerve." White-hot anger seethed through Biloxi. "No."

"She can't know about your *situation* with Chantel."

"Just when I thought I might be able to trust her, thinking the past was behind us—after all, she did help a few times in the garden since the storm—now this. How long has Chantel known of Cat's whereabouts?" Waves of anger punched from her gut to her throat, burning on the way up. She sipped ice tea, hoping to dampen the mounting rage. "This can't be happening!"

"Sit," Greta ordered.

Biloxi growled. Sinking into the chair, she blinked when Greta rolled close until they were nose to nose. "You're not thinking straight. If Chantel knows, she certainly hasn't said anything to anyone, including Nick. Maybe her intentions are good. Maybe she doesn't want to be involved—this has two potentially extreme outcomes. One, Nick hates Cat or Aurélie, or whatever she calls herself, and never sees her again. Or two, he's totally renewed by reconnecting with his mother. Chantel's in a bad spot. She works for him. Either way, he's going to need your support, not Chantel's. I don't blame her for remaining silent. She probably wants to remove herself from this mess. It has all the earmarks of disaster."

"Except that she hasn't refused to be involved. *She's* the contact. The go-between."

"Who else could Catherine trust? If she gave you the name of a realtor or some other stranger, you probably wouldn't believe the authenticity of the note. She used Chantel for a reason."

Biloxi's shoulders slumped. "This whole thing could be a trap."

"I believe you can trust Chantel enough to ask her about this," Greta said. "And maybe the reason Nick wasn't able to find his mother before now was because

Cat lived abroad. The letter suggests she thinks y'all are already married. She's not trying to ruin your wedding."

"Okay." Biloxi sighed deeply. "Maybe I'm overreacting. He said no one could find even a trace through her Social Security number until recently, so maybe that's the truth."

"You won't know unless you investigate." Greta rose. "Eat your lunch. It'll probably help your headache. It will definitely give you the strength to go groveling," she chuckled. "I can't wait to see what you're going to wear to meet his mother."

Turning toward the desk, Biloxi held her head in her hands and rested her elbows on the desktop. "I don't know... My headache is back full force. I can't believe I'm going crawling on my hands and knees to ask for Chantel's help."

When Greta reached the door to leave, Biloxi asked, "What does one wear to meet the enemy?"

Chapter 4

"I would've preferred The Old Coffee Pot," Biloxi grumbled, making her way from the parking lot next to the mall at the old Jax Brewery to Café Du Monde in New Orleans. The light blue, cotton-jersey dress was cooler than jeans and a blouse in May's humidity. Walking on uneven bricks and sidewalks, she picked her way at a slower pace than her usual brisk steps to ensure the wedged heels didn't cause her to trip. Regular heels were out. Not safe footwear in the French Quarter where, even stone-cold sober, someone could trip. Sunglasses protected her eyes from the peek-a-boo sun shining between buildings and allowed her to observe others without making obvious eye contact. She needed anonymity, even the tiniest bit, to tamp down her rising vulnerability.

What she was walking into?

Navigating around and through the throng of tourists, she sidestepped a woman in a caftan and turban. One of the many street vendors, she assumed, setting up tables in front of St. Louis Cathedral.

"Chantel could've chosen someplace more out of the way. But nooo, not her."

Tourists never seemed to mind the heat and humidity. Just another excuse for walking around with a frozen daiquiri in hand. The worst of the summer was yet to come. Locals went into hiding then, except at night when cool breezes blew across the river and bands cranked up for their musical sets. Then locals ventured out. Maybe that ambiance gave credence to the theory that New Orleans was a haven for vampires. That, and stories by author Anne Rice.

She dodged a woman walking three dogs.

"At least I'll be close to Dutch Alley," she muttered. There she hoped to find pearl earrings as special gifts for each of her attendants. The artist co-op displayed photography, paintings, jewelry, pottery, and fabrics, all wonderful original works by local artisans. If she lived closer to the city, she'd consider trying to show her own photographs at the gallery.

She selected a seat under the mostly empty green and white striped canopy with an open view, easy to spot Chantel, then checked her phone for the time. Fifteen minutes before the scheduled meeting. Just enough time to enjoy a treat.

Folding a ten-dollar bill into her palm, she scooted closer to the table, crossed her legs, and sat upright, hoping to strike a relaxed yet bored pose, as though the meeting carried little significance. When she caught herself drumming her fingers on the table, she rested one hand on top of the other to cover any signs of anxiousness.

"Order?" a waitress asked.

"Beignets and hot chocolate, please." She held up cash to pay.

"Thank you. Back in a moment."

After forcing herself to breathe, Biloxi turned her thoughts to Nick. If he had any idea where she was and why, his anger might finally show. The man always remained in control of his emotions…except when they were in bed. She chuckled.

But he wasn't like other men she'd cared about in the past. He never showed anger. Never shouted or got drunk. Would he consider this rendezvous deceptive? The last thing she wanted was to give him a reason for mistrust.

Her conscience took only a small hit when she agreed to meet Chantel without his knowledge. Thankfully, she hadn't lied when she explained to him about her day. The trip to the city allowed her to checkoff a line item on her wedding to-do list. But when and how she'd share about this meeting with Chantel and its outcome hinged on a lot of different maybes.

Last night, they'd had sweet make-up sex during their picnic in bed. As of this morning, everything between them appeared normal.

But it wasn't.

She was meeting a woman she didn't trust—Chantel had tried to steal Nick away and caused heartbreaking pain—to conspire to meet Nick's mother. But it had to be done to protect him. Who knew what reason this woman claiming to be his mother had in mind. She held the power to hurt Nick. Biloxi would do nearly anything to prevent him from suffering more pain.

"Where is she?" Biloxi checked her phone again for the time. "Leave it to Chantel to arrive fashionably late. I'll wait ten minutes, no more." Her shoulder muscles cramped.

"Your order." The waitress set a plain mug and a plate of fried puffed dough covered in white powdered sugar on the table.

Biloxi's mouth watered. Beignets would make the time pass tolerably while she waited. "Thank you. Keep the change," she told the waitress.

For an added distraction, she tasted the warm sweet dough and sipped her hot drink while perusing photos she'd taken on her phone of several Royal Street addresses.

"Which one is Cat's?" A flush of self-consciousness washed over her. She managed a quick look around. While she'd been taking photos, had the woman been watching her from behind the slats of a shutter or peering around drapes? Could she be hiding in plain sight somewhere in the crowd? Anxiety ramped up. Maybe Chantel told Cat of this meeting, and she was watching now. Biloxi dabbed the corner of her mouth with a napkin.

Nick's mother had the advantage. Cat knew what she looked like from the engagement photo in the paper, which had identified the engaged Biloxi Dutrey and Nicholas Trahan. She had taken the photo herself. Whereas, the only image she had of Cat was her wedding photo from thirty-plus years ago. It was dubious as to whether or not the blurry one Suzette captured of a woman in a scarf was truly Nick's mother.

"There you are."

Biloxi looked up when she heard Chantel's voice and grinned halfheartedly.

Chantel waved. The woman looked like a model for summer seersucker suits. White and light blue stripped slacks and jacket and a soft white silk blouse with the opening plunging nearly to her waist. It wasn't hard to hate Chantel with her long legs, long flowing hair, and perfect model figure.

"Same," Chantel said to the approaching waitress as she swirled her finger over Biloxi's food.

"You eat like a real person?" Biloxi felt the expansion of her curves. She slid the plate—minus one beignet—away.

Metal legs scraped the concrete when Chantel pulled out a chair directly across the table. She grasped Biloxi's offered hand and kissed the air beside her cheek. "See," she said smiling. "We can get along."

"As long as you remember who's engaged to marry Nick."

"Ah, well then, we'll dispense with the pleasantries and get down to business. Shall I begin or do you want that honor?"

"You start." Biloxi didn't intend to reveal anything. Better to let Chantel spill her news before picking it apart with questions. She sipped her cooling chocolate drink trying to appear utterly nonchalant.

"I can only assume—"

"Don't assume anything. Just say what you know, what you've been instructed to tell me," Biloxi insisted. She wanted the facts, only the facts, thank you very kindly.

Chantel paused as the waitress placed her order on the table. She paid the woman, then clutched the cup, her blood-red fingernails a stark contrast against the white of the mug. Biloxi blinked and took a second look—Chantel's hands were shaking.

"I did not ask for this job. I don't like being a messenger. However, I agreed to help because I know of Nick's longstanding desire to find his mother."

"How were you recruited?"

"A priest called me."

Biloxi *harrumphed*. "Don't try to suggest this is heaven ordained."

"He said he placed the call at Cat's request."

"Cat, is it…very chummy of you. I understand she's more comfortable going by Aurélie Dubois." Maybe if she tossed out a nugget of knowledge, Chantel would think she wasn't totally in the dark about the longtime missing Mrs. Trahan.

"I'm told that's her mother's name," Chantel said, appearing completely unruffled. "I don't know anything about her time in France. I don't know much beyond the one conversation I had with her. In fact, if the family attorney hadn't vouched for her, I wouldn't have taken her call, wouldn't be here discussing this with you." She reached across the table and placed her hand on Biloxi's arm. "I am on your side in all of this."

Biloxi looked down her nose to the spot where Chantel's hand rested. "We shall see." Every nerve in her body urged her to fling Chantel's hand aside, but rudeness wouldn't solve anything. How else would she find Mrs. Trahan? It irked her to know the family attorney, a priest none them knew, and Chantel had contact with Cat—when Nick had been waiting for years to hear from her.

"The instructions I've been given are to deliver you to her house on Royal Street."

"When?"

"Today." Chantel smiled megawatt bright.

"What? No…This makes no sense."

"Let me finish one beignet and a sip of my…what is it we're drinking?"

"Hot chocolate."

"Then we walk."

"How far?"

"Two blocks up St. Ann to Royal, take a right, and our destination is near the Gallier House. You know. The museum."

Biloxi shook her head. "None of this feels right."

Chantel reached across the table and plucked Biloxi's sunglasses from her face. "There, now I can see the truth in your eyes. You'll be safe. I'm not going to leave you alone. Nick would kill me, feed me to gators, and no one would ever find me. He'd commit the perfect crime—for you. You and I are going together. I'm here for your support."

"Still—this is just crazy. Why are you involved?"

"I don't know *why* she's involving me. Shall we ask her together?"

"I'm calling Nick and telling him what I'm doing *and* where I'm going."

"If you thought that was wise, he'd already know. You would've told him before you came." Chantel stood. "Let's go."

Biloxi pondered her sanity while her nerves screamed *disaster*. Maybe if she managed to reunite Nick with his mother, maybe he'd not cause a rift in the family by asking her brother to step aside as his best man. "Let's get this over with." Rising, she headed for the exit and slipped her sunglasses back in place.

Chantel did nothing to hurry her along as they trekked toward their destination. On Royal Street, the clop of horse hooves and the chatter of guides in carriages carrying tourists through the French Quarter punctuated the air, along with the music of the calliope on the riverboat docked on the banks of the Mississippi

River. Biloxi navigated the uneven sidewalks—banquettes—and the brick streets, musing all the while that never in her wildest imaginations did she dream she'd be meeting Nick's mother before him. Slowing her lead, she turned to Chantel. "I'm not sure this is a good idea. Let's not go."

Chantel halted. "You don't want Nick hurt. I understand. If you go ahead with this, you could be protecting him. If she's nuts, and she might very well be crazy, he'll never need to know unless you decide to tell him. You, not me, are the go-between. I'm just the escort. You're her ticket to Nick." Chantel ran her hand down Biloxi's arm and gently squeezed her wrist. "I understand your reticence to trust me, but please, I assure you, I'm here to help."

The sincerity of her tone struck a chord. Biloxi sighed. "All right. Let's continue. "

As they walked, Biloxi doubted her sanity. No one knew where she was or what she was doing. Not even Greta. If something happened to her, how long before Nick would begin a search for her? And what about the PI? Did Nick's mother know the reason for the meeting he'd set up with her? Her letter had been written after the appointment was set, and she was under the impression Nick had already married.

Biloxi winced. Confusion swirled in her mind like a slow-moving hurricane. In another block, in a matter of minutes, she might have all her questions answered by the one woman she never thought she'd meet—Cat Trahan.

"We're almost there," Chantel said, slowing. "Let's pause here for a moment."

"Which house?"

"The one with the dark blue shutters." Chantel pointed across the street to a two-story yellow house with iron posts supporting a second-floor balcony.

"I think someone's watching us." Biloxi slanted her gaze upward. "The curtains moved. Upstairs window." She chewed her bottom lip. No turning back now. Her palms moistened. Her heart pounded double time. What if Cat was crazy? How could she deliver *that* news to Nick?

"I meant what I said. I won't leave you alone…unless once we're inside, you want me to step out. Just say the word. I'll wait for you right here." Chantel linked her arm with Biloxi's. "Deep breath. Let's go."

Together, steps in sync, they crossed the street. Chantel used the fleur de lis knocker to announce their arrival.

The door opened. A teenager in white walking shorts and a white cotton blouse with at least ten silver bangles dangling from her wrist greeted them. She smiled shyly. Her asymmetrically cut blue-black hair fell to her jawline on one side, the other side ended over her ear. Her lips were red and her nails matched, a fashionable look for someone who probably hadn't celebrated a sixteenth birthday. "I'm Biloxi Dutrey. I'm here to meet Mrs. Trahan."

Biloxi tried not to stare. The girl had Nick's mouth and his eyes. Who was she? A relative to be sure, but what was the exact connection?

"Yes. I know who you are."

Biloxi noted her French accent.

"My *maman* is waiting to meet you."

"Mother?" Biloxi and Chantel said in unison.

"This way, *s'il vous plaît*."

Biloxi followed her through a living room with high ceilings to a hall where double doors opened onto a brick patio shaded by a beige sailcloth canopy that offered protection from the sun. A woman in a tailored red and white print dress and red shoes rose from a chair. Beside her was an iron bistro table with four tall glasses of lemonade, complete with thin slices of lemon floating with the ice. In the center of the table, a three-tier cake holder displayed pink petit fours with tiny white roses and green leaves. Cloth napkins had been neatly placed on the table in front of each chair. The setting was inviting, as though they did this often.

"I am Catherine Trahan. This is my daughter, Sophie." The woman's accent was clearly southern. She moved five steps to Biloxi. "You must be my daughter-in-law. I recognize you from your photograph." She grasped Biloxi's hands, leaned in, and kissed the air beside her cheeks. "And you must be Chantel. *Merci beaucoup*. You brought my family to me."

Stunned speechless, Biloxi blinked. No one could ever doubt this woman was Nick's mother. They had the same smoky topaz eyes. The ones that had hypnotized Biloxi from their first meeting. The sparkle in Nick's eye matched the one she spied in this woman. Biloxi sucked in a quick breath. Nick had a mother *and* a sister. And they lived less than an hour from home. That news would devastate him. What was she going to do? A hurricane of mental confusion whipped faster, swirling so quickly dizziness made her sway.

"Oh darlin', I'm afraid the shock is too much." Cat assisted Biloxi to a chair and motioned for the others to sit.

Biloxi sank, her legs about to give out. "If you're really Catherine Trahan, why haven't you contacted Nick?" she blurted, manners be damned.

Sophie offered a glass, but Biloxi waved it away. She wanted an answer from the woman who claimed to be her fiancé's mother. "He has a sister? There's nothing more dear to Nick than family. Why haven't you contacted him?" Her heart ached for him. He had a younger sister he'd never met.

"It's complicated," Cat began.

"No. It's. Not," Biloxi insisted. "Edward came back into his life more than a year ago, after Claude died. Where have *you* been?"

Chapter 5

With a lighthearted bounce in his step, Nick slid into the seat of a shiny new white convertible. The Infiniti's red leather interior added a sexy vibe. The price of the car was worth every cent just to see *surprise* on Biloxi's face when they departed for their honeymoon after the reception.

He'd heard through the family grapevine how she expected they'd take a ride in Captain Jack's carriage before flying off somewhere, the same carriage he borrowed when he proposed to her, but also the one Branna and James used in their wedding celebration. For his bride, he wanted something unique, something special. After much contemplation, he settled on the perfect wedding gift—and with the help of Biloxi's brother, Linc, the car would remain out of sight in a storage unit in Picayune until the perfect moment.

Pulling out of the dealership in Metairie with the top down on the car, Nick headed for a barbeque joint famous for its sliders. His mouth watered. He was meeting the PI for lunch at a food truck parked in a permanent spot where the locals flocked. A TV station featured the place on the evening news as a highlight in the rebuilding of New Orleans, which still moved at a snail's pace. Reconstruction had a long way to go. So many people weren't returning.

His stomach rumbled. He couldn't live on a diet of

only gumbo, jambalaya, and fried shrimp po'boys. He craved variety when it came to food. Lucky for him, marrying into the Dutrey family meant he sampled the best home cooking in the county. Biloxi once joked that the only reason he proposed was to gain regular entrance to Greta's cooking at family dinners. He hadn't bothered to argue.

Navigating surface streets rather than the interstate, he put the car through its paces. Stop. Go. Blow through a yellow light. Exhilaration thrummed through his body. He gripped the steering wheel, then relaxed his hands. Zipping along, shifting gears, Nick headed eastbound. He chuckled remembering his past visits to New Orleans—drinking parties with his college buddies while they roamed Bourbon Street and the times he carried packages for his grandmother on her shopping trips to Magazine. Adrenaline rushed. He couldn't wait to meet with the PI before heading home. The man had photos of a woman documented to be Catherine Trahan and a scheduled meeting with her next week. The question remained—was this Catherine Trahan indeed his mother?

Certainty beat a steady rhythm in his chest. His spirits soared. Could it be that his grandfather in heaven had worked his charm to bring his father and mother back together again? There could be nothing greater than having his entire family at the wedding. Photographs of his side of the family mingling with Biloxi's. Together they could field a football team including second and third-string players. Family meant everything.

"But..." he said aloud, "too much, too soon could be disaster." His enthusiasm for reuniting his family needed tempering. The woman might not be his mother. But if she were—he hesitated to quickly reintroduce her to his father and grandmother. At the wedding wouldn't work. He couldn't risk a family blowup on that special day. Biloxi would kill him.

Flipping on satellite radio, he stopped the shuffle on Maroon 5's "Woman." Linc had made him listen to the band, 'to break your country music rut,' he'd said. The song teased his brain and made him think of his bride-to-be. She was a woman above all others. But what was it about her? Her artistic eye. Her curvy body. Her kindness. Beyond her strength and sweetness, he'd peered into her vulnerability, even when she fought to hide it. In his dictionary, Biloxi was listed under family—His. Yeah, she came with a big one attached to her hip, but he never minded that. She turned balancing all the aspects of her life into an art, always making him feel as though he came first—before Fleur de Lis, before her large extended family, even before photography. She made him a better man. He trusted her completely.

After he pulled to the curb on Esplanade, he snagged a coveted parking place, put the car in park, then flipped a switch, and robotic arms moved the hardtop of the car into place.

"That's slick as shit," a man said, leaning against the side of the building, his Panama hat pulled low. Sunglasses hid his eyes.

"Thanks." Nick sized up the guy. He had an air of familiarity. In a white button-down shirt and navy blue slacks, the man could've been anyone attending a business casual lunch.

The man pushed off from the building, grabbed a

brown bag at his feet, and took a step with his hand extended. "Clete Thibodeau."

"That's right," Nick said, pumping the man's hand. "I guess this is the real you, rather than the one I met incognito."

"This is my tourist look," Clete chuckled.

"Can't be. They wear Hawaiian print shirts two sizes too big and ball caps."

"Why don't we find a seat?" Clete pointed halfway down the street to the open courtyard with wooden picnic tables.

Nick allowed the man to order first, then gave his, and paid the bill. "I'm not going to lie. I'm excited about the news you have," he said, turning toward Clete.

"Curious thing"—Clete took a seat and opening the bag, he pulled out two bottles of beer, handing one over to Nick—"all the while we've been watching the house, no visitors ever. Yet just a while ago, she had two. I drove by the residence since it was on my way here and managed to take some shots. I have the prints I told you about, but the new pics, I didn't have time to run back to the office and make copies before our meeting."

"Order up!" the guy at the window called.

"Just a sec." Nick headed to pick up their food. Returning to the table with a tray laden with pork sliders, chips, and potato salad, Nick noticed eight-by-ten pictures covering the top of the table. He placed the tray on the bench next to him. "Wow." He picked up the first photograph and stared into the face of a stunning woman. Blonde flowing hair, blue eyes, pink shiny lips, tight white dress, pink stilettos. A stunner. Maybe over fifty. Nothing familiar struck a chord with him. His response to the photo—nice-looking woman—that was it.

"That's not her," Clete said, hustling the photo out of sight. "She was passing by, and a guy just has to look." He stated it matter-of-factly, as though every man would gawk. "This is her." He pulled a photo from the bottom of the pile of splayed photos.

The woman in this photo was the antithesis. Shoulder length, thick dark hair, dark sunglasses, red lips, fitted black dress, and black heels. Polished and elegant, down to her painted fingernails. She might pass for the woman his grandmother photographed, but without a side-by-side comparison, he couldn't be sure.

"Catherine Trahan, aka Aurélie Dubois. Lives on Royal Street. Title to the property is Benson Bressler. Very rich. Married. New York City primary residence, but houses in several places. Including one in France. Big fan of the Saints."

"And..." Nick prompted. Football mattered, but not in relation to his mother or his wedding.

"There's one hitch."

"Only one? That's a relief." Nick stared at the picture, hoping for some glimmer of recognition. Nothing. No spark, no hint of remembrance.

"Bressler died recently. The property on Royal is up for sale."

"You're giving me data, which I appreciate, but how about sharing the information between the lines," Nick said dryly, picking up another photo. This one he recognized. It was the same scarf as the one in the photo his grandmother had taken. Only the woman in this picture wasn't old enough...a teenager, probably not yet eighteen.

"This is all speculation. I think the girl in the photo is her daughter—"

Shock hit Nick. "Daughter?" He'd never seriously considered he might have a sibling, even a half one.

"Sophie Dubois. I'm working on confirming the father part. But I'm confident it's Bressler. They lived as family whenever he was in France. He owned the house where Catherine and the teen lived. I think Catherine returned to the U.S. because the house in France was sold about the time Katrina hit here. Catherine has no obvious means of income—that is, she isn't on anyone's payroll for taxes."

Nick studied the photo. That could be the reason he didn't recognize the woman his grandmother insisted was his mother. Because the person she saw was his half sister. Surely, after everything Edward explained about the past, the girl couldn't be a full-blooded sibling.

"Are you saying you believe this woman is Bressler's mistress and the kid is his? But do you think she's my mother?"

"Yes and yes. I see the family resemblance."

Examining each photograph, Nick tried to hit on a memory, something to convince him of his relation to this woman. He needed concrete evidence. To trust, to believe, based on a vague photograph…that could lead to a world of more pain.

"Grocery shopping," Clete said, sliding that photo closer. "Store in Metairie. This one"—the woman stood beside a cab—"was taken when she returned home. See the house in the background. That's where she lives."

"I've been down Royal Street several times since the storm. You think she came before it? What evidence do you have?"

"Credit card receipts I uncovered."

"Do I want to know how?"

"No. No, you don't. What you want to know is *why* she's here now. She hasn't contacted you for the duration. But I'll have answers next week."

The man had summed it all up in one sentence. Why now?

If his mother had arrived in New Orleans before Hurricane Katrina, she'd obviously survived it. Schools were closed after the storm. Where had the teen attended? Was the girl family? Hopefulness took root. Not only was he getting his mother back, but he was getting a sister, too.

If so, Biloxi would probably beat him senseless if he asked to increase the wedding party to include his sister as one of her bridesmaids. If these photos proved his mother and sister were in town, he had to know their plans. They had to stay for the wedding. He'd make his father and grandmother understand.

"Oh, before I forget, take a look at these. I just took them. Do you recognize this woman?" Clete handed over the camera.

Nick peered at the screen. "Chantel. She's my business partner. That's outside the house." Nick shuffled through the printed photographs and found one of Catherine standing almost in the same spot.

"Flip the screen. Chantel didn't make the visit alone. There's another woman with her."

"What!" Nick stared at the camera. "That's my fiancée. What the hell!"

"Uhhh, guess you didn't know your business partner and fiancée are acquainted with your mother."

Uneasiness punched him. Why hadn't she mentioned she knew where his mother was? A list of questions flashed through his mind, each one ratcheting up his anger. "I can't believe this," he said, keeping his voice deadly calm. He trusted her. She knew what finding his mother meant to him. Why would she keep it a secret? Was his father somehow involved? Were they conspiring to keep him from seeing his mother?

Nick clenched his fist. "What I do know is this—someone's got some explaining to do."

Chapter 6

Biloxi sipped lemonade. Holding on to the cut-crystal glass prevented her from tossing the beverage onto her hostess. She glanced at the folder of documents on the edge of the table. Picking it up, she flipped it open again. "You have to forgive me. This is a lot to take in." Her stomach churned. She hated secrets. Never kept one from Nick. Ever. Until now. The result of this innocent meeting was like riding the Scream Machine and plummeting more than a hundred feet in under six seconds. How could all of this be true?

"All I can say is 'holy shit.' Lady, you don't know the can of worms you've opened up." Chantel pushed her chair away from the table, crossed a leg over her knee, and bounced her foot. "Your son is very old-fashioned when it comes to family values. Believe me, I know. I also know he's been looking for you, but a relationship with him, after he learns what you've done? I just don't know…"

"I don't wish to make this any more uncomfortable than it is." Biloxi reached across the table and grasped Sophie's hand. "I'm sorry for your loss, for your father's passing. It's hard to lose a parent. But think about Nick. When he was ten, he lost both his mother— she just disappeared—and Edward, his father, left Nick with his grandparents, who raised him. Family is *the* most important thing in his life because of that."

Sophie hung her head. "I didn't know I had a brother until a month ago. Family is important to me, too."

"It would only be a temporary stay," Catherine insisted. "If family is so important to him, won't you at least discuss my request with him? We need a place to live. Sophie needs to attend school. I can't register her until we have an address."

"You thought Nick and I were already married, which is why you thought you'd recruit me to help you. No, I'm sorry. You may come to the wedding if Nick insists, but the two of you cannot live with Nick and me after we're married."

"It would be only until legal issues can be settled with Bressler's attorney."

"His wife, you mean," Chantel snorted. Shaking her head, she said, "Nick's not going to like any of this news. Besides, Bressler's wife could tie things up in court for a very long time. She's now in control of his fortune."

Biloxi glanced at Chantel. Gratitude welled in her heart. Her former nemesis provided much needed support. The shock of Catherine's revelations had Biloxi's mind turning like a whirligig in the wind. Over the last hour, she and Chantel had combed over the paperwork Catherine offered as proof of her identity, and that of her daughter—Nick's half-sister.

"May I take this with me?" Biloxi closed the folder again. "We need to be going."

"Certainly," Catherine said.

"I need to understand something. Why did you write to me at Fleur de Lis? Who left the note tacked to the kitchen door?"

"Well," Catherine began.

"No, *maman*. I will tell her." Sophie straightened in her chair, composing herself. She placed her folded hands on the table. "I searched the internet and found out about the Trahans. Claude's passing. Then I discovered your engagement notice. It mentioned Fleur de Lis, and I looked up that. It's a big house. I found an article about the restoration on the house—an interview with a construction foreman, Jared Richardson—"

"He's engaged to my cousin Camilla. His grandfather owns the architectural firm overseeing the accuracy of the historical details," Biloxi explained.

"Mr. Richardson mentioned Nick in the article. *Maman* and I decided we wouldn't interfere with your wedding. The shock of meeting both of us...so we waited until after the wedding date."

"Only Nick and I didn't get married then. My cousin Branna and James married instead. Our wedding day is in about two weeks, June third."

"We rented a car and drove to Fleur de Lis, but as you know, lots of workers around. So we went to Mobile for a hotel. Then before dawn the next day, *Maman* waited while I ran up to the house and left the note. No one saw me. I promise. I had to see where my brother lived." Her brows crinkled. "I admit, I had hoped to run into someone, just by accident. But I saw no one."

An ache opened in Biloxi's heart. Poor Sophie. No one could see her. Her father kept her a secret—he had another family with children in New York. Her mother kept her hidden. All along she had a brother and couldn't reach out to him. Catherine had robbed her children. While Nick's mother deserved whatever she got, Sophie, on the other hand, was an innocent victim.

"Sophie, there's only one problem. Nick doesn't live there. Fleur de Lis is *my* family home."

"But with a home so big, isn't there room for two more?"

"Where does Nick live?" Catherine frowned. "Where will you live after you're married?"

Catherine," Biloxi began, purposefully ignoring the woman's questions, "how long do you estimate *temporary* to be?"

Catherine's face lit up. "You'll help us?"

"Maybe. I don't know yet. I need to discuss all of this with Nick. He's not going to be happy—I didn't tell him where I was coming today."

Chantel waved her finger back and forth like a metronome. "No. No. Nick's not going to like this. You've never seen him mad. I have. Don't tell him about all this before the wedding, Biloxi. I'm warning you. Don't."

Biloxi rubbed her temples. "Please, Chantel. Let's not complicate things. If I don't tell him before the wedding, about meeting his mother and sister, he'll be livid. That's not the way I will begin my marriage."

"Please," cried Sophie, "Don't argue. I don't want Nick to be mad. *Maman*, we'll manage some way."

"How?" Catherine wailed. "Your father was rich. He promised to take care of us, but he didn't. I never had my own money. I never questioned anything. Now we must vacate this house in a week. I have sold all my jewelry. There's enough money for me to enroll you in private school for one term. Housing is scarce in the city. I don't know where else to go." She covered her face with her hands. "I'm a horrible mother, but—"

"No buts. You are. You've even got me beat in the horrible department," Chantel said.

"—I don't want Sophie to suffer. I didn't have any choice about Nick. They took him from me. I—"

"No. I don't want to hear the details of what happened back then," Biloxi snapped. "You must tell Nick before you tell me. He deserves that much."

"Yes, you're right." Catherine sat up and brushed her hair from her face. "I am at your mercy." She put her hand on top of Biloxi's.

"We are at your mercy," Sophie said quietly.

Pulling her hand away, Biloxi picked up the folder, pressing it to her chest. "I'm not making any promises. I'll tell Nick we met. If he wants to talk or meet with you, that will be his decision. He needs time to process this news. Unless he's adamant about not wanting anything to do with you, which I doubt will be the case,"—Sophie brightened for the first time in an hour—"I'll leave it up to you to share with him all you've told me. I will, however, give him this folder."

"I wish I could be at your wedding," Sophie whispered as she stood, her expression imploring.

Chantel sighed, shook her head. "We can find our way out." She stepped to the door and opened it. "Let's go, Biloxi. We've lived an entire day in just the last hour."

Catherine's pain pierced Biloxi's heart. How could she not help them, even if Nick refused?

Once outside, she pushed on her sunglasses. This end of the Quarter was mostly empty, not crowded with tourists like the area closer to Canal Street. Quiet soothed her nerves.

"I'm in shock," Chantel said. "I've known the

Trahan family for a long time, but I never bothered to understand Nick's situation."

When Biloxi took the second step in the direction from which they'd come earlier, Chantel reached for her hand and squeezed. "If you need me, girl, I'm here. If Nick gets mad and you want to vent, I'm here. But don't do anything that will cause either of you to need mouth-to-mouth, because I don't do that."

Biloxi chuckled. Tension began to lessen with each step they took farther from the house. Taking in the surroundings, she mused about the plain walls and unadorned doors lining the sidewalk. Much happened beyond the ordinariness of those walls. New Orleans was famous for its luxurious hidden courtyards where secrets played out.

"Thank you," she told Chantel. "This was quite a shock." If Chantel weren't walking beside her, she'd wonder if she hadn't dreamt it.

"That's what friends are for," Chantel replied.

Ahead, the skyline of modern New Orleans, a city of contrasts, stretched tall above the historical French Quarter. She contemplated asking Chantel to accompany her to have her fortune told in Jackson Square, but she'd had enough surprises for one day. Any more challenges and she'd crawl into bed and stay for a year.

From behind, the rev of an engine startled her. She stopped. Chantel halted her progress, too. As Biloxi turned to look over her shoulder, a shiny white sports coupe came roaring down the street. Glare on the windshield and darkly tinted windows made it impossible to identify the driver. When the car passed beside her, the horn honked. Biloxi jumped and dropped the folder of papers. They drifted to the ground.

"How rude!" Chantel shouted, bending to help retrieve the documents. "And we think tourists are impossible. That car has a Louisiana temp tag. For shame."

Picking up the scattered pages, Biloxi sighed. "This is the picture of my life. Between the hurricane, Fleur de Lis, and now this, mess describes my life."

After leaving the artist's gallery with wedding attendant gifts in hand, Biloxi stewed about what, when, and how to tell Nick the truth about her day. Would he understand?

Chapter 7

Biloxi drove up the long drive to Nick's house. As the driveway curved, his truck came into sight. Her palms began to sweat. Why was he home?

With Sophie's sad eyes haunting her, Biloxi searched her mind for the best possible way to tell Nick about meeting his mother and breaking the news about his younger sister—so polite, so pretty, and so French.

Distracted, she slammed to a stop and threw the car into park. Taking the front steps two at a time, she reluctantly pushed forward to the door. When she shoved the key into the lock, the door opened. Nick stood there shirtless. His tanned broad chest tapered to a narrow waist. His arms stretched overhead and his fingers gripped the top of the doorjamb. He leaned carelessly, as though a model for one of her shoots. Her heartbeat shot upward. Her initial panic dissolved. Desire bloomed. The man never failed to excite her. Mesmerized by him, she swallowed.

"You're home?"

He took her hand and guided her inside. "Yes."

Confusion swept over her. "Why? You had a full day…"

Nick pulled her into his arms and lowered his lips until they barely touched hers. It was the lightest kiss. An invitation.

Forehead to forehead, he said, "I had to see you."

His whiskey-smooth baritone voice sent soothing vibrations through her. He was the Pied Piper, and she had no choice but to follow his tune. He massaged her shoulders before his strong, warm hands traveled down her arms. When his hands met hers, he laced their fingers together.

"Did you get what you went for in New Orleans?" He planted another light kiss on her lips.

Mood kill. Did he know? Guilt clogged her throat. She swallowed against it and nodded. It was a lie. She'd never told him one before.

"Great. Did you have a good time?"

A second ago, she wanted nothing more than for him to carry her off to bed, but now? She couldn't make love to him until she confessed what had taken place.

"Nick…"

"*Chèr.*" His husky voice confused her senses.

"Wait," she said, tugging back. "We need to talk."

He pulled her close. "And we will," he whispered. The warmth of his breath brushed her ear, sending shivers down her back. "After I tell you how much I love you and trust you. After I show you how much I worship your body—with my hands, lips, and…"

"I love it when you call me *chèr*," she said. "But I do have something important I need to tell you." Why did he bring up trust?

"Something like you love me, can't live without me? I believe in you. Believe in us. Nothing will ever come between us."

How did she fight charming and sexy? Confessing now would punish them both. He deserved her attention. Anything else would ruin the romantic mood. "It can wait."

Her news could wait a little while longer. He cared about her feelings, had a talent for making her feel so special and loved. He could coax her mind into letting go of any distractions. Her body responded to his touch until her insides curled deliciously tight. He had a gift for sending her to the end of the universe, riding an incredible high.

She dipped her chin and looked up at him. "Darlin', I'm feeling it." She pushed past him, grasped his hand, and pulled him along. Why had they ever thought waiting six months after they married to start a family was the most responsible thing to do?

She smiled. At least practicing now would only make it perfect then. If they had a girl, she hoped to convince Nick to name her after her many-great grandmother, Bridgette, an old-fashioned name to be sure, but honoring her ancestor was important. Nick wanted something more modern like Toni or Tessa. If they needed a boy's name, he insisted on Alexandre, named for one of his relatives from the 1700s.

"Biloxi Dutrey, I think I know what you want," Nick said, once they stood beside the bed.

Hopping up, she perched on her hands and knees, giving Nick a peek at her cleavage. She straightened, put the tip of her index finger on her bottom lip and fluttered her lashes innocently. "And what might that be Nicholas Trahan?"

"Come closer, *chèr,* and I'll show you."

Their lips met. Shivers and tingles raced through her.

"I'll worship your body," he whispered, pushing his fingers into her hair.

Delighted, she nodded. Desire and need rolled into

one. Giddy anticipation bloomed into craving. A second later, Nick sat beside her. Her clothes went flying, her bra and panties landed on top of the pile on the floor. When she reached for his shirt, he playfully pushed her hands away and yanked off his clothes.

Biloxi giggled. "I think that's a record. I've never seen you strip so fast." Her hand traveled slowly down his chest, inching closer to the prize.

He grabbed her around the waist and flipped her on her back. "We're not going to hurry with the rest of this. He peppered her face with feathery kisses, then licked from the hallow of her neck up to her ear, setting her core on fire. Squirming beneath him, she arched her hips, offering herself, then reached for his hardness, but he drew back just beyond her grasp.

"Slow, *chèr*. I'm not going anywhere."

With gentle caring, he touched her, his palms brushing her skin so tenderly. He stroked her breast. Need ricocheted through her body. She strained to reach him. When she sank back into the bed, she tried again to guide him to her spot craving connection, but he resisted. He moved as his tongue traced a line down her stomach. He sucked her fingertips. Trembling, she tried to keep from fighting him to give her body some relief. Coiled tension in her core tightened more.

"Nick," she moaned, clutching the comforter as though that would keep her from exploding. "Please, please."

"What do you want, *chèr*? What more can I give you?" He slid his finger from her belly button, dipping lower until he reached her hidden nub.

"Nick," she moaned. "Baby, now. Please. I can't hold on. Don't make me go without you."

His body covered hers. His hardness slid inside her. Joy washed over her as she tightened around him. The first wave of bliss hit her at his first deep thrust.

"Again," she commanded. She wrapped her legs around his hips and hung on. His motions were fluid. His strength rocked her. Her body tightened and relaxed.

"Faster, Nick. Fast." Her body hungered for satisfaction. As she rocked in rhythm with him, heat rolled through her. Her mind blanked. Waves of sensations flooded her, taking her higher. A deep moan escaped from her lips. Nick's moan joined hers. Glorious sounds filled her ears.

Slowly, she drifted down, down, back to earth. Awareness became reality. The weight of Nick's body on hers.

"Ahhh," she sighed.

Nick rolled to his side, taking her with him. He nipped at her breast. "I love you."

"Oh, Nick," she whispered. "I love you."

He rested his hand on the curve of her hip. His eyes closed. "You hold my heart in your hands."

Her heart tripped from the cocoon of love back into reality. "Nick?" she whispered. No answer. "Darlin' I need to talk with you."

"Hmm?" he mumbled. "Later."

Sighing, Biloxi wiggled close to him. She flipped the comforter over them, wrapping them in a cocoon of bedding. There was no crime in afternoon delight or Nick napping. It would give her time to find the right words to tell him about meeting his mother. He trusted her. He had to understand. Besides, family meant everything to him. Someday, they'd make one of their own.

Family…the ache of missing the Old Aunts surfaced and seeped into her heart. Their presence had been the life-beat of the clan at Fleur de Lis for…forever. Family meant everything to her, too. But as a new bride, under no uncertain terms, would she allow Cat to live with them. She'd waited a very long while to marry this man. The reward for that—serenity, which would come after she and Nick married and just the two of them lived in his house.

No sister-in-law.

No mother-in-law.

But would he agree?

Chapter 8

When the weekend rolled around, a limo pulled under the portico of the casino in Tunica, Mississippi. "We're here," the chauffer announced. "If you'll wait a moment, I'll unload your bags."

Nick stretched his legs and bumped the plastic bowl resting on the floor. The poker chips inside clattered together. His bachelor party weekend provided time for him to think, stew really, on the story Biloxi told him last night about his mother. It had taken several days for her to get up enough courage to tell him. He'd waited, given her time to share what he already knew, because he trusted her. But the waiting had torqued his patience.

If he hadn't seen her and Chantel leaving the Royal Street address, he might have been tempted to disbelieve her, but the truth flashed brightly like a red neon sign in the middle of a black desert night. He hadn't seen Cat in over twenty years, and she'd invited his fiancée to visit her before him. It stung. Plus, she lived so close, yet hadn't sought him out for nearly a year. That pain soured in his stomach. Soon he'd have more answers. The PI was meeting with Cat at that exact moment.

"Stop your frowning, Nick. You won every hand of poker on the trip over," Linc, Biloxi's brother, complained. "If I didn't know better, I'd say you cheated. It would've been cheaper for me to rent a plane and pay for fuel than play poker with you."

Nick slowly smiled wide. "You'll be flying for hire soon enough. It's not the same as going up for pleasure. Besides, isn't it one of the rules of a bachelor party—to let the groom win?" He eyed James Newbern, Branna's husband, Carson, Branna's brother, Jared Richardson, Camilla's boyfriend, and Linc.

"Watch it now," James cautioned. "You're marrying into a volatile family. No need to create additional problems."

"You're telling me? I'm officially ending the Trahan-Dutrey feud. No one ever hated a Trahan more than a Dutrey."

"I, for one, can't wait until the wedding is over," Jared chimed in. "Camilla insisted we wait until after you're married to set a final date for ours. Now, she's saying after your wedding"—he punched Nick in the arm—"she wants to head to Cody for the summer. Help her friend Haley with her new riding business since it's going to be another six months of construction to finish Fleur de Lis Café. I don't want to wait. I want to marry that woman tomorrow."

"Riding? Camilla doesn't ride," Carson interjected. "Send me video of her on a horse. That'll go viral," he chuckled.

Jared leaned back, putting his hands behind his neck. "Son, you don't know how fine your sister looks atop a horse." He appeared to think on memories of his soon-to-be bride.

Nick picked up the bowl of poker chips. "Shall we take a bet on which one of us has the most tempestuous mother-in-law?"

The limo driver interrupted the betting when he opened the door. "The doorman has your bags on a cart waiting at registration for you."

Nick insisted his party exit the vehicle before him.

"Thanks," Nick said, handing the man a hundred-dollar tip. "See you Sunday afternoon."

"Sure thing, Dr. Trahan."

Sliding glass doors *whooshed* open as Nick approached the lobby. *Ding. Bing. Clink.* Sounds of slot machines in the background created a thrum of excitement, offering the promise of great wins.

Once registered and checked into their rooms, Nick gathered his group in his room. Pouring a shot of whiskey into five glasses sent up from room service, he lifted his. "To some of the finest men I know. I really lucked out with Biloxi. Smart, talented, and so family oriented. I never thought when I took a wife, I'd gain a band of brothers. To you, gentlemen."

They clinked glasses and drank.

"As best man, I've got the schedule planned. Golf, then dinner, then gambling." Linc passed out cards with the itinerary. "Tomorrow is a repeat of today. Sunday is sleeping in, then male spa time."

Jared and James groaned.

"Hot shaves," Linc continued, ignoring the two. "Massages and haircuts for all." He grinned wide. "And just for Nick—a *man*icure. Your hand's gotta look good when my sister slides the ring on it."

Nick rolled his eyes. He was about to retort when the phone rang. Carson, sitting closest to it, answered. "Yeah. Okay." Then he hung up.

"Shit. It doesn't pay to eavesdrop on you," Jared said.

"The van is downstairs ready to take us to the golf course. Plantation Oaks has agreed to allow us to play as a five-some. Two carts. Linc and I are driving."

"Yes, Capt'n." Nick saluted. "Let's go."

They arrived at the resort course a half hour later. "I need to replace my putter," Jared said. "Once you get the cart, pick me up over here."

"That's not a bad idea," Nick said. "I'll join you."

Inside the large golf shop, Nick pointed to the display of putters. A sand wedge caught his eye, "I'll be over there." He kept Jared in sight as he tested a club.

Jared selected a new putter, dropped a ball from a bucket, and then took a swing, sending the ball into a hole in the floor.

"Nice," a man said, approaching Jared.

Nick tensed. He'd never been properly introduced, but was familiar with the face of the man whose picture often landed in the local paper. Steven Sterling. Branna's ex-fiancé. Whatever caused Branna to call off the wedding remained a mystery still, but the name Sterling brought out an aloofness in her like no other.

Jared took another putt, made it on the first try.

"Hello," the man said, offering his hand. "I'm Steven."

"Nice to meet you." Jared shook his hand. "Jared."

Nick marched into the conversation. "Jared, we need to go. Think that putter will do?"

Jared raised an eyebrow. "Just a minute more. I want to try out a few more."

"That's *exactly* what I did," Steven said before turning and leaving without acknowledging Nick.

"What was that all about?" Jared asked.

"I don't know. Pick a putter. I'll be outside with

the guys waiting."

When Nick reached the golf cart, Linc pulled him aside. "I need to get something off my chest. I've been waiting for you to say something about it, but nothing." He shook his head. "Biloxi told me you want your dad for your best man. I want you to know it's cool. I can do that. I understand he wasn't around most of your life, and now you're reconnected." Linc shifted his weight from one leg to the other. He lifted his hands in surrender. "I promise. No hard feelings."

Nick frowned and raked his fingers through his hair. "Look, I didn't say anything because some other things have come up, *and* I don't want to start another family feud."

"If it will make things easier, I can always say that I withdrew."

"Nope. That's not going to happen. I want you as my best man. There may be a surprise guest at the wedding…and I don't want my dad to lose it if he sees her."

"Her?"

"Linc, you're my best man." Nick slapped him on the back. "Let's go play golf and not worry about anything else."

The afternoon sun beat down as Nick took his place at the first tee. "Drive for show. Putt for dough. We're playing best ball. The person with the most strokes on each hole buys drinks tonight." After placing the ball on the tee, Nick planted his feet and set up his swing. In his mind, he was stepping up to the altar to marry his bride.

"Come on, Nick, take a swing," Carson urged.

Pushing aside the daydream, Nick focused on the

task in front of him. He hit the ball.

Wack.

It flew straight down the fairway at least two hundred yards.

"Shit. Is there anything you aren't good at?" Carson asked.

Jared used the handle of his club to push up the brim of his hat. "Damn."

"Yep, guys. Damn. I'm good."

But in his mind's eye, his father as his best man crashed to the ground before the wedding ever began. Standing at the altar allowed a straight-arrow shot of Cat in a pew. No matter how Nick imagined what happened next, there was no good outcome. Nope. He only needed one best man. Linc had been there from the beginning. From the first night he and Biloxi met. He would have one best man, three groomsmen, one father, *and* one mother at the wedding.

This time the feud would be contained to only those with the Trahan name. But what would that mean for Biloxi, once she became one, too?

Chapter 9

Biloxi paced Nick's living room while he talked on the phone. The end to their weekend surprised both of them.

Something about Cat had made her question setting a time for an introduction. Instead of ruminating on the problem, she pushed ahead with wedding festivities. Her bachelorette party weekend had gone off without a hitch—almost.

Branna, Camilla, Nola, Evie, Melony, and other cousins roamed the streets of the French Quarter in boas and tiaras, making appropriate spectacles of themselves. Those not underage sipped on frozen daiquiris. They played silly games of truth and dare. Sophie kissed a mime on his box. The man played dead. Camilla had danced in the street like a wild woman to music from a sidewalk band.

All of the women in the family, especially her sister, Nola, had taken Sophie under their wing. Cat had been a no-show, which was no big deal. None of the other mothers were allowed. Biloxi had only extended the invitation to Cat as a courtesy.

Then, on Sunday evening, the big blow came.

Branna had hired a limo to deliver everyone safely home. The driver made Sophie's house on Royal Street the first stop. The limo had barely pulled away from the curb when the girl screamed and chased after the car.

Biloxi sighed. Now she had a teenaged, almost-sister-in-law, sleeping on a cot in the office at Fleur de Lis. The poor girl hadn't even met Nick yet. There was no other place to put her after her mother packed up the Royal Street house, sans Sophie's belongings, and disappeared. Poor Nick. His mother took off again.

Only this time, she left the best part of her behind. Sophie.

In time, Biloxi hoped Nick would come to understand that.

Cat didn't deserve a son like him. Clearly, Sophie and Nick had a bond, something significant in common. A runaway mother.

"What!" Nick shouted over the phone at the PI who had more news for him. "Just great!"

Nick ended the call and flopped on the couch. Rolling angry energy emanated from him. She'd never seen him like that before. Chantel's warning niggled the recesses of her brain. No matter—they'd weather any problem together. She would never walk away from a fight. Neither would Nick. They'd proven that to each other when their families threatened to disown them for dating.

She sat next to him and ran her hand down his arm. "Tell me. How bad can it be?"

"She filed divorce papers."

"Nick, that's not necessarily a bad thing."

"She's left the country."

"What? To go where?"

"France."

"But…but…"

"It seems my mother is not at a loss for suitors. According to the PI, Mrs. Trahan hopped a plane for

France. The furniture and her belongings are in storage here. My mother's nickname is so fitting. She's a cat with nine lives, always landing on her feet."

"Yeah, but only after she's tries to kill her young, metaphorically speaking, of course," Biloxi said, disgusted.

"We're getting married in five days," Nick groaned.

"You say it like it's a bad thing."

"No, *chèr,* but I never wanted my family to cause problems for us." He kissed her forehead. "I want you to have the wedding of your dreams. Drama-free."

"And *we* will," she insisted. "Nick, it's *our* wedding, not *my* wedding."

"Thank you for including my sister in your bachelorette party. That came as a bit of a surprise."

"I like Sophie," she said, kissing his cheek.

"So you've met my mother. I only remember her through the eyes of a child. And now I have a sister I never knew existed. Your mother's going to kill me if any of this messes up the wedding."

"I'll say it again. It's *our* wedding. If we're fine with it, she'll be fine with it—well, we'll just ignore her. But first things first. Tomorrow you need to meet your sister. How do you think your father is going to take all of this news?"

"My father?"

"Yes. Edward."

Nick rose and paced back and forth in front of the fireplace. He stopped and leaned against the mantel. "I haven't told him about Cat. He knows nothing about Sophie."

"Nick!"

"I know. But until I could meet her and get answers to my questions, I didn't want to involve him. Can you imagine? Married for thirty plus years and never setting eyes on each other for over twenty? Then she had a child with another man?" He huffed out a deep sigh. "That's not the kind of marriage I want."

"Nor I. Are you going to tell him?"

"Not unless I have to. Damn Grandmère and your grandmother. If they'd never set eyes on her, no one would ever have to know about any of this."

"Except…there's Sophie. Cat came back for a reason, which we may never fully know. But I believe she wanted to see you. I think she wants you to take care of Sophie. Maybe there's more to the story. Maybe she really is sick."

"Abandoned by Cat. It's something Sophie and I have in common."

"She's part of the family. If anyone sees her, it's clear she's related to you."

"She's not a Trahan."

"But she's your sister, nonetheless."

"What do you want me to do?" Nick sank into the seat beside her.

"Tomorrow, you'll meet her. We have to decide where she's going to live and go to school. Do you trust me?"

Nick pulled her onto his lap and she straddled his hips. He settled his hands on hers. "I trust you with my life." His mouthed nipped at her lips until they parted. When their lips met fully, she sagged against him. Tingling desire bloomed, and heat raced through her veins. He was definitely a drug. One she'd want forever.

"Leave everything to me—about the wedding—and this." She slid back and moved off the couch. "Follow me, *chèr*." She tried to sound mysterious and alluring.

"Upstairs?" Nick asked.

She tugged on his hand and pulled him to standing. Tossing the couch pillows on the floor, she said, "The first time we made love was right there"—she pointed in front of the fireplace—"and it seems appropriate to revisit old times." She winked and began to undress.

"You take care of the wedding," Nick said, pulling her close. "As for tonight, leave everything to me."

She loved it when he took control.

****

The next day, Biloxi escorted Sophie to the front gallery of Fleur de Lis. The teen rubbed a worry stone while marching back and forth. She looked like any other American teenager in jeans, pink t-shirt, and sandals.

"Sophie, sit," Biloxi insisted, pointing to the chair next to her. The teen's pacing was about to wear a pattern in the new boards. She didn't want Sophie to sense her own worry. What would she do if Nick didn't take to Sophie? She seemed younger and more innocent than her age. It wasn't like they could ship her off to France. No one had a new address for Cat. And that's probably exactly as she planned it.

Biloxi sighed and settled into a chair. She took in the sounds of hammers and saws. Construction continued on the café. Jared had somehow found a way to speed up the completion of the project. She looked forward to his walk down the aisle with Camilla. The growing family at Fleur de Lis meant more joy and love to spread around. It marked a new beginning, one without the presences of the Old Aunts, but their wisdom and love she would always carry in her heart. As for Nick, the thing he cherished most—family—had gifted him with a half-sister. At least their mother had given them each other.

Sophie finally flopped into the empty rocking chair beside her. "But, what if he doesn't like me?"

Biloxi's heart clenched. How could Cat have abandoned her child?

"Not possible." Biloxi squeezed her future sister-in-law's hand, trying to allay her fears. "He's tall…with broad shoulders. He looks imposing, but I promise, he's a marshmallow." She crinkled her nose trying to make the girl laugh.

"I only saw him in a picture from the newspaper." Her shoulders slumped.

"I've been talking to his grandmother, Suzette. I think we've worked out a solution for you for the fall."

"Really?" The hopefulness in Sophie's expression strengthened Biloxi's determination.

"Suzette speaks French, which will be a help for you. We've found a wonderful private school for you in Baton Rouge."

"So, you'll send me away?"

"Oh, no." Biloxi kneeled beside Sophie's chair. "That's not what we're doing. Schools aren't up to full capacity—the hurricane we had did so much damage. You can't *not* go to school. Suzette has a big house, and she'll provide a good home."

"But I like it here. I won't be a bother."

"You'll come home on the weekends—when you want to. I know once you get involved at school, you'll make friends." She laughed. "You won't want to come here every weekend. And when you don't, we'll come to you. I'll need my Sophie fix."

"But I have the summer here?"

"Absolutely. Oh, look. There's Nick's truck." She pointed at his pickup coming up the front drive. She giggled to herself about the first night they met. She'd demanded that he not drive to the front, but to the back. She'd had a silly idea about sneaking into Fleur de Lis and making a grand entrance. Someday she would share that story with Sophie.

Nick parked and climbed out.

Biloxi and Sophie stood at the railing. Biloxi blew him kiss.

"*Mais*, if I ain't a lucky one. Two beautiful women waiting for me."

Before Biloxi could turn toward the stairs, Sophie was running down. She launched herself at him. Biloxi held her breath. Clearly startled, Nick opened his arms and caught the girl.

"Nick!" Sophie cried. She clung tightly to him.

Biloxi raced down the stairs. She paused a few feet away. Nick's eyes opened wider than she'd ever seen them. When Sophie hugged him tighter, his expression softened.

"Nick, this is your sister, Sophie."

"Hello, Sophie." He set her on her feet and wrapped an arm around her shoulders. "It's nice to finally meet you."

Suddenly shy, Sophie took a step away. "I am so happy to have a brother."

"Yes, well," Nick stammered. "We have a lot to learn about each other."

"And y'all don't have to do it all in one day," Biloxi interjected, reaching for Sophie's hand. "Let's go have some lunch. I know Greta has fixed something special. Fried chicken. Just for Nick. It's his favorite."

"But you said he'll eat anything," Sophie said.

"Ah. Well…he's really marrying me, so he can get Greta as part of the package."

Nick frowned at her. "What I failed to understand before is, there are so many of y'all around that I'm getting a band of brothers, too. I'm not the only male addition to the family. I'm in damn good company with James and Jared."

"Do you swear much?" Sophie asked as she climbed the stairs.

Biloxi laughed. Nick appeared perplexed.

"Not a lot," she told Sophie.

"Good. *Maman* always told me cursing shows a lack of culture and intelligence."

"A good lesson for all of us to learn." Biloxi smiled. The girl channeled the Old Aunts.

"Nick, I love animals. Do you treat horses? Someday, I want a horse."

"Oh, Sophie, do I have a story to tell you about Nick, Captain Jack, and his horse and buggy," Biloxi said.

Together, the three of them entered the house. "I think with Sophie here for the summer, Fleur de Lis will be complete," Biloxi said, happy to have unease that had been shadowing her finally gone.

Chapter 10

Biloxi rolled over to shut off the alarm. The nap had revived her. Excitement ramped up to warp speed. Her day had finally arrived. In only a few hours she would officially be Mrs. Nicholas Trahan. Fingers trembling, she picked up the framed photo of Nick from the nightstand next to her bed. "I love you," she said, then closed her eyes and clutched the picture to her chest. "Our new life is about to begin."

She imagined him standing tall and proud in his black tux and light gray vest. He and his guys picked out the tuxedos—alone. He did say his handkerchief would be lavender, to match her flowers, while his guys were made to wear deep pink pocket squares to match her attendant's dresses.

"Knock, knock," Branna called.

"I'm up," Biloxi shouted.

Branna entered with Greta, who beamed as though she were the mother of the bride.

"I'm here to help you with your hair and makeup," Greta said.

"I'm sure it will go smoothly," Biloxi chuckled. "We've practice it at least ten times."

Greta made her way to the closet and pulled out a folding chair. Next, she opened the top drawer of the dressing table, taking the makeup bag from it.

"I'm herding the girls into my room to dress,"

Branna explained. "I think Sophie is…not quite sure what to make of all of this. She seems a little reluctant."

"Just be gentle with her," Biloxi insisted. "Weddings are busy, noisy, and overwhelming, even for me, and it's *my* wedding."

"Sit," Greta ordered Biloxi. "Branna, go."

"You heard the boss." Branna backed out of the room bowing.

An hour later, with her hair pulled back in cascading loose curls and wearing demure makeup, Biloxi stood in front of the mirror. "I don't think I've ever felt so pretty. I hope Nick likes it."

Harrumph. Greta snorted. "He'd marry you regardless of what you had on. That man is as smitten as they come."

A knock sounded at the door. "We're here," Camilla called out.

Biloxi turned toward the parade entering her bedroom.

Branna, Camilla, Nola, Evie, Melonie, and Sophie, all in full wedding regalia, marched into her room.

"The florist just delivered these. The house is decorated. Flowers and candles and crystals everywhere." Branna, the matron of honor, carried the bridal bouquet of pink and lavender roses, baby's breath, greenery, and soft pink ribbon trailing the floor. The elegance of the bouquet stopped Biloxi's breath. It was more regal and elegant than she imagined, having only seen it in photographs.

The rest of her entourage showed off their flowers—three pink roses and baby's breath wrapped in a white lace cuff with pearls. The tea-length deep pink bridesmaid dresses flared out from the layered crinolines hiding underneath, a fifties-inspired creation. The strappy white sandals with rhinestones offered the perfect bling.

"Happy wedding day," Nola cried. She came to the bed and kissed Biloxi's cheek. "You are going to be a gorgeous bride. Momma is being a good girl. She has *asked*, though I won't say it was entirely polite, to come up and see you."

"The photographer is downstairs, waiting for the word to begin," Branna said. "As you instructed, we'll start the photos of us on the stairs. The lighting in the upstairs landing is perfect, just as you said it would be for photos of the bride and her girls."

"I'm going to get ready," Greta said. "I'll leave you in Branna's hands. She's the wedding expert."

"Ladies," Biloxi announced. "Please assemble outside and down the hall on the landing. Branna is going to help me slip into my dress after my mother comes up. The room is too crowded for all of us."

A few minutes later, Deidre entered. Her hand flew to her chest. "You are breathtaking."

With Branna's help, Biloxi slipped into an ivory silk organza and French lace gown. Branna gingerly moved the full circle skirt so neither she nor Deidre would step on it. Biloxi adjusted the long sheer lace sleeves.

"I was so mad at you for not allowing me to help you pick out your dress." Deidra reached for a chair as though standing a minute more might cause her to collapse.

"While I appreciate that choosing a gown is supposed to be an event, with everything going on since the storm, I did it all on my own. I knew exactly what I wanted. Momma, would you button up the back?"

Branna stepped aside and snapped a few photos of Deidre assisting Biloxi.

"The dress is stunning. I love the lace and the open back."

Biloxi nodded. "I love the way it flows. This is the perfect dress for me."

Once the dress was buttoned, Biloxi went to the full-length mirror to examine her image. "It's hard for me to believe this is really me."

"Branna, would you be so lovely as to give me a moment alone with my daughter?"

"Sure, Aunt Deidre. Biloxi, I'll be right outside."

Deidre went to the closet and retrieved a box. Biloxi's wedding heels. She bent before her daughter and helped her slip on the shoes. When Biloxi stood to her new height, Deidre stood behind her. Together they gazed into the mirror.

"I'm so proud of you." Deidre rested her chin on Biloxi's shoulder. "You're absolutely beautiful. But do you know the best part?" She stepped from behind Biloxi and faced her. Pushing a curl over Biloxi's shoulder, she said, "You are even more beautiful on the inside."

Biloxi drew back. Who was in habiting her mother? Had Momma just paid her a compliment? "Ah…I don't know what to say."

"You have a truly golden heart," Deidre insisted. "You work hard to get what you want, but you're not unwilling to compromise. You did a wonderful thing last night at the rehearsal dinner."

"I did? Which part?" Biloxi asked suspiciously. If she waited a bit, the other shoe would drop. Her mother had to have something negative to say.

"You introduced Sophie to Edward. When you took him aside and explained Sophie's plight, I was convinced Edward would walk out—after all, his wife had a child with another man, and now had dumped that child on their son. Yet, you convinced him to show compassion. He never had a daughter. He missed out on so much of Nick's life. Here was a chance to have another connection to Nick."

"I didn't think of it as a sales pitch," Biloxi explained.

"I know, darlin', but nonetheless, you did the trick. And then Suzette. She now has a girl to spoil. You found the perfect school in Baton Rouge for Sophie."

"Momma, I'm not trying to shove her off on Suzette. It's the best place for Sophie. They have an international student body with dozen of languages spoken. Sophie is fluent in both French and English."

Her mother grasped her hands. "Biloxi, you aren't listening to me. I'm saying I am sooo proud of you. I know if there was a good school for Sophie here, you'd send her there, but you're doing what's best for her. Any news from her horrible mother?"

Biloxi narrowed her eyes and pursed her lips. "Don't go there, Mother."

"Mother? You must be mad at me."

"Momma," Biloxi sighed. "Thank you for seeing my deeds as a kindness to Sophie." She hugged her. "Thank you even more for not making a big deal about me adding one more bridesmaid to the party. And thank you for being so warm and welcoming to Sophie. You keep this up, and we'll have to downgrade Hurricane Deidre to a tropical depression."

Together they laughed.

"I only wanted the best for you. Nick is it." Deidre said, standing back and looking Biloxi over head to toe.

"Wait just a minute. You tried to dissuade Nick from dating me."

"Honey, if a man is so easily put off by a girl's mother, then he doesn't deserve her. It was my reverse psychology." Deidre winked.

"What am I going to do with you?" Biloxi kissed her mother's check.

Deidre shrugged. "I don't know? Help me find a good woman for Linc when it's time? Right now, we're going to have pictures made, and then get you to the church for the wedding."

****

After the priest proclaimed Biloxi and Nick husband and wife, Nick held out his arm to escort his bride down the aisle. Tucking her hand in the crook of his arm, he said, "I can't believe this day is finally here. I have the perfect wife. Dreams do come true. And, I have a special gift for you."

Biloxi lifted her chin and looked up. Her expressive eyes twinkled and conveyed her feelings. Just a look from her made his heart race like a randy stallion.

"I love you madly," she said. The softness of her tone, along with the conviction it carried warmed him. He'd been right to wait for the perfect woman. She was everything and more. Because of her, her compassion and understanding, his immediate family had begun to heal after his grandfather died. Now with his half-sister appearing, only to be abandoned by her mother again, Biloxi had smoothed the way, opening her heart and arms with love to the teenager. His love for her swelled.

"You know, *chèr.*" He paused when they reached the church doors. "We're a southern Romeo and Juliet with a happy ending." He kissed her soundly. The crowd in the pews behind them burst into applause as they began to file out of the church around the couple.

"Guess we get to write a new ending to that story." Biloxi grinned. Her face shone with joy and love.

"Let's go," Nick said, crossing the threshold. He couldn't wait to see her expression. Linc had parked the car at the end of the sidewalk. Would she recognize it?

She laced her fingers through his, then stopped suddenly. "What's that?"

Nick grinned. "That, Mrs. Trahan, is your chariot."

"I don't understand."

"Rather than getting you a horse and carriage, I'm giving you horse power. Do you recognize the car?"

She paused. Their eyes locked, then she stared for a moment at the car.

"In the French Quarter, that was me in this—the day you went to visit my mother. I never mentioned it. I wanted to confront you, I wanted answers, but I couldn't give away this surprise. And that's all in the past. Think of the fun we'll have driving along the beach with the wind in our hair, the stars shining overhead, and the sound of the surf to relax us."

"I...I never dreamed..."

"I love you." Nick pulled her gently into his arms as though none of the cheers and chatter from friends and relatives was taking place around them. In that moment, only they existed in their own cocoon. After placing a kiss on her lips, Nick said, "Our future awaits."

Linda Joyce

Camilla

by

Linda Joyce

Dedication

This book is dedicated to those who strive
to make their lives better
and love those around them unconditionally.

Prologue

Tired, dirty, and smelling like a sweaty construction worker, Camilla Lind parked at Fleur de Lis and dragged herself from the SUV. The space next to her was open. Jared hadn't arrived home yet. Her heart sank. Work had become his mistress. How did she compete with that? It was one of the reasons she delayed setting a wedding date. They'd been tossed into turmoil…since they first met. Was true love enough to ensure a lasting marriage when these days they scarcely had a relationship?

Dusk was falling, and a few stars twinkled in the September evening sky. She worked most days until there wasn't enough light to see, and one more step was impossible. But it was a good tired. Her aching muscles complained. It was as though they shouted through a megaphone in her ears, but helping others gave her a sense of worth. With a weak wave of her hand, she motioned to Greta who waited at the top of the steps of the back gallery.

"I feel guilty coming home to a completed house and a nice bed." Camilla trudged up the stairs. When she reached the top, Greta pushed a cup of hot tea into her hands.

"So many people still need so much. We've passed the one year mark. I never thought recovery would take this long." Camilla sipped the warm beverage, hoping it would revive her enough to climb the stairs to a shower and her bed. Otherwise, she'd be zombified in the morning. She wondered if Jared would make it home before she zonked out for the night. Once asleep, there was no waking her. Their schedules didn't permit much time for lovemaking, let alone romance.

"Your volunteering is a full-time job," Greta said. "People are grateful for your time and expertise."

"I need to do something. I'm not needed here. I can't find a job. I don't want to go back to school." She shrugged. "And Jared is so busy—I'm really missing him. As for our business, you and I have already perfected all the recipes for the café—whenever we do finally get it opened. Nothing else for me to do, but help others until then."

She and Greta sat side by side in rocking chairs. Camilla took in the evening quiet only broken by the occasional squeak of a chair rocking. If she stayed another ten minutes, she'd be asleep.

"It's very different around here," Greta said wistfully.

"Yeah, with the Old Aunts gone… Sometimes I still forget."

"I had hoped Branna would move back. I could care for baby Anaëlle while she helped Biloxi keep things straight with estate business."

"Everything's changed, Greta." Camilla shook her head. So many things she'd taken for granted when she first left home with her head hung in shame were different. After working so hard to reform herself, to grow up and be a respectable and responsible adult, she had counted on coming home to the traditions and security that family and Fleur de Lis offered. But a monstrous storm changed everything.

On the plus side, Jared had not returned to Wyoming like she thought he might. When he arrived and rescued her during Hurricane Katrina, and even for a while after that, she expected him to leave. But the timing of the storm helped him launch his construction business in a big way. His expertise in new construction and restoration, including antique elements of historic homes and buildings, had put his services in high demand. In the last few months, she went several days without seeing him while he traveled for work.

Weary, she wanted a break from the constant battle of trying to make things right in the world. Taking Haley up on her invitation to come for a visit, to once again see the blue skies of Wyoming, grew daily in its appeal.

"Mr. Sterling called for you again today. I took his number *again*. What's going on, Camilla?"

"Nothing."

"That's a lie. Why is Branna's ex-fiancé leaving messages for you?"

"Next time he calls, please ask him to stop. There's nothing here for him. No one wants anything to do with him."

"But why? No one's ever told me what's lurking in the shadows. Not you. Not Branna. I'm guessing your momma knows, but even she hasn't confided in me." Greta sounded hurt to be excluded.

"Momma doesn't know. Believe me on that, but you know how you can't unring a bell? Well, I did something I can't undo. I will regret it all my life. Let's just say that Counselor Sterling had a hand in it. Now he needs to move on with his life. With that, I'm going to haul my body upstairs for a soak in the tub."

"I'll call up to you when dinner is ready."

"Don't wait on me. If you wouldn't mind, just put a plate in the oven." Camilla rose and kissed the top of Greta's head. "You're very good to me. I used to be jealous of Branna because she is firstborn. I was jealous of Biloxi because she's your favorite. Now, I'm happy to be me, and I'm thankful to you for taking care of me."

Greta squeezed her hand before she left to go inside.

Climbing the stairs, she wondered what Jared was doing that moment. An ache from missing him added to her weariness.

The irony of men in her life. When she wanted to be single and unattached, she had men hitting on her all the time. Now that she only wanted one man in her life…he was rarely around. Could she be losing him? Would their relationship die of boredom before it ever had a real chance to bloom? They needed some sort of excitement in their love life. They needed to do more than work all the time. Maybe she could entice him to come home earlier—like before she passed out from exhaustion. Maybe…a shopping trip to Mobile was in her future. Where was the best place to buy sexy lingerie?

That would entice any man, right?

Chapter 1

The October air brought lower humidity, but Mississippi temperatures remained warm compared to most everywhere else. In the comfort of air conditioning, Camilla paced the upstairs hallway. Any minute she hoped to hear the roar of Jared's truck. She missed him all week. Usually, work took him away for a day or two or four, but this time it was longer. His absence made her world incomplete, like gumbo without rice or bread pudding minus bourbon sauce.

Giddiness and nervousness blended into a cocktail, one she couldn't drink, but she enjoyed the feeling while daydreaming about him. After their last chat about Wyoming—he'd been adamant that his business was taking off, and he couldn't go—how would he respond to her decision to take a short vacation without him? She needed time away, and Haley offered the opportunity for an escape.

When the doorbell rang, she raced downstairs. "Jared!"

"Hello." A young man barely old enough to drive stood at the front door holding a large vase of pink roses nestled in a cloud of white baby's breath and wrapped with a satin green ribbon. A stunning arrangement.

"Well, hello, yourself," Camilla said, drawling out the words. The flowers melted her heart. Jared had missed her, too.

"For Miss Camilla Lind."

"That would be *moi*." She brought her hand to her chest. The new charm bracelet Jared had started for her dangled around her wrist, and the tinkling sound brought a smile to her lips. Her body shimmered with excitement. True love made each day brighter. Jared made the moon glow. He possessed a generous heart. Whenever he was away for any length of time, he always brought a gift. "A reminder," he'd said, "of how special you are."

The delivery guy handed over the vase, then picked up a device from the small table near the rocking chair. "Please sign showing receipt."

Camilla scribbled her name. "Wait, let me give you a tip."

"Not necessary. I've been well paid for this order."

"Then, thank you." She closed the door and set the vase on the table in the foyer before plucking the card from between the flower stems. Smiling, she did a quick happy dance as she opened the note.

Miss you. See you soon.

~Lover Boy

The signing of the card struck her as odd, but Jared had been away for nearly a week. Maybe he was feeling especially amorous? Any moment he would pull around back by the kitchen, climb the stairs to the back gallery, and drop into one of the rocking chairs. In a flash, Greta would be out the door with a glass of sweet tea and an offer of bread pudding.

Her thoughts wandered to after dinner when they would stroll together through the garden, then later after Greta had gone to bed, they'd dance—she giggled at their secret euphemism—at the *garçonnière* in private. Despite the passing of the Old Aunts, the legacy of their family traditions, carved by generations at Fleur de Lis, remained ingrained.

Picking up the vase, Camilla carried it to the dining room before heading upstairs to her room. After slipping into a denim dress and donning the turquoise leather cowboy boots Haley, her friend from Wyoming had sent, she brushed her hair and applied lip gloss, checking the mirror for smudges. Surely, Jared would arrive on time. She checked her phone. Still no call or message from him.

Ding. Dong.

She raced back downstairs, her heart racing faster. With a short hop, she planned to launch herself in Jared's arms. This weeklong separation had been the longest since before the storm last year. She ached for the feel of his lips pressed against hers and his fingers in her hair.

Grabbing for the doorknob, she flung the door open. "Hel—" Her words halted. Her brain screeched to a stop. She blinked. Swallowed hard.

"Hello, Camilla." Steven Sterling stood on the opposite side of the threshold.

She drew back to close the door, but it refused to shut all the way. Camilla pushed harder.

"Would you pause for a second? That's my foot you're trying to murder, which is still a capital offense in Mississippi."

Opening the door just enough for him to remove his foot, she ordered, "Leave."

"Now, Camilla, is that any way to greet an old family friend?"

"Friend!" She jerked open the door. "You arrogant, self-centered, ego-maniacal—"

"Wait. Give me a chance. You've changed. So have I." When he grinned his silver-dollar smile, she clenched her fists, her nails biting into the palms of her hands, to keep from punching him. There was a time when that smile meant something, but now it made her stomach knot.

"What do you want? You're not welcome here." She'd managed to avoid him since returning home. Thankfully, Branna's impromptu wedding had quashed his impertinent self-invitation to attend her wedding. Afterward, news got around that he had taken a job in the attorney general's office up in Jackson. And he'd left town with a new fiancée.

"The storm changed so many things. It changed me." He stepped closer. "And I want a chance for you to see the new me."

"Why?" She folded her arms over her chest.

"Because I've realized that you're a free spirit, able to break away from"—he huffed out a deep sigh—"all the chains of tradition, to live, really enjoy your life. I admire that about you. I've been watching from afar. We could be good together. And I want a second chance."

"There can't be a second time because we never had a first. We did a horrible thing. Horrible thing to my sister."

"But we were good together."

Crack! Her open palm made contact with his cheek. She shook out the sting. "You haven't changed."

Steven's eyes sharpened. "I'm sure I deserve that." His voice was low and even. "I'll take my licks for now. All I'm asking is that you give me a chance."

"No. Leave. If you don't, I'll get Greta to make you."

"You're home alone."

The smug grin on his face made her want to kick him in the crotch. Taking a few short breaths, she frowned and tapped her toe. "Greta is in the kitchen waiting for our company to arrive."

"No, she's not. I waved at her as I came from town."

She couldn't outmaneuver him, a professional liar, with a lie. The truth always worked better anyway. "Steven, I will accept that you may have changed. But that doesn't open the door for you to enter my life." Anger and disgust hit like a tsunami. All her muscles tensed. She counted the seconds it would take to grab the lamp on the table and hit him if he took another step closer.

"But you did—you opened the door for me. I want to make amends. All I'm asking for is a chance to show you how I've changed, and what you mean to me."

Sincerity from Steven? Laughable. She stepped forward, pushed him back several steps, and closed the front door behind her.

"The past is the past. You don't exist in the present."

"Camilla, I've been engaged twice." He winced as though he was sorry for his past. Had she been too harsh? Maybe he had changed. Even so, he wasn't welcomed at Fleur de Lis.

A pang of guilt gnawed at her. Her manners were inhospitable. Their illicit relationship had ruined his first engagement to her sister. She wondered what ended his second.

"I've been with a lot of women," he continued, "and so it is with good authority and an aching heart, I confess, I've never wanted a woman, any woman, like I wanted you. Want you."

"I'm engaged."

She wanted to wipe away his grin.

"Now, there's engaged and there's *engaged*. I've heard that about you for months now, even when I was up in Jackson, but no word of a wedding date. So"—he stepped closer and took her hand in his—"that must mean there's trouble in paradise."

She jerked away. To prove she cared nothing for him, to reinforce her earlier words, she sat in a rocking chair on the porch and folded her hands, left one on top of the right to show off her engagement ring. "Shows what you know, counselor. I'm very happy. Completely in love. Now will you remove yourself from the porch and don't come back? There's nothing here for you."

Squatting beside the chair, he put his hand on the armrest for balance. Camilla kept her eyes straight ahead, staring down the long drive to the road. Steven leaned in. The heat of his breath touched her cheek.

"You can't deny what we shared."

"I have no reason to bring it up. No need to deny or confirm—because it isn't a topic of conversation." Her patience stretched like a rubber band about to snap. "I'm asking politely. Please leave." The last thing she needed was for Jared to arrive and find Steven parked on the front gallery with her.

"Won't you give me a chance? If nothing more than just a friendly lunch. I'm back to stay. We're going to be moving in the same circles again. Let's make nice.

I won't take 'no' for an answer."

Worry stirred in her mind. Jared was due back any minute. She had to make Steven leave. "Will you go away if I agree to lunch?"

"Yes."

"Then, I agree. Now go." She had no intention of ever meeting him, especially alone, but in the moment, she'd say anything to get him gone. Even if it made her a liar, too.

Steven drew closer. For a second, she anticipated a kiss on her cheek, but with a quick movement, he turned her chin in his direction and planted a kiss on her lips.

"Stop!" She shoved him. He wobbled like he might lose his balance but remained upright. Drawing back in the chair, she wiped the kiss away with the back of her hand.

Steven chuckled. "God, woman, you make my blood hot. I'll call about lunch. Don't disappoint me. Or I may have to tell your fiancé about you kissing me."

"I did not!" Camilla shouted. Jumping up and nearly knocking him over, she ran for the front door and slammed it shut. Cowardly of her, but scorched pride and past humiliation made her retreat from any encounter with him. She would never voluntarily kiss him. Jared would know that. He was confident of her faithfulness. Her love for him had no room for temptation. She would never kiss another man, least of all Sterling.

Steven's laugh picked at her like a vulture picking at roadkill. "You like the game, Camilla. You like me. You loved what I used to do to your body. But, like you, I've changed. Give me a chance to show you. It could be you and me. Forever. You want excitement, not some damn boring cowboy contractor."

She peeked through the side glass window next to the door. Steven did a soft-shoe tap dance down the stairs. When he looked back toward the house, she ducked out of sight.

After a minute, she checked his progress. Her unwanted visitor slid into his Mercedes and drove down the long driveway in the direction of the road. Halfway, he passed a truck, beeped and waved.

"Oh, no." Camilla groaned and sank to the floor. "What do I tell Jared?"

Chapter 2

Ahead on the driveway, a car moved toward Jared, and he slowed. The other car's horn honked. The other driver waved. Jared waved back.

"Wonder who?" The man looked familiar, but in the moment, he couldn't place him or the pricey, silver luxury sedan. He shrugged. No matter. Only space for one person in his brain—Camilla.

He'd missed her all week. She'd blossomed since moving home. Thoughtful and helpful to everyone. It was as though she reabsorbed all the southern sweetness she'd left behind before taking off several years ago to cleanse her soul of guilt and shame. He never imagined she would grow even lovelier, but she had. He was a lovesick man. From her long hair and smiling eyes to her mischievous smile. He loved that lately she wore dresses more than jeans—she had sexy legs, long and coltish. And while he'd never admit it to Greta, Camilla cooked as good or better. "Happy wife equals happy life," he said, relaxing to the New Orleans jazz playing on the radio in the background. "If only my wife-to-be would set a date."

Bone-tired after a week on the road—his grandfather had him visiting abandoned antebellum mansions to determine the cost of renovations—Jared craved alone time with Camilla and his bed. Daily he thought about what it would be like once they married.

How sharing the future with her surpassed anything he thought possible.

When the last FEMA trailer left Fleur de Lis after the storm, he'd been relegated to the bachelor quarters—the *garçonnière*—since he and Camilla were unmarried. The Xbox left behind by her brother might have been a perk, if he had time to play it. Usually, he just crashed. Except for those occasional interludes when Camilla visited him during the night.

Approaching the front of the house, he swerved right, taking the new driveway linking the front with Loblolly Lane and leading to the rear of the house. Camilla burst through the front doorway and waved. As he continued his trek around to the back, he caught her movement. She pointed and took off in that direction to meet him.

"Honey, I'm home," he called, climbing down from his truck.

Camilla blew him kisses. She bounced down the wide stairs to meet him. "Lover Boy! I've been waiting!"

Scooping her up, he twirled her around. Every day, he offered a short prayer of thanks to his father for pushing him to go after Camilla. Like the full moon, she possessed a gravitational pull he couldn't resist. Gus, he'd decided, knew a lot about women. He couldn't imagine his life without her. She shined brightness into his world and added sweetness the way sugar made southern tea sweet. When he set her back on her feet, she kissed him soundly, nipping on his bottom lip. His hands reached for her butt, cupped her there, and pulled her close. "Woman," he murmured. "Look what you do to me. Nothing about me says, boy."

A Chevy Tahoe pulled around to the back of the house, and Camilla moved. Jared captured her cheeks when she started to break their connection.

"Jared," she whined, her lips still touching his. "I want you, too."

"Excuse me!" Greta called out. "There are groceries in the back. Camilla, I could use your help." The housekeeper sighed and shook her head. "You would've never carried on like that in public when the Old Aunts were alive."

Jared released his hold on Camilla. "Aw, Greta, this isn't exactly public." When Camilla took a step away from him toward the parked vehicle, he followed, not wanting her any more than an arm's length away. "I'll take the groceries in. I want a beer. What's for dinner? Who's home?"

"Just us," Camilla squealed. "The three of us."

"No, make that two," Greta said. "It's Friday night, and I have a date." She slid her purse strap over her shoulder and sashayed up the stairs.

"A date?" Camilla followed Greta. "With whom? Do we know him? He's picking you up here, right? We have to meet him, young lady."

Jared chuckled. "Don't mind me," he said, hoisting four bags of groceries. "I'm just the lowly grocery boy." Neither woman was paying him any mind.

"Camilla, put the food up. I'm going to get ready. There's gumbo in the fridge and salad. French bread is still in the oven. And in one of those bags your man is carrying, you'll find nut-free pralines—I didn't have time to make them for you."

"Yes, ma'am." Camilla bobbed her head. "Got it

covered."

At the top of the steps, Camilla turned back to him and smiled, soft and sexy. "Don't you worry. I'll tip you real nice tonight. I'm looking forward to my time with Lover Boy."

"Promises, promises," he teased, but wondered why she had suddenly tagged him with the nickname.

Once Greta departed and the groceries were stored in their rightful places, Camilla handed him napkins and silverware. "Will you put them on the table? Then grab the salads from the fridge."

As instructed, he moved to the dining room. "Nice flowers on the table. Who sent them?" Jared called out.

"Let's share a bottle of red wine tonight," she hollered from the kitchen. "Pick your favorite from the rack. And you know where to find the glasses."

Obviously, she hadn't heard him.

"Wine is open," he called out a few minutes later.

When she appeared in the doorway to the dining room, he poured dark liquid into both glasses and offered her one. They *clinked* their glasses together.

She sipped. "Hmmm, that's nice. Dry and fruity."

Taking the glass from her, he deposited it on the table. "About these flowers," he said. "There's a card here."

"Are you fishing for a compliment? You *know* who sent them."

"Know?" Jared asked. She wanted to play a guessing game?

"Okay, I understand." She stopped and made a slight curtsy. "Thank you, darlin', for the flowers. I should've said that the minute I saw you, but you…sort of distracted me. They're lovely, and I adore you."

After blowing a kiss in his direction, she went to the stove where she placed sliced bread on a plate with a small dish of butter. "Take this, please. I'll ladle up the gumbo."

"Honey, I love you bunches, but I didn't send the flowers. I bought you a gift, but it's still in my truck."

Camilla pivoted on her cowboy heels and eyed him suspiciously. Her mouth turned into a frown. "What do you mean you didn't send them? They were delivered to me." Her eyes took on a wild fright. She dropped the ladle back into the pot on the stove. Pushing past him, she went to the dining table and plucked the card from the holder.

"Miss you. See you soon. Lover Boy," she read.

Jared pulled the paper from her fingers. "Camilla, I didn't send them. Looks like you have a secret admirer." He grinned. He could think of a dozen workmen who had become infatuated with his spunky southern belle during the restoration of Fleur de Lis. When her face paled, he stepped closer. "You all right?" he asked, growing more worried. "Why don't you sit down? Want some water or wine? Shall I call Greta? Camilla, what's wrong?" She tottered as though she might fall. He pulled out the Queen Anne chair from the head of the table and helped her sit.

"I…I'll be fine. Maybe I'm just hungry. I forgot to eat lunch."

"You're sure that's all? You sit. I'll get the gumbo." Uneasiness ate at the edges of his mind, an old familiar and unwelcome feeling. She'd never lied to him before. He wanted to believe her, but his bullshit meter went into overdrive, causing the muscles between his shoulders to spasm. Since they'd met, this was the first time he'd ever doubted her. Her lie threw up a roadblock as monumental as the Hoover Dam, bringing back memories of his dead wife, Cheyenne, and her repeated pack of lies.

The image of the man in the car that passed him flashed in his mind. What business did he have at Fleur de Lis?

Rather than press Camilla into a confrontation, he decided to give her time to come around. After a week away, he wouldn't allow a mysterious flower delivery to ruin their time together.

But what was Camilla hiding?

Chapter 3

A week later, Camilla stopped in the hall to examine the large framed photograph recently hung on the wall. The entire Fleur de Lis family had gathered on the porch for the photo shoot, compliments of Biloxi, on the first anniversary of Hurricane Katrina—that was when Jared officially proposed. The gathering was bittersweet. She touched the glass in the spot where the Old Aunts would've sat. She missed them and wished she had them for guidance. They wouldn't like learning about her past, but she believed they'd overlook it because she'd changed—and because they'd loved her unconditionally. Staring at Jared's image in the picture, she hoped it was an omen—that they'd get past the current bumps in the road they were experiencing, and a lasting future awaited them.

"Camilla?" Greta called from the ballroom, her voice echoing down the hall. "Is that you? Your momma and I are in here."

"Yes," she answered, heading in their direction. "I'm coming, notebook and tape measure at your service." Her heels tapped against the wooden floor until she reached the ballroom.

"Hi, darlin'." Her mother walked toward her, hugged her, and kissed her forehead like she used to do when Camilla was a girl. "It's exciting! The Halloween Ball is in thirty days. If we start now, we won't have to rush to complete it all last minute. And your idea for tiny twinkling lights will be the perfect touch for the Stanton-Dorset wedding between now and Halloween."

Camilla handed the notebook to her mother, pulled out the tape measure, and began measuring the first column. "Fourteen feet," she said.

"Ten columns." Macy jotted in the notebook, then tapped a pen against it. "Lights down each column. Drape the columns with tulle. Add wide soft pink and mint green ribbons—the bride will love it. Will you calculate the number of strings we need?"

"Your idea of crisscrossing lights on the ceiling is a great one," Greta said.

"The wires from the lights will create a grid. We can weave tulle and have a canopy covering the ceiling," Camilla added.

"Then, later, after the wedding, we can change it out with black and orange tulle for the Halloween Ball," Macy said.

"Momma, be sure to remind Branna and Biloxi that I'm doing their job."

The telephone ringing in the office interrupted the meeting.

"Excuse me. I'll be right back." Greta left them to themselves.

"Camilla, honey," her mother began, coming to stand in front of her, "I'm worried about you. Has something happened between you and Jared? You've been dragging around zombielike for a week." Camilla started to step back when her mother grasped her hands and pinned her with a stare. "When are you going to set a wedding date? I'm not trying to nag, but the man deserves an answer."

"Has he said something to you?"

"No. Jared never complains. About anything. He just digs in and helps where and how he can. We would've never made it through the repairs—he was our white knight in a pickup truck."

"Yes, he saved the day, but Nick did a lot, too. Momma, Jared said he would wait until I was ready. Falling in love can't be helped, but a wedding, a marriage—that requires a certain state of mind. As much as I love Jared, I needed more time. 'I do' has to be forever. After all, he and I didn't know each other well when you met him." Camilla scrunched her face, wrinkling her nose and frowning.

She had told Jared repeatedly, he didn't know her. The fact was, after her wild ways, trusting herself proved challenging. Marriage was a risk. Jared had been hurt once before, and she needed certainty about herself before walking down the aisle. It was only fair. A grand passionate love affair didn't necessarily translate into a stable marriage. Not for someone with her history.

"I do want to talk with you more about this. I'm hoping for a wedding here. Traditional. Fitting of Fleur de Lis."

Camilla groaned inwardly. Of course, Momma wanted traditional. "I'm really close to setting a date. My engagement has been under...unusual circumstances. Not many fiancés today move in with the bride-to-be's family. Besides, I know you're not going to like what I want in a wedding when I tell you, but I'm going to ask you to respect my wishes."

"Don't be so quick to judge me. I've changed some, too. I just want to help you have the best wedding ever—in the style of wedding you want, but keep in mind all the brides that came before you. The tradition I want to uphold is you being married here."

"How about an Addams Family themed wedding?"

Her mother nearly choked. "I'm not going to be baited today. When, Camilla, when do you want to get married?"

"I thought when everything slowed down, after the building frenzy. I don't have a month or day in mind. But now, since the café will open in time for the Christmas season…I've been thinking of making a short trip to Wyoming to see Haley." Could she divert the topic from wedding to Wyoming?

"What about Jared? Doesn't he want to see his family?"

"Jared's business is taking off. He barely has time to sleep. He wants his family to come here for the holidays. His sister-in-law is all for it."

Macy sighed. "Do you think you'll need to move to the city after you marry?"

"I…I don't know. It would be a hardship for Greta to manage the whole house alone—Auntie Deidre is back in New Orleans. Biloxi and Nick, living across the road, are here all the time, but it's not the same as living here. We can't count on Branna and James—she says they're staying in Florida for another year. I don't know what we'll do."

"Well, the house will survive. We've all seen to that. Carson and Linc might be coming home to start a business…they'd live here. But things are okay with you and Jared? You've been pensive and sad for the last couple of weeks."

Maybe if Momma finally understood all her

relationship history, then she could understand the delay. She motioned her mother to one of the settees lining the wall. Together they sat. "There is something bothering me. I want to take you into my confidence, but you have to promise you won't get upset. Promise, or I won't tell you."

"This sounds serious." Her mother stared at her as though she might discover a secret without being told. "I promise."

"Macy," Greta said, reentering the room carrying an envelope. "We're having guests for lunch today. Mrs. Sterling and her son are on their way over."

"That's odd. I know what she wants, but what on earth does he want? That's fine with me, Greta, as long as it's not an inconvenience for you."

"I've got it covered, but I need to finish in the kitchen and set the table, so I'll leave this party planning to you two." Greta handed an envelope to Camilla. "This was on the counter. I forgot to give it to you. It's from yesterday's mail."

"Thanks," she said. Greta was already heading out of the room.

When Camilla read the handwriting, her stomach dropped freefall. It was as though hands encircled her throat. She forced a swallow. Never did she want to see Steven Sterling again. She certainly didn't want mail from him. She rose. "I don't want to have lunch with them."

"Mrs. Sterling is coming to discuss hosting an event here."

"That's Biloxi's job, not mine. If you want me to help with the ball, we discuss it before lunch, and then, I'll excuse myself."

"Sweetheart, you're as much a part of this business as any of us now. Biloxi runs things mostly, but she can't do it alone. That's why we're here. Besides, I'm certain Mrs. Sterling's event will need catering. You and Greta will be cooking. You can't run out just because you don't like someone. This is business. Now what did you want to tell me?"

"It can wait for another time."

"That's fine. I'll see you after you change for lunch."

"What? I have to change? Jeans are completely appropriate."

Her mother looked up at her, one eyebrow raised.

"Okay. I'm five again. What do you want me to wear, Momma?"

"That blue and brown dress." It was an order. Not a request.

Frustration dredged a moat in Camilla's gut and filled to nearly overflowing with guilt. Maybe she needed to seriously consider giving up Fleur de Lis Café—let Biloxi and Greta run it—and move to New Orleans to make things easier for Jared…and herself. She could work in any top-rated restaurant in the city. That would make life less difficult. Steven had said they'd be moving in the same circles again. She just hadn't expected them to be on her home turf. "I'll be down when they arrive—"

"Before. So I can see what you're wearing. I don't understand your immense dislike of the Sterlings. Branna's attitude I get. What is wrong with you?"

She smiled wide. "Whatever you want, Mommie Dearest." Turning, she wanted to stomp her heels and punch something. She reined in her inner child and strode from the room as gracefully as she could muster.

Upstairs, in the safety of her bedroom, she flopped on the chaise and opened the envelope. A card. On the front, a beautiful arrangement of red roses with glitter. Inside, a handwritten note:

Second chances. Take a risk. I will part the seas and lasso the moon for you. Let me show you I've changed.

All my love,

Steven

Why couldn't he understand? She loved Jared. Planned to marry him.

But nothing—not Jared, not Momma's nagging, and certainly not Steven's unwanted pursuit—would force her to the altar before she was ready. She wanted what all of her married relatives had—forever love.

****

Camilla laid her fork on her plate. She'd spent the entire lunch pushing food around. It was bad enough her mother insisted on a specific dress, but she hinted as only she can, which pieces of jewelry and which shoes to wear. Each trip up and down the stairs shored up Camilla's resolve. She could be the demure, dutiful daughter her mother wanted while attending to business because that's all lunch was—a simple business meeting over food.

But Momma couldn't force her to eat. She'd choke if she tried to swallow. During the meal, Steven sat across from her. He rubbed his foot on the inside of her leg. She had tried to avoid him without drawing attention to herself, but when his toes tickled the inside of her knee, she almost threw her knife at him.

"Mrs. Sterling," Camilla said, "I'm confident that your ladies tea to raise money for the library will be a success. If you'll excuse me, I have other business to attend to." She smiled and rose from the table.

"Camilla, would you mind a word out front?" Steven asked, rising, too.

She couldn't refuse him without causing concern. To mask her anger, she smiled again and nodded. On her way to the front door, Steven grasped her elbow, slowing her pace. He held the door open and gestured for her to exit first.

Wanting to be beyond earshot, she walked to the far end of the front gallery. She perched on the corner railing where the side and the front joined. She squared her shoulders. Anger simmered, but she wouldn't allow him to know it. He had killer instincts and would exploit any weakness. That would give him the upper hand. She had to display complete emotional control. Calm aloofness. Because, after all, he was of no consequence in her life.

"When did you get such a tough shell?" Steven sank into a rocking chair.

She looked across the front lawn. The oak trees lining the driveway to the road had sustained some damage from the storm. Mother Nature's resiliency impressed her. Over the last year, the surviving trees had taken on new growth.

"Camilla, to Earth. Where are you?"

"Mr. Sterling, what did you wish to speak with me about?"

Steven left the chair and stalked toward her as though she might be prey in the crosshairs of his sight. She met his gaze. He couldn't frighten her. She grabbed for the corner post when he placed his hands on the railing on either side of her, blocking any movement unless she touched him.

"What do you think you're doing?"

"Getting a good look at the woman I love."

She shook her head. "Steven, you don't love me. You love the chase. I'm the one that got away. Let's be adults. I'm willing to be on polite terms, but there's nothing between us."

His hands moved to her hips.

"Stop that!"

"Then kiss me," he urged. "Convince me you have no feelings for me. I know a woman wants a man who's willing to fight for her. To be a fool for her—"

"Oh, Steven." She shook her head. "I *never* loved you. It was a game. You always knew that."

"It was a good game. And it can be more. I've changed."

"So you keep telling me," she responded dryly.

"I was here when the storm struck, helping people survive. I've taken stock of my life. I know what I want in a woman."

"Okay." She shrugged. "I have no evidence you've changed, but I'll believe you if it's important."

"Then give us a chance. You're strong and determined. I love everything about you. You look more beautiful now than you did then. You have all the social graces, even if you don't choose to use them, to help me launch a political career—"

"So that's what this is about?"

"No. I said it wrong. You're a prize package of a woman. I don't deserve you. But I want you. I won't give up until—" He leaned in and kissed her. She wobbled backward. He grabbed her around her waist, pulling her forward and off the railing.

Shoving him away, she slapped him and raised her knee fully poised to kick him.

"I love it when you're feisty, but I won't allow you do that again." He rubbed his cheek. "You know what physical foreplay does to me." He cupped his crotch. The bulge in his pants was unmistakable.

"You're disgusting."

"I've got it bad for you, Camilla." He moved closer to her.

She backed up, her backside against the corner post. "At least, call it what it is—lust, not love."

"So maybe"—he raised an eyebrow, his mouth puckering near hers—"if you come play with me, I'll be able to get you out of my system."

The front door opened. Mrs. Sterling and her mother exited the house together. Steven turned and leaned casually against the railing next to her.

"It's nice to see the two of you together," Mrs. Sterling said. "I always told Steven that of the Lind girls, you would've been a better match."

Her mother eyed her with obvious confusion.

"I'll see you soon, Mrs. Sterling," Camilla said. She pushed off from the railing, crossed the gallery, and went into the house, heading straight for the powder room. "I think he's tetched in the head from the storm," she muttered. Gazing at her reflection in the mirror, she was satisfied nothing about her appearance tattled. Never again would she agree to be alone with him.

"Camilla?" her mother called. "Where are you? We need to talk about what's going on."

After a deep breath, she held her head high and went to face her mother.

"Momma," she said, meeting her in the hall, "I

think you and I need a glass of lemonade and a shot of whiskey on the side. I've got a story to tell you." She took her mother by the hand and led her back out onto the front porch. "I'll be right back with our drinks."

When she returned, her mother shook her head. "I'm not going to like what I'm going to hear, am I?"

"Nope, most of it not. But...I think it's time you knew the truth. You need to know what an honorable daughter Branna is. She's done so much for this family and to protect me...especially when I didn't deserve it. However, I'm hoping you'll like the ending."

Macy sucked in a long slow breath and blew it out. "I'm as ready as I'll ever be."

Taking her time, Camilla began the sordid tale, hitting the high points of her behavior and omitting the detailed blow-by-blow descriptions, all the while making it clear she bore all the responsibility for what happened when Branna broke off her engagement to Stephen.

Shock, surprise, sadness, and confusion flashed across her mother's face. "I'm...it's a lot to take in. You always marched to your own tune. Maybe I should've been stricter with you." Her mother hugged her and kissed her forehead. "I failed you."

"No, Momma. I acted out even when I knew better. It's my fault, and my fault alone."

"Not quite. You had a seducing accomplice. So, are you and Branna good? Your relationship is fine, now?" Macy asked, hopefulness flitting across her face. Camilla couldn't let her down, and thankfully, it was the truth.

"Yes."

"And you're in love with Jared. Completely. Ready

to be a wife?"

"Yes."

"But Steven is pursuing you…and you haven't told Jared?"

"Yes."

"This can't go on. Steven may have changed since the storm, but you know what your grandfather always said—"

"Yes. 'A leopard doesn't change its spots.' I can't buy that. I changed. Maybe he has, too. The thing is, it doesn't matter. He's of no consequence in my life."

"He's preying on you. I won't have it. To think, all I've done for his mother. Their family. And the way they treated us when Branna broke off her engagement to him…it just sickens me." Her mother's hands clenched into fists.

"I won't be bullied or threatened," Camilla said. "And if I leave now, he'll think he's getting to me, wearing me down. I won't risk him following me to Wyoming, so, I've decided to bring Haley here for a visit at Thanksgiving."

"But Camilla, why not marry Jared now? It will make everything simpler."

"I am going to marry the man." She smiled. "It's going to be a party like we've never had at Fleur de Lis. It's going to be perfect for Jared and me. And it's all going to be done my way."

Macy nodded. "Fine. When?"

"I'll announce the date at the Halloween Ball."

Chapter 4

Camilla covered her body with a bath towel before escaping from the steamy bathroom. Tonight marked the first big public party at Fleur de Lis. Family weddings didn't count. The party buzz had taken over Bayou Petite. Everyone from the mayor down had sent an RSVP to the Halloween Ball. The Sterlings hadn't been invited.

All week, she'd worked tirelessly with Biloxi, Branna, and Momma to ready the estate for the party. Stacked bales of straw and huge pumpkins filled with flowers decorated the driveway. Mechanical decorations added dimension—ghosts flying in the trees, witches stirring caldrons with steam rising, and an army of Frankensteins standing guard on each step leading to the front door. The night held promises of a spook-tacular time.

Securing the towel, she stepped into the large second-floor hall.

"Finally," said her cousin Evie. "The princess is finished."

Children. What did they know? For the first time ever, she pulled rank on the other girls in the family by insisting on the first shower. "All yours," she called to Nola, Biloxi's sister, next in the pecking order.

"That's okay. I'm going to let Sophie go first."

"Really?" Sophie asked, her French accent still

thick. "*Merci*! I'm about to pee myself."

Camilla laughed. Nick's half-sister, visiting from Baton Rouge for the weekend to attend the Halloween Ball, scampered into the bathroom and closed the door. "So exciting," she squealed.

"Never heard French and southern together quite like that, let alone a French girl say she's about to pee herself," Evie muttered. "Why does she get to go before family?"

"She *is* family. That was very nice of you, Nola," Camilla said before taking refuge in her bedroom. Closing the door, she twirled, dreaming of dancing with Jared. They'd enjoyed many dances since their first meeting more than a year ago at the Lucky Seven. Their relationship had its highs and lows, but the flower incident had cast a pall on the bond between them over the last month. She intended to fix that by making Steven confess to sending the flowers. The news had to come from him. And if he dared to suggest she'd kissed him as he'd threatened, she'd flat out deny it—she had truth on her side. The jerk had manipulated the whole scene.

She would do whatever it took to remove the shade of doubt in Jared's eyes. Life with him had changed her in so many ways. Meeting him had been a stroke of luck. Biloxi had said it might be karma—she deserved a good man because she'd changed so much.

Their first meeting, first lovemaking, first words spoken of love, filled her with fluttering excitement and anchored in her heart. He was more than she'd ever dreamed—no betting person would've put good money on her to ever fall in love.

Heat spread through her. Tensing energy

thrummed. Desire hit in her core. Too bad Jared wasn't home yet. Not only did she want to share with him her news about finally choosing a wedding date, but she'd sneak him upstairs in the house and into her bed to celebrate. Later, she'd pray for forgiveness to the Old Aunts for breaking a generations-long house rule—no single men allowed in the private family quarters, but she couldn't very well go traipsing off to the *garçonnière*. There the walls were paper-thin, and her brother Carson and cousin Linc would hear every last moan she'd make.

And oh how Jared made her moan. In the most delicious way.

"Where are you?" she muttered.

Tonight she planned for them to announce their wedding date at the party. All this while, he'd never pressured her, said he understood she needed time. However, Momma had continued to harass her to pick a date. Momma reminded her of her responsibility—a wedding brought out the best of everyone at Fleur de Lis.

Camilla raked her fingers through the ends of her long hair. She purposefully kept everyone, including Jared, in the dark about the special date. She wanted a courtship. Wanted all the perks of being in love. Plus, though she'd changed, a streak of rebellion still resided in her heart. What no one knew would surprise them. She had already planned her wedding down to the last detail. Everyone, including Jared, would be surprised when she announced the date and details.

Slipping on the soft pink silk robe, the one Jared's sister-in-law gave her for Christmas, Camilla lay on the bed. "Why haven't you called?" She scowled at her cell phone. He'd been gone another whole week in New Orleans working on a project for his grandfather. Restoration of mansions in the Garden District required painstaking attention to detail. She never worried about Jared with other women. Fidelity grounded him, and that offered her security...but had work truly become his mistress?

"Jared," she groaned. "Come home. This is the most exciting event since I've been back. I want to share this with you."

She hummed, "Here comes the bride." Branna's intimate wedding had provided family bonding after the storm, and Biloxi's elegant and extravagant one returned the family to their social prominence in the county. But hers had to be different. Unique. Fitting of her true personality. And tonight was the perfect night to reveal her wedding plans. Only where was her groom-to-be?

"Knock, knock," Biloxi called. "I'm here."

"Enter," Camilla said loudly. "I haven't done my hair yet."

Biloxi entered. "Branna and James just rolled up in the motorhome. Good thing they bring their house on wheels. We barely have room in the house anymore." She stretched out on the chaise in front of the window.

"That gives me an idea. I'm thinking...I want a party bus for my bachelorette party," Camila told her. "We can take the drive on Highway 90 along the coast and into New Orleans. I want to go to that burlesque show, you know, the one with the dancer we met at that awesome boutique in the French Quarter."

"Cousin, that's all well and good, but first you have to set a date."

Camilla sat up and smiled wide. "I want to tell Jared first. Then, I'll tell the family."

"And your attendants? Matron of honor? Maid of honor? Bridesmaids?"

"You'll just have to wait and see," she teased.

"Well, things are looking up. We're booking more events...so if you're getting married here, you might want to let me know when, or your date may be taken by someone else."

"Idle threats. Nice try. You forget. I work here, too. I know the calendar as well as you. Well, almost."

Biloxi wrinkled her nose. "Remember. It's their wedding. It's your marriage. Anyway, when is Jared arriving?"

"He was supposed to be here for lunch, but couldn't make it. New client meeting. Plus he had measurements to take and an estimate to write."

"Is that your costume?" Biloxi asked, rising from the chair.

"Yep. You're the first one to see it."

"I can see why. This is supposed to be a PG-13 party. Your momma is going to pitch a fit." She fingered the lace of the corset. "At least the cups aren't see-through. As it is, you're going to attract a lot of attention."

"Trust me, it will be just fine. Momma won't say a word."

Biloxi sat on the bed next to her. "It's not a matter of trust. Anyway, get your hair dried, and I'll fix it for you. Then we'll get you dressed."

"What about you? Where's your costume?"

Smiling, Biloxi shook her finger. "No. No. It's a secret. Let's see if you recognize me at the ball. I'll be the one in the mask."

"Everyone"—Camilla laughed—"will be wearing a mask."

"I know! Isn't it wonderful?"

"I'm wondering what our mothers will be wearing. They've been very secretive this year. Seems they've grown closer since the storm." Camilla went to the antique dressing table and pulled out a blow-dryer, several brushes, and a curling iron. "Will you check on the girls while I dry my hair? I want to call Jared. That man better not be late." She checked the time again. Worry formed a pit in her gut. Had something happened to him? She never interrupted him while he worked, unless it was an emergency. Instead, she always waited until he phoned her.

"Wipe that frown off your face. I'll go check on the girls. This is Sophie's first masquerade ball. She's excited to dress up as a cowgirl. Short denim skirt, boots she borrowed from you, Stetson from Nick, but no guns."

"She'll have to visit the Rockin' R up in Cody where Jared's from. The good thing about tonight is Sophie won't smell like a sweaty horse."

Ring.

"It's him." Camilla's finger tapped the button. "Hello?"

Biloxi pointed at the door, then left Camilla alone.

"Hey, honey," Jared said, his voice full of affection. "I'm sorry. I'm going to be late."

"Noooo. Not tonight. You can't be."

"It's unavoidable. Work has tied me up. I'm meeting that new client at the country club in Slidell on my way home."

"I'm going to have Sophie tie you up," Camilla said.

"What? I couldn't hear you. Connection isn't that great."

"I said," she cooed, "if you want to be tied up, I'll be happy to do it for you."

Jared chuckled. "Can't wait. Look, I'll make it there before the party ends, and I'll be staying over, but...have to get back to New Orleans in the morning."

"Jared, everyone's home. You know how my family is—tradition. We go to church and then have brunch."

"I know. I know." He heaved out a sigh. "What if we have our own church service in the morning? I could worship at the altar of Camilla."

As much as his teasing tickled her, she worked hard to not disappoint anyone since returning home. If the family went to church, she went to church. If the family had brunch, well, she was never late to the table. "We'll discuss it when I see you tonight. I have some news, and I'd like to tell you before I tell everyone."

"Baby, I promise. I'll be there before the party is half over—"

"Costume is required for entry," she reminded him.

"Complete in costume. One certainly to impress. Christ. Who knew I'd have males-in-law—James, Nick, Carson, and Linc—to compete with. I won't disappoint you." His insistence placated her a bit, but only a bit.

"I'm the one who should be fashionably late. Now I have to arrive unescorted. That's not going to look good."

"Maybe not, but woman, I know *you're* going to look good. Can't wait to see you. Gotta go. Love you."

"I love you, Jared Richardson. Get your arse here as soon as you can—safely."

Ending the call, she dropped back onto the bed. She pulled the towel from her hair and draped it on the hook by the closet door. "I'm going to dance with every male at the party. That's my mission tonight."

Maybe that would make Jared sit up and take notice.

And if it didn't…maybe he wasn't ready to commit to a wedding date after all.

Chapter 5

Jared entered the private golf club's pub and selected a seat at the bar. He settled on a tall barstool and ordered a drink.

"Thanks," Jared said to the bartender when a glass was placed in front of him.

Reaching for the whiskey, neat, he waited for the new client to arrive. The Bayou Historic Home Foundation owned an antebellum property near Donaldsonville, Louisiana, and said they'd heard of his expertise. They were sending their attorney to start the preliminary talks. He preferred to deal with architects and craftsmen, but a meeting was a meeting. Potential business was always good.

Jared took in the dark paneling and golfing paraphernalia in the clubhouse. It had been rebuilt from the ground up after Katrina. Swirling amber liquid in the highball glass, he sighed. The last thing in the world he wanted was to don a ridiculous costume for a masquerade ball. Camilla insisted he not come dressed as a cowboy. "Just too predictable from you," she'd said when his spurs arrived in the mail from his brother. He'd argued that no one in Bayou Petite knew him as a rancher, just a contractor and builder.

A musketeer costume, complete with gray shirt, black britches, polished black knee boots, saber and pistol, and a hat with a fluffy feather, hung in the closet at Fleur de Lis. Camilla selected the theme. Greta sewed most of it. They were thrilled when he tried it on. "It looks better than the one I saw for rent at the costume store."

He went along with it to make her happy, trying to fit in with her family. But costumes and parties didn't suit him. His idea of Halloween? A horse race. A shooting match. Beer and a big steak on the grill.

Camilla had warned him about the idiosyncrasies of the Linds and Dutreys. Shit. They had a party for everything. At first, he'd assumed she exaggerated, but nooo…the lack of understanding about the level of celebrating rested clearly with him.

"Hello," a man said, taking a seat next to him at the bar and scrutinizing him. "I'm guessing you're Jared."

"Yes."

"I remember you," he said. "You were with Nick Trahan up in Memphis. Golfing. What a coincidence." The man offered his hand. "Steven."

"Jared." He shook the guy's hand.

"How's your game today?" Steven asked. Then he turned to the bartender. "Scotch on the rocks."

"Just played nine with a client. Not bad, but not good. I don't play much." Jared shrugged.

"I saw one of your drives. For not playing much, you're a natural."

Steven had watched him play? "I'm better on a horse. Or at the gun range."

"Interesting. A man's man."

Something about the guy's tone and the compliments triggered wariness. Jared eyed him. He exuded a commanding confidence, gave off the vibe of enjoying the power of control. A spasm hit Jared between the shoulder blades. Always a warning sign he heeded.

When the bartender set the scotch on the bar in front of Steven, he picked it up. "What shall we drink to?"

"Surviving in the south," Jared said.

"Surviving in the south," Steven chimed in.

They clinked glasses. Jared sipped. Steven knocked back half the liquid in his glass.

"Your accent gives you away."

"Oh? Where am I from?"

Steven smiled. A snake couldn't look more pleased after swallowing prey. "It's not where you're from," he said. "It's how you speak that labels you an outsider. Not from here."

Jared set his jaw and nodded. "I can 'y'all' with the best of them."

"Maybe." Steven continued to smile.

A dislike for the man slithered down Jared's spine. He leaned his forearms against the bar and cradled the highball glass. If this was a business meeting, somewhere it had taken a wrong turn. It would suit him fine if Steven slithered away.

"So you do work for the Bayou Historic Home Foundation?" Jared asked, wanting to get to the task at hand.

After several moments of quiet, Steven said, "We have a friend in common."

Jared shrugged, trying to discourage any further personal conversation.

Steven downed the rest of his drink and pushed the glass away. He turned in the swiveling barstool and faced Jared. "We have the same taste in women."

Jared stared straight ahead, focusing on the shelves of liquor bottles. He hadn't been in a bar fight since he finished college. Every fiber in his body screamed that whatever else Steven had to say, he wasn't going to like it. He kept his hands on the glass in front of him. Who was Steven? The woman in question had better not be Camilla.

The man leaned close. Jared's jaw ticked.

"I remember the taste of her lips," Steven said.

"I think you must have me confused with someone." Jared shifted in his seat. He'd had enough. He turned in the chair to climb down from the barstool. Steven grabbed his forearm. Jared stared hard into the man's eyes. "Take your hand off me." He kept his voice calm and even. "Don't touch me again."

The man smiled. His eyes glinted. "But I've touched her."

Standing tall, Jared shook his head. "I don't know who you are. What the hell are you talking about? You drunk?"

Steven laughed. The sound curled a knot in Jared's gut as he turned to leave.

"Jared Richardson. I know all about you. Wyoming rancher. Father married too many times to count. Money in the bank. But I know Camilla better. I let her get away once. I won't let that happen again. You've been leaving her alone. Too much business on your part. Your work and no play makes Camilla a horny woman. I've been by to see her several times. I guess she never mentioned it. And now"—Steven saluted— "I'm about to carry myself over there. She's grown up while she was away. Maybe I have you to thank for that. She's a fine-looking woman. She needs a man who pays attention to her. One who knows how to satisfy *and* keep her in line." He slapped Jared on the back. "I'm the man to give it to her."

Jared grabbed Steven's shoulder. Spun him around. Drew back his fist. "No. Not with my woman." He punched Steven in the stomach. The man wheezed, doubled over, grabbed for the barstool, and missed it, landing on the ground.

"Hey!" the bartender shouted. "Take that shit outside."

Jared leaned down close to Steven's ear. "Don't ever touch what's mine."

"Go to hell," Steven coughed out. Rising up, he leaned on the edge of the bar. "I had her first."

"I just put two-and-two together," Jared said. "You're less than shit. And just remember, I'm a damn good shot, Wyoming rancher and all." He turned to leave the bar. "A private club. Guess they'll let any riff-raff in here. I'll have to cancel my membership." He walked to the front double wooden doors and pushed one open. Outside the sky glowed pink, orange, and lavender. The colors not nearly as brilliant as in Wyoming. That's where the connection between him and Camilla had bloomed. A slow ache burned in him. He'd been too busy since the hurricane to think about the ranch, about Wyoming. He'd failed to give Camilla the attention she deserved. That would change now.

But had she really spent time with Asshole? She never mentioned it. Could he trust her? The flower incident and now this. How many times in the past had she said he really didn't know her? How many times did he refute that claim? Then there was the lie about the flowers. But if she cheated with Asshole when he was engaged to her sister, would she cheat with him now? A slice of doubt opened a vein of hurt. He tried to squelch the pain. Trust, that's where he needed to land. What choice did he have? She had become his life.

"Listen up," Steven yelled from the doorway as Jared walked to his truck. "Say good-bye when you see her tonight, because by tomorrow, she'll be mine."

Chapter 6

"A cowgirl. A mermaid. A princess. And Wonder Woman." Camilla named all the girls' costumes. "Y'all look wonderful. Greta's in the kitchen, and she could use some help with the caterers, so scoot!"

"We're going," grumbled Nola. She pointed to the door, and the other girls filed out orderly.

Biloxi burst into laughter after the group hustled down the stairs. "We need more boys in the family. We were never that sweet and obedient when we were their ages. I guess you and I are going to have to increase the boy population in this family."

"Maybe," Camilla said noncommittally. "Jared's gone all the time these days. I'm glad business is taking off for him, but what about us?"

"The café will be done soon. We'll be really busy when it opens."

"Yes, but I'll probably see even less of Jared then." Camilla adjusted her black lace body corset and pulled on a black and orange tulle skirt, short in the front, long in the back. She created the costume as hint— Halloween Bride. Would Jared get it?

"Hmm," Biloxi murmured.

"What?"

"In that outfit, everyone will be seeing a lot of you."

Camilla pointed one toe and ran her hand from her

shin to the top of her leg. "I love fishnet stockings."

"Yeah, but showing the garter is a bit much."

"Lordy, when did you become such an old maid?" Camilla shot back. "You're covered head to toe in that princess costume, but it shows every curve. Are you sure it's appropriate to flash so much cleavage?"

"Let's not argue."

"Hey there!" Branna called from the other side of the closed door. "May I come in?"

"It's open," Camilla called.

Branna entered dressed as Morticia from the Addams Family.

"Let me guess. James is Gomez?" Biloxi asked dryly.

"I already know what Nick's wearing," Branna shot back. "Your King Arthur is cooing at my baby with my husband in the motorhome." She turned to Camilla. "Sister dearest, I love you, so please take this in the light in which it's intended"—Branna made circles in the air in front of Camilla as though waving a magic wand—"but this thing you want to call a costume is just too over the top. A little cleavage like hers"—Biloxi took a bow—"is fine. A little leg"—Biloxi pointed to the slit up the side of her dress as Branna narrated—"is fine, but this. Not so much. Too much cleavage. Too much leg. Too much risqué for a PG party. Momma's going to pitch a fit."

"Not if she doesn't see me until the party is almost over. She won't recognize me with my mask on."

Branna laughed. "Darlin', you wait until you get to be a momma. We have a second sight when it comes to our children."

"Speaking of mothers," Biloxi interrupted. "Have

you seen ours? Flappers! They look too cute!"

"Why don't y'all go down and see to everything. Would you send up one of the girls with something adult for me to drink? Jared's running late, and I want to wait for him to arrive so he can escort me down."

"You miss part of a party?" Branna asked. "I'll say it again. Sister, you've changed."

Camilla waited for Branna and Biloxi to leave before removing her skirt to keep from wrinkling it. She lay on her bed and reached for her cell phone.

"Jared, where are you?" she asked when he answered the call.

"I'm on my way there. I have to make one more stop. I'll find you at the party. I promise I won't be too late. Less than an hour."

Camilla sighed. "I want to enter the ballroom with you."

"I know, baby. I won't fail you again. Forgive me? Want to tell me what you're wearing? Just in case someone else has the same costume?"

"No," she pouted. "It's a surprise. Though Branna and Biloxi both gave it a thumbs-down."

"What do they know?" He laughed. "They're old married women now. You'll be stunning, I'm certain. I'll change and be over to the party to dance with you. Don't have too much fun without me."

"I'll be toasting with champagne. I do have some good news to share."

"I'm already speeding. Be there soon. Love you," Jared said.

"I love you, too."

Sighing, she closed her eyes, drifting off to dream about Jared. These days, that was the best way to have him all to herself.

A little while later, she woke. Twilight greeted her. She went to the chaise in front of the window. High in the sky, stars sparkled as the sun's last halo of light descended below the horizon. Laughter filtered up from the back garden. A group of people dressed in costumes and masks wandered the paths lit by lanterns. Tonight candles created ambiance, transporting guests back to a simpler time. Aunt Macy planned the Halloween Ball to be reminiscent of the first one ever held at Fleur de Lis, the details of which were discovered in an old diary after the storm.

Settling in, Camilla caught a glimpse of a Musketeer leaving the *garçonnière*. Her brother? Her cousin? Jared? Had he been teasing her? He'd made it home! Excitement urged her into action. Hurriedly, she examined her reflection in the full-length mirror. After adding deep orange lipstick, she slid into the tulle skirt. The black mask, decorated with sparkling crystals around the holes for her eyes, lay on her dressing table. She slipped it in place before adding the final touch to her costume— the tiara with a floor-length veil trimmed in black lace, then tucked its combs securely into her hair. When she adjusted the sides of the veil to cover her bare shoulders, it formed a cloak. She turned from side to side and took several steps to ensure the costume allowed easy movement.

Three hours to go. At ten p.m., she would have the orchestra play a waltz that would make everyone notice. Especially her groom-to-be.

She left her bedroom with a flourish. Her heart fluttered like a thousand tiny cymbals shimmering simultaneously. The night held every promise.

At the top of the stairs, she glanced down. A few people mingled there. Waving as she descended, she noted the werewolf pawing a belly dancer's arm, a ballerina in black stretching on the railing, and someone dressed as a racecar driver—by the jumpsuit, she guessed it was a guy, but she couldn't rule out that it could be a woman. At the bottom of the stairs, leaning on the newel post most cavalier-like, a Musketeer. Black hat with a single long, white feather. Red coat, gray shirt, black breeches, and black boots. Saber dangling at his side. A black mask with a dusting of silver glitter covered his entire face. In the dimness of the candlelight, she couldn't make out the color of his eyes. She would recognize Jared anywhere by the color of his Wyoming sky-blue eyes and the thin scar that made his face even more rugged. But the costume this man wore revealed nothing. The Musketeer had to be him. Who else would be waiting for her?

"I'm so happy to see you." She reached the bottom step, paused, and turned in a circle to give him a complete view of her outfit. Shrugging one shoulder seductively, she winked. "Let's dance."

The Musketeer bowed. He took her hand in his gloved one, and kissed hers, the smooth mask brushing the top of her hand. He offered his arm. Entranced by his elegance and good manners, wordlessly, she followed his lead. Giddiness rippled through her, flowing as swiftly as the mighty Mississippi.

As they approached the ballroom, strains from Carrie Underwood's *Cowboy Casanova* spilled out of the room. Through the arched opening, Camilla spied her sister and James. They danced together like a couple twirling on top of a music box, dominating the center of the floor. Near the edge of the crowd watching the dancers, Biloxi and Nick stood. Her head rested on his chest. He held her close. They swayed in place as though entranced; what they did could barely be called dancing.

"Champagne, please," Camilla whispered to her Musketeer. He nodded and left her side. "So mysterious," she whispered. Jared made her insides sing.

A tap on her shoulder, and she turned. A Musketeer folded one arm at his waist and bowed low. Behind him, two other slightly shorter Musketeers gave slight bows. Then the two from behind stepped beside the first one and clasped him on his shoulders.

She giggled. "Three Musketeers."

"At your service." She recognized her brother's voice. Leaning close to the lead man, she said, "My champagne, Jared? I thought you went to get me a drink." He departed. The remaining two bowed again before leaving her alone.

The coolness of glass touched her back through her veil. With a slight turn, she looked up to find a Musketeer offering a flute of champagne. A strawberry rested at the bottom. "Thank you, Jared." She lifted on her toes to kiss the cheek of the mask. "Let me drink this, and then we dance." He lifted his gloved hand to his chest and tapped there, imitating the beat of a heart. She tilted back the flute to claim the strawberry resting at the bottom. As it slid down, she caught sight of the identical Musketeers.

"I haven't had enough to drink to see double."

The two men were of equal height. Dressed identically. One man stood at attention and more rigidly.

"I don't get the joke." A prickling sensation inched up her spine. When a passing waiter offered her another glass of champagne, she accepted. She sipped the chilled bubbly, then saluted the two men before draining the glass.

One Musketeer reached for her hand as the other took the glass from her, and he, too, held her hand, growling and elbowing the first Musketeer out of the way.

"While this is flattering, Linc and Jared, this is quite enough," she scolded, guessing at the identities of the men behind the costumes. Pulling away from the two, she caught sight of her brother—minus his mask—dancing with Sophie. She turned back to the men standing behind her. Until that second, she never considered that either of the men facing her wasn't Jared. She'd just assumed his comedic streak was a show to throw her off. Warily, she scanned the room. Where was Jared?

The music slowed. A country ballad played. The mirrored ball turned, casting prisms of light. One Musketeer came forward, bowed, and offered his hand with a glance toward the dance floor. The other man folded his arms over his chest, feet planted in a stance, clearly not intending to let them pass.

"This isn't fun anymore," she said. "I don't believe either of you is my fiancé. Please leave me alone."

Pivoting, she wove her way through the growing crowd. She needed air. Passing her mother, she asked, "Have you seen Jared?"

"Is everything all right?"

"Yes, just some pranksters playing a joke on me."

"Do I need to get your father to remind them how to behave?" her mother asked.

"I'll ignore them. I just need to find Jared."

"Isn't that him over there?" Macy pointed to the dance floor where a Musketeer's feathered hat could be seen above the crowd.

"The man's costume is identical to his, but that's not him. I feel like I'm going in circles."

"How can you be so sure?"

The crowd parted. A Musketeer danced with Chantel, who was dressed as a black cat in body-hugging leather.

"I guess it better not be Jared." Her mother's tone turned disapproving.

Camilla glanced at the dancing couple again. Locked together in a kiss, their bodies swayed to the music. The gloved hands of the Musketeer roamed over Chantel's backside.

"Who is that masked man?" Camilla asked, fully intending a bit of levity. "I counted four men dressed as Musketeers. Who knew there'd be so many? I thought pirates were more popular."

"I'm sure Jared will show up, hon." Her mother shimmied away in her flapper dress.

With her nerves pinging like popping corn, Camilla headed for the dining room. A few nibbles of finger food and another glass of champagne would satisfy one of her cravings. The other couldn't be fed until her lips were pressing against Jared. Where was he?

Pounding music rocked the house. Camilla made her way to the dining room. Taking a plate, she added cucumber rounds topped with sour cream and caviar, celery filled with spicy baby shrimp, and a few mushrooms stuffed with crabmeat.

"This is the last one tonight," she said to the bartender. "Don't give me any more. No matter if I beg or not."

"Yes, ma'am."

But she doubted he'd remember her instructions if she decided on a fourth or even a fifth glass of champagne.

After dodging a half dozen people, she finally reached the butler's pantry, seeking its peace and quiet. "Let Jared find me," she muttered. The party didn't excite her the way others had. It wasn't any fun without him. It didn't matter that she was acquainted with nearly everyone on a first name basis attending the event. She wanted to share it with him. Wanted to show him off.

As she balanced the glass and plate of food, she slid the partially open pocket door aside with her little finger and entered. She placed the items on the counter, freeing her hands. Then she pulled up a wooden barstool for a seat. The screech it made crossing the wooden floor was barely heard over the music. Moonlight lit the room in a soft magical glow. "I should've made a faery costume," she mused. After eating one of the cucumber rounds, she sipped her drink. Raising the glass to the moonlight filtering in through the window, she stared at the champagne's bubbles rising and imagined them as fireworks—just like those Jared set off in her heart when they made love.

Setting the glass down, she reached for a mushroom. A gloved hand reached from behind her and covered her mouth. She tried to scream. Another hand snaked around and grabbed the front of her neck, pressing her backward against a brick wall of a body. Her legs flailed. She nearly toppled from the stool. Shiny black boots kicked the stool away. She remained upright on her tiptoes. The grip on her throat caused her to gag.

"Be quiet. Be still. I'm not here to hurt you," a voice she didn't recognize snapped. "I'm here to tell you Steven wants you. He sent me to find you."

She kicked, hitting the man in the shin with her heel. She slammed him with her elbow, once, twice, three times. The man wrangled her. His arms looped upward, catching her in a shoulder lock. "Settle down, Camilla. I promise, I won't hurt you," he hissed. Still, she couldn't place the voice.

A cloth wrapped around her mouth, biting at the corners. Rage exploded inside her. She screamed again against the fabric, but the sound came out muffled. Over the music and the din of guests, no one could hear her. Wiggling, she tried to shimmy, to break the man's grasp. From behind, he shoved his knee between her legs. Forced her forward, bending her against the counter. She resisted, pushing back. Her attacker reached around. His hands slid between her legs, grabbing her between her thighs.

She screamed.

His hand quickly covered her face.

She fought back. What did he plan to do next? She would not be raped in her own home.

"Stop," he barked. "I said, I won't hurt you."

She stilled.

"That's better. This was intended to be a bit of fun, but honey, you way overreacted. I'm a friend of

Steven's. He wants to see you. And if you want to see Jared unharmed, you had better show up."

She nodded. Did they have Jared? She trembled with panic.

The man removed his hands, but his body still trapped her against the counter. The hardness of his arousal pressed into her backside. She swallowed back fear and nausea.

"Meet Steven at the river, the private dock. Midnight. He said you'd know what he meant."

Again, she nodded.

"See, that wasn't so bad."

A cold metal barrel pressed into her side. She tried to draw in a breath, but the cloth around her mouth allowed only a slight amount of air to pass. Light-headed, she panicked. Would he really shoot her?

"If you don't show, I'll use this on Jared. I won't kill him, just make him hurt. Maybe I'll just take out a knee. I'm going to leave. Don't look at me. Stay where you are. I'm going to back out of here. If you turn, I will shoot you."

At least, he didn't intend to kill her, she hoped.

A grunt was all she managed.

Coolness brushed her backside when the man stepped back. She grabbed for the cloth at her mouth, gasping for air as it dropped away. She turned just in time to see a person dressed as the grim reaper with a hooded cape silently slip out of the room.

"Stop!" she screamed. "Help!" she shouted, bursting from the pantry, pointing. "Stop that man!"

The crowd in the kitchen and the hallway turned to look at her. Some looked around. She ran after the man, but when she turned the corner into the foyer, she lost sight of him. Sinking onto a step on the stairway, she rested her head in her hands.

"Camilla?" Branna called, running over. "What's the matter?" Branna sat beside her.

Camilla lifted her head. Whatever commotion she caused, the party guests all appeared insouciant, as though the screaming and chasing and running were all part of a Halloween drama.

"Someone just assaulted me. I don't know who. But the person behind it all is Steven." She barely managed to control her seething rage.

"What?" Branna snapped.

"He's crazy. I mean literally. He says he wants to marry me." She didn't know how to handle this level of crazy.

"What?"

"Now you sound like a parrot. He's been sending me flowers and cards. He came to see me. Even showed up with his mother. His mother! For goodness' sakes. Let's go outside. I need to tell you something."

She rose and tugged on Branna's hand. Once they reached the fountain, Camilla motioned for her sister to keep walking farther away from the house. "I need to be sure no one hears me."

"James is going to wonder where I am," Branna said, glancing back at the house.

Camilla stopped and took her sister's hands in hers and squeezed. "I must tell you something."

"Make it quick. Evie is watching the baby. I need to go check on her."

She huffed out a breath, then grimaced. "It all started a few weeks ago. I received flowers anonymously. I thought they were from Jared. Then I discovered Steven sent them. I think he even said something to his mother because when they came for lunch—"

"For lunch!?"

"Yes, ostensibly to talk with Momma about a ladies tea and the next Valentine's Day ball charity event and this party tonight. He tried to play footsie under the table with me. His mother said, and I'll say this slowly, that she always believed I was the one for him, not you."

Branna drew back as though she'd been slapped. "I don't want to talk about this. You said you were assaulted. Tell me about that. What exactly happened?"

"I went to hide in the butler's pantry with a plate of food when a man, I don't know who, gagged me, pushed me against the counter—" She shuddered over reliving the assault.

"What!"

"Nothing happened, so don't go there. He threatened me. Said I had to meet Steven or he'd shoot Jared." She wouldn't tell her sister about the man's groping.

"We have to tell Momma and Daddy. Call the police."

Camilla shut her eyes tight and scrunched her face. "No."

"Yes."

"I'm saying no. Steven will not ruin my plans. I have a big announcement. I planned it for ten o'clock, provided I find my fiancé. After that, I have a plan. Here's what we're going to do…"

Chapter 7

In the *garçonnière*, Jared dropped his feathered hat in a chair. Camilla would kill him for being late, but he'd make it up to her with a little surprise. He mentally congratulated himself. He had discovered ways to get through Camilla's outer shell. Each challenge had brought them closer together. He counted on this one winning him big points.

"Haley, you go ahead inside. I'm sure you'll find Camilla. I'll be along in a little bit. I'll give the two of you a few minutes before I show up to claim the glory." He opened the door and pointed. "Just walk through the back garden. You can enter in the kitchen. Ask around for Camilla. Everyone knows her."

Haley flung her arms around his waist. "You rock, Jared." She scurried down the stairs in a fortuneteller's costume. He went back inside. The airport limo had dropped Haley at the golf club, and he'd driven her to Fleur de Lis all for the purpose of bringing a smile to Camilla.

"She's gonna love this." He understood her better than she realized. She showed steel strength to the world, but he saw her tenderness tucked away to avoid being hurt.

Gathering his mask, he pulled it into place. Next, he adjusted the feathered hat on his head. With a glance, he checked the full-length mirror Biloxi had mounted for her photography clients. Satisfied with the costume, he struck a Musketeer pose, saber drawn. "You'll win the damsel not-in-distress." He chuckled, thinking about the rest of the night he had planned. "A little role-playing never hurt anyone."

Before opening the door, he snapped off the light.

Bam!

A slamming blow to his upper back sent him to his knees. He fought for breath against the pain. A hard shove pushed him to the ground. He rolled. Curled to protect himself. A black boot impacted with his side. He rolled again. Tried to stop the attack. He managed to grab the booted foot, but the attacker stomped on the side of his neck. Shocked, Jared let go and reached for his throat. The attacker kicked his side again. For once in his life, Jared wished he carried a gun.

Jared remained still when the intruder bent over him, the man's masked face near his ear.

"End it with Camilla! Go back to where you belong." Whoever spoke used a voice modulator. The scent of musk combined with sweat made Jared hold his breath. He might not know the person, but from the strength and the kind of blows, it had to be a male. When the man opened the door, light from the porch streamed and illuminated the room. He caught a brief glimpse of a black hood and black boots as the man slammed the door on the way out.

"Ohhh," Jared groaned. "Shit." Lying on the floor, he clutched his side.

Breathing deeply, he felt his ribs. He'd suffered fractures before, back when he was rodeoing. "Sore. Not broken." Hoisting himself up, he flipped on the light. No traces of anyone having been in the room.

Nothing appeared out of order. "He vanishes into the night like a ghost." He shook his head to clear it. Then fear slammed him. "Camilla!"

He jerked opened the door and flew down the steps, wincing in pain.

"Camilla!" He shouted for her again. If the intruder harmed her, he'd hunt the man down and extinguish him with a single shot.

The partiers on the back gallery turned when he hollered for Camilla again. Some shook their heads. A few shrugged. None were the woman he sought. His heart pounded double time. Panic pumped in him like a piston out of control. He had to find her.

"Camilla," he shouted over the sounds of the band playing the chicken dance song. He pushed his way through the throng of guests flapping their arms and wiggling their butts. "Where is she?" he gritted out. Maneuvering through to the ballroom, he spotted Haley beside Linc, but no Camilla.

"Have you seen her?" he demanded, standing in front of Haley as she danced.

"Yes." Her hands went to her underarms. She flapped as though she had wings. "She's outside with Branna."

"Don't just stand there, dance," Linc commanded with a laugh. "Get in line with us."

Jared grabbed Haley's shoulders. "She's okay?"

"Hey." Linc stopped dancing. "What's up?"

"Someone may hurt Camilla."

Jared shoved between other dancers. Haley and Linc followed behind. When he reached the screen door, he spied Camilla and Branna coming toward the front steps. Relief washed through him.

"Camilla!" he shouted and waved. He shoved open the door and ran to meet her.

At the bottom of the stairs, he scooped her up in a bear hug. "You're all right," he said, nuzzling her neck, breathing in her scent with an urgency as though his life depended on it. His side ached, but he ignored the pain. "Thank God. You're not hurt." A wave of relief slowed his thudding heart. He set her down, pulled her close, and brushed his hand from the top of her head, down her back, taking the lace veil and tiara from her head.

"Jared, what's wrong? You've got a cut there." She grabbed for the tiara as she pressed a finger to his neck.

He sank to a step and felt the spot. "I was attacked. Luckily, the guy waited…" He paused at the sound of footsteps behind him.

"Haley?" Camilla sounded shocked. "What's going on? What guy, Jared?"

Haley shrugged. "Surprise? I flew out with Jared's help. I saw you talking to Branna"—she pointed down the driveway—"so I decided to dance. Your cousin found me." She nodded in Linc's direction.

Camilla turned to Jared. "Are you okay? Do you need a doctor?" She sank down on the step with him.

"After I sent Haley to find you, someone hit me from behind," he explained, taking in slow breaths. "I was scared shitless that someone had hurt you. I'll be fine. My side hurts, but I can breathe."

"I'll call an ambulance," Linc said.

"Is everyone else all right? Was I the only target?" Jared asked.

"Well…" Branna's expression turned to concern.

"What?" Jared stood between Camilla and Branna. "Tell me."

"Camilla?" her mother called from the gallery above. "It's almost ten o'clock. What's going on down there?"

"Nothing, Momma." She turned and smiled at her mother, then turned back to the group. "Jared, if you're sure you don't need a doctor…"

"I've got anger and adrenaline on my side. If I fall over later, call an ambulance then."

"I have a surprise. If you're up to it, let's go inside. The band is set for a break at ten. I'm making an announcement." Taking a corner of the lace veil, Camilla wiped Jared's neck. A drop of blood stained the lace. "I think the cut is superficial, but I can wait to make the announcement. I really want you to see a doctor."

Jared pulled her into his arms. "I'm okay, but we need to talk."

"I'd like to make my announcement. Can we talk right after that? Are you up to this?"

"Announcement?"

"Yes," Branna chimed in. "I think we need to attend to the two attacks first."

Camilla started up the stairs. "I'm going to put an end to all of this with my announcement. Come on. Trust me." She held out her hand. Jared laced his fingers with hers. "And you, Boo," she said to Haley. "Let's go. We have some catching up to do tonight."

Haley marched up the steps and hugged Camilla. Jared continued, entourage in tow, to the ballroom. The gawking crowd parted.

"There she is." The band's guitar player pointed. "Here's the lady of the night." Snickers circled the room. "Aww, get your minds out of the gutter," he joked. "Presenting, Miss Camilla Lind."

Jared stood off to the side and assisted Camilla up three steps to the stage. Maybe taking her back to Wyoming for a while would be a good thing. There he could keep her safe. If he shot an intruder there, everyone would agree his actions were warranted. The idea steadied his thudding heart more. He'd put on a holster and strap on two six-shooters if that's what it took to keep Camilla from harm. He couldn't have been more right than when he'd raced against time to catch up with her before Katrina hit. He'd protected her then. He'd do anything to protect her now.

"Lovelies and ghouls. Flappers and Musketeers. Cowboys and cowgirls. Thank you for coming tonight. Usually the Keeper of Fleur de Lis makes these sorts of thank-you speeches." She pointed to her sister and cousin. "But tonight is special."

Jared smiled back at her when she smiled at him. Then he turned to scan the room, trying to identify his attacker. No one dressed all in black. No one with a cap or hood he didn't recognize.

"How special?" someone in the crowd shouted. Camera flashes flickered throughout the room.

"So very," she said. "Many of you have come to know Jared Richardson. And y'all know what a party girl I was before…I came home. I was lucky to find purpose to my life during my quest out West. I was luckier still when Jared refused to take 'no' for an answer." The crowd applauded.

Jared shifted his weight and forced a smile when Macy and Charles Lind came to stand beside him. They had no idea the danger Camilla was in.

Then the others came. Branna and James. Biloxi

and Nick. Haley and Linc. Even Deidre and Sean Dutrey, Biloxi's parents, rounded out the growing group. Silently he urged her to finish her speech. He wanted her out of sight and away from anyone who wanted to hurt her.

"The storm took stuff away," she continued. "Changed our way of life. But we're southern strong. We bounce back." Tears began welling in her eyes. He stayed rooted with her family, though he wanted to pull her down from the stage.

"I'm so proud to stand here with all ya'll and announce I have finally set the date to marry Jared." She lifted her left hand and flashed her engagement ring. "I'm breaking with tradition. I'm not marrying a southerner. I'm not waiting a year to plan a wedding."

She motioned for him to join her. Jared climbed up next to her. "We'll be sending out invitations for our February wedding. But if you want to come, you won't be selecting fish or chicken for the reception. You'll be noting what kind of Mardi Gras float you'll be riding. That's the way I roll. Jared and I are going to have a parade! Ya'll are going to be in it!"

Applause broke out. The crowd chanted, "Kiss! Kiss!"

Stunned, Jared blinked. A Mardi Gras wedding? The din in the room swirled around him, making him dizzy. Camilla dropped the microphone, grabbed his shirt, and jerked him closer. "Kiss me, fool. You said you wanted me. Now you have me. All tied up with a date."

He wrapped her in his arms, kissing her, pressing his lips against her soft warm ones. His tongue flicked. She opened her mouth slightly. He deepened the kiss.

An electric current ran between them. He'd never love another woman the way he loved Camilla.

Around them, chanting continued. "Kiss! Kiss!"

Breaking the kiss, he dipped her back. She lifted one leg, and her hand drifted to the floor with a flourish. She might not sit well in a saddle, but she could wrangle a crowd.

Then the band appeared on stage. "This one's for the bride and groom to-be." The band picked up their instruments and tuned.

Jared handed Camilla off the stage into her father's arms. Well-wishers rushed around her. He hopped down, wincing from the jarring of hitting the ground.

"Carson," Jared said, waving him over. "After this dance, gather the family by the garage." Carson nodded and began to whisper to family members.

Reaching for Camilla, he twirled her and pulled her to him when the band's lead singer belted out *At Last,* the song made popular by Etta James years ago.

They swayed together in the middle of the floor. He lifted her arms around his neck, pulled her close, holding her around the waist. "I love you."

"I love you more," she whispered against his lips.

They moved as though one. He scanned the room. Was their attacker watching? Was there more than one?

"Woman, Branna's words aren't lost on me. She said, 'two attacks,' when we were outside. Tell me what happened. Are you okay? Did he hurt you?"

"Shhh." She put her finger to his lips. "Not now. I'm dancing with my future husband. Let's just enjoy this."

"That's fine," he said. "But just so you know, I'm going hunting. Someone is going to get hurt."

Chapter 8

"Jared, please. We have a house full of guests," Camilla pleaded. "Let's not involve the whole family in this." She feared they'd look at her and shake their heads, thinking how like a crab to bait, she always found trouble. After working so hard to change, she wanted to handle it quietly on her own—the only way to deal with Steven.

"We're not stopping them from having a good time."

"Wait. Let's talk about his." She followed him as he tugged her through the kitchen and out the back door with guests paying her no mind.

"No deal, woman." He continued tugging her along.

By the garage, a dozen of her family members waited under a bright floodlight. Strains of a ballad drifted on the night breeze. She'd just announced the biggest news of her life, and all she wanted was a happy groom and dreams of a future. But with her family, it was more like a judge and jury waited rather than a celebration.

"I wasn't hurt." She had to convince him of her point.

"Doesn't matter. No one puts their hands on you. Hello, everyone," Jared called out.

"Jared's overreacting," she insisted. "We can take

care of this situation ourselves." Faces of all her loved ones stared back at her, a mood of unease settling on the crowd.

"Steven Sterling threatened Camilla. She was assaulted in this house." Jared pointed. "I was attacked in the *garçonnière*. All of this tonight. Someone, not Steven—he's too crafty for that—has invited her to meet Steven at midnight. I think we should consider this a hunting party." Jared made eye contact with all her male relatives. "She'll go. But not alone. We'll all be there to protect her."

"And the police!" Charles Lind inserted.

"Sir, respectfully, I think we can handle this—as a family matter," Jared replied. "No need to spook our prey with red flashing lights."

She tugged on his sleeve. "Darlin', this isn't Wyoming."

"That's right," Linc chimed in. "We're civilized here. A man can't just walk into our home and hurt one of us. I'm in, Jared."

"Not without the wrath of all of us to deal with!" Carson proclaimed. "I'm in."

"Jared," Charles interrupted. "I appreciate how much you want to protect my daughter, but I think if we talk with Steven, we can clear up this misunderstanding."

"Time for talking is over." Jared raised his fist. "He's out of control. He set me up this evening posing as a potential client. Made it so I couldn't meet Haley at the airport to bring her here. I had to hire a driver."

"He what?" Camilla asked.

"Let's just say, he must have sent someone to do his dirty work tonight after the exchange he and I had earlier."

"Go, Jared!" Haley cried.

Jared high-fived the girl.

Camilla frowned and shook her head. Sheepishly, Haley lowered her arm.

"Camilla, exactly what happened in the house?" her mother asked, stepping forward.

As Camilla sought words to explain, to be truthful, but not rile Jared more, a realization came to her. Steven counted on her being too intimidated to tell anyone, especially her family, what he'd done. He counted on her past sins to keep her in line, to maintain silence. "I needed some quiet from the party noise. I was pouting because Jared was late. Taking a moment, I went to the butler's pantry—the only quiet spot. A man came in from behind, gagged me, bent me over the counter"—her mother gasped—"and pressed himself into me."

Her mother rushed to her. "He didn't?' She brushed hair from Camilla's face and tucked it behind her ear.

"He didn't touch me beyond that."

"A man knocked me to the floor, kicking me. I was threatened—ordered to leave Camilla," Jared added, lifting up his shirt and revealing bruises forming on his side. "This craziness has to stop."

"But—" Camilla argued.

"No buts." Jared folded his arms on his chest.

"Steven said to me that I hadn't set a date. I think that's why he's kept on pressing. He didn't believe I was serious, truly serious about Jared. I've made my intentions public. I think he'll shrink away now."

"You set a date—to marry me—to convince an

idiot to leave you alone?" Jared faced her. A storm roiled in his eyes. She'd never witnessed anger like this from him before. "So, I'm what…your excuse?"

"No. It's not like that," Camilla wailed.

Macy went to Jared, placing her hand on his arm. "I promise you, she announced the date tonight because she's ready to be your wife." She smiled at Camilla. "My daughter and I had a long talk. I'm so proud of the woman she's become."

Jared frowned but remained silent and shifted his stance.

"Jared, you know by now how stubborn Camilla can be," Charles Lind added.

"Dude, she only does what she wants to do. An ass like Steven can't make her do something she doesn't want to," Linc said, nodding to everyone.

Jared scrubbed his face with his hand. "Yeah. You're right."

"But Steven has to be stopped. He's injured Jared and assaulted my sister," Branna insisted. "I vote we call the police."

"Want to know what I think?" Haley said, stepping forward.

Camilla smiled and hugged the teen close to her. "Sure, tell us."

"I think this Steven guy is outnumbered. I say we all—"

"Macy! Branna! Biloxi!" Greta shouted from the back gallery.

"Yes?" Macy called back.

Greta stormed out of the house and flew down the steps. The angel wings on her costume flapped as she ran. A white feather came loose and floated on the air, landing in one of the shrubs. "The police"—she panted—"are out front."

"What?" Branna asked.

"They're here to question Jared."

The news startled Camilla. "No. He's not done anything wrong. He was the one attacked. Get them over here." She pointed to the spot in front of her. "We're going to give them a report. We're filing charges against Steven." How dare the police even think Jared could do any wrong. Anger rolled inside her like a boulder gathering speed. She locked her jaw. She'd never considered shooting anyone before, but she'd like to give it a try now. Just one target—Steven.

"Camilla," her father said, putting his hand on her shoulder. "Why don't you and Jared come with me? Let's talk to the police in the *garçonnière*, and the rest of the family—please return to the party. We have guests that need tending to. Gossip is going to spread like an oil slick. Let's try to contain the spill."

"I should stay," Linc said. "I saw Jared first, after the attack."

Jared shook Linc's hand. "Thanks. I appreciate the support, but I think Charles is right."

Camilla wrapped her arm around Jared's waist. "I'm sorry about all of this." Even when her imagination worked overtime, she could've never considered Steven coming unhinged. That had to be the only answer for his bizarre behavior. "Why do they want to question you?"

Jared pulled her close, lifted her face, and pressed his lips to hers. "Together we can deal with anything. Nothing to worry about."

Though she wanted his words to put her at ease,

they didn't. Steven was an officer of the court. About to make a bid for Congress. He carried clout. If it came down to her word or Steven's, she doubted she'd win. Given her past wild ways, her credibility was thin.

"Follow me," Charles said. "Let's get this over, and get back to our guests. Costume judging is starting with the winner to be announced at midnight."

"Gee," Camilla mumbled. "Too bad Steven didn't come. He'd win best scumbag in town."

"You can't win unless you have a costume," Jared pointed out. "He's always a scumbag, so that doesn't count."

"Touché."

Once inside the *garçonnière*, two police officers joined them. The taller of the two hitched his holster and stepped forward. "We're investigating an assault. Give me your full names."

"Charles Lind. I'm her father. Soon to be this young man's father-in-law."

"Camilla Lind. Daughter to him." She pointed. "And his fiancée."

"Jared Richardson."

"You're not from around these parts," the shorter officer said. "I need to know your whereabouts at ten p.m."

"That's rich. We"—she pointed to herself and Jared—"want to file a complaint. An assault complaint."

Jared glanced at the clock. "Eleven now. I don't exactly know—"

"I do. We were in the ballroom. I made the announcement about the date of our wedding. In front of an entire room of people. Exactly at ten p.m. Guests took pictures. Lots of flashes went off. Or ask the band. That's when I scheduled their break."

"Can you tell us what this is about?" Charles asked. He motioned the officers to the two chairs. Camilla tugged on Jared's arm. They sat on the couch next to her father.

"Tell me about the assault you mentioned," the second officer said. He leaned forward as though genuinely interested, but she believed it was a ruse.

"I was in the house. Shoved from behind. A man pinned me against the counter. I never saw his face. He shoved his knee between my legs. Pressed his…man parts into my backside, then reached around and grabbed me between the legs—all while he had a gag cutting into my mouth."

"I'm sorry, ma'am." The first officer took out a small notepad and jotted in it. "I don't mean to be indelicate, but was it a sexual assault?"

"No," she snapped. "But I was threatened. If I didn't agree to meet Steven Sterling at the boat ramp on the river at midnight, he would hurt my fiancé, who was attacked in here."

"After I finished dressing for the party"—Jared flicked his hand over his costume—"as I was about to leave, just turned out the lights, someone hit me from behind. Knocked me to the ground. Kicked me several times."

"Look," she said, pulling Jared's collar open. "A cut on his throat."

"I think you should seek medical care. We can call an ambulance now, if you wish."

"No," Jared and Camilla said simultaneously.

"You're both acquainted with Mr. Steven

Sterling?" the taller officer asked.

"Yes," Camilla answered.

"He was found badly beaten by the boat ramp. We got a 911 anonymous phone call. His face is pretty messed up. A broken arm. He, too, was kicked a number of times."

"Know anything about this?" the second officer asked.

"Couldn't happen to a nicer man," Jared offered.

"He's been harassing me for several weeks. Making accusations. Threats." Camilla stood. "We're not friends. We have no relationship."

"He says you"—the officer pointed to Jared—"jumped him at the country club, says there's a witness. Then you asked him to meet you tonight, and you finished the job by beating him."

"Lies," Jared said. "All lies. Look at my hands. I haven't hit anyone."

"He said you wore gloves, that you're pissed because you found out your fiancée, Miss Lind here, was having an affair with him."

Camilla sank to the floor beside Jared. "You know that's not true."

"We found a bunch of cash on the ground. He said you threw it at him and threatened him to stay away from Miss Lind."

"Officers, our family has known the Sterling family for generations. It is unbelievable that anyone in our family would hurt him like that."

"Which is why we're investigating. What with Mr. Richardson being an outsider. Not from here."

"Jared." Camilla turned his chin to capture his full attention. "You know Steven lied, don't you? I need you to tell me you don't believe what they're saying." Tears welled in her eyes. His image blurred before her. It would crush her, destroy her heart, if Jared, for one second, thought she had cheated in any way. She would never betray him the way Cheyenne had.

"Babe, you're not that kind of person. You would never hurt me like that. Officers, that accusation is completely false." Jared spoke matter-of-factly. "As my fiancée explained earlier, we have a hundred or more witnesses in the house to testify to our whereabouts at ten p.m." Jared rose. "What do we need to do to file a harassment complaint against Mr. Sterling? What about Camilla's attack? No one puts their hands on her disrespectfully. No one hurts her."

"We'll take the info, but you never said it was Sterling who did these things."

"The message I was given while being assaulted came from someone other than Sterling, but the demand was to meet him at midnight," Camilla explained. "He said he'd shoot Jared." She wanted to shake them. Why couldn't they see beyond Steven's snakelike smile and slithering ways?

"I was told to break it off with her. Which, of course, is nonsense."

"Were there any witnesses to either of your attacks?"

Camilla glanced at Jared. "No. It was in the house, but I was hidden in the butler's pantry. It's a small space. By the time I got the gag off, the man was gone. He had a musky cologne."

"I was alone," Jared explained. "Never got a look at his face. I smelled the same thing."

"Oh, God! It had to be the same man! To think I

may have danced with him at the party…"

"Look, officers, you're upsetting Camilla. She is the victim here." Jared held her hand.

"I hate to bust up your party, but we need to talk to a few witnesses at least."

"And I want to talk to Steven with the two of you present. I'm telling you, he's harassed me for the last time." Camilla stood and looked down at the seated officers.

"Is that a threat, Miss Lind?"

"No, Officer"—she peered to read his name on his uniform—"Miles. It's a promise."

"What if you speak to the guests on the front gallery? I'm sure you'll gather enough proof that my daughter and Jared weren't in two places at once."

Charles led the police away.

Jared sank onto the couch. "Come here, please."

She went to him. He put his arm around her shoulder and held her hand. "You sure you weren't hurt? You'd tell me all of it, wouldn't you?"

"Yes."

"Good," he said, claiming her lips. A soothing heat radiated from him. For the first time all evening, she could truly breathe calmly.

The evening hadn't gone as planned. But she'd be damned if she'd allow Steven to ruin everything. "Let's go make the rounds and congratulate the costume winner. Let me get Haley settled in for the night. My cousins will look after her. Then I'll meet you back here in an hour."

"I'd love to take you away tonight. We need a break. I need you."

"Jared, I can't leave, now. And you have work

tomorrow."

"You're a wise woman." Jared nodded. "Okay. We'll go play host and hostess. But tomorrow night, I've got other plans for us."

Chapter 9

The moon cast a silvery glow as it rose just above the horizon. Jared drove Camilla with the top down on Biloxi's convertible. The cool night air had a greater chill as the breeze rushed past while they rode. Jared reached behind to the back seat and grabbed a large beach towel.

"Use this to keep warm," he told Camilla.

After she draped it over her shoulders like a shawl, he held her hand.

"Where are we going?" she asked. "It was so nice of Biloxi to lend you her car. Clearly, she likes you a lot. She hasn't let anyone else drive it."

"She's feeling generous...and sorry for me. She apologized for the attack several times. Nick, I think, convinced her to suggest it. I'm guessing a peace offering. Something about family being glue, yet sometimes too sticky for its own good. I don't understand, but couldn't say 'yes' fast enough. And here we are."

"Biloxi's going to be an amazing matriarch. But where are we going?"

In Picayune, he turned onto Highway 43. "For a ride. And then a private dance."

"Really?" She brightened.

"We haven't had a full night alone together since we left Wyoming." Jared rubbed his thumb over the silky smoothness of her hand. Want and need heightened his arousal. In less than four months, she would be his wife. It had been a long road to get to this moment—her committing to a lifetime with him.

"It wasn't like I planned it to be this way. I came home from Wyoming and was thrust into a battlefield. The storm ripped away all that was normal. Fleur de Lis had to come first." Her tone carried a defensive hitch. Trying to avoid an argument, she lifted her arm and caught the wind.

"Understandably so, but I stopped sneaking around when I hit my twenties. Camilla, we're engaged. You sleep in the house. I sleep over the garage, and the only time we've made love is when your brother and cousin aren't in residence there, and then, only during the middle of the night when you sneak out of the house. I admit, secret rendezvous for steamy quickies kept me going. But the storm is over. Life has changed. You're not the same party girl who left home several years back."

She squeezed his hand. "I know. I'm just very…self-conscious. When we first came back, I was focused on all the repairs. Everyone dropped into bed at night exhausted—in those awful trailers. I wanted so much, needed for everything to look and feel like it did before I left—before I had made such a mess of my life and ruined my relationship with my sister. As Fleur de Lis was repaired, it was like I was, too. My family and friends saw me as a contributing adult, not some flaky party girl. Then we brought the Old Aunts' home…"

"Really, Camilla? You're going to blame our lack of love life on them?"

"You don't know how it was. They were so strict

when I was growing up. I was far more afraid of them being disappointed in me than I was my parents. Before the storm, they were tyrants."

"Maybe so. However, tonight we start a new chapter in our life. It's the official countdown to the wedding. Less than four months, we're getting married!"

Camilla leaned over and kissed his cheek. "Yes, dear." Her quiet submissive behavior caught him off guard.

"You okay?"

"Just sleepy." She tilted her seat back and closed her eyes.

Flipping on the radio, Jared heard the haunting sounds of Chris Botti's trumpet. His mind turned to recent memories. Becoming part of Camilla's family had taken some getting used to. Never before had he been surrounded by so many women. Bossy and demanding. Taking charge, doling out orders. Women outnumbered the men of the family, who welcomed him immediately, especially Nick. With Linc and Carson back in college, both graduating in December, James still in Florida, that left him and Nick to help Sean Dutrey and Charles Lind do the heavy lifting. If it weren't for Nick's money, connections, and influence, Fleur de Lis' recovery after Katrina would've taken even longer.

"Jared?" Camilla interrupted his thoughts.

"Hmm?"

"I promise you, I didn't set a date to get Steven to leave me alone. I am truly ready to get married."

"Your sister and your cousin both contemplated eloping to Vegas."

"Is that what you want? You don't want to wait?"

"No. I want us to be married at Fleur de Lis. I think it means a lot to both of us. I don't want you to even consider the idea of an elopement." As he spoke, the bright lights of Biloxi, Mississippi came into view.

"Aww, darn! There aren't any drive-through wedding chapels here." Camilla put on a pout.

"There's a nice bed-and-breakfast down the street. A lovely couple has owned it for years."

He cast a glance at Camilla. Chin down, she looked up at him. "You are so good to me. I love you."

"And I'm never going to let you go a minute without feeling loved." He squeezed her hand. "I actually owe Steven a thank-you. But for him, you and I might not have met. I would've missed the love of my life. We won't start our life together harboring any ill will."

After settling into a comfortable room at the inn, complete with polished antiques and a brand new bed, Jared slid a CD of classical music into the player while Camilla changed in the bathroom. After lighting a few candles, he turned out the lights. He plucked a red rose from the bouquet on the dresser—the owners of the B&B managed to have a florist deliver them before their arrival that night. He laid the flower across Camilla's pillow. The soft sheen of white satin set off the deep red of the rose, the flower of love.

Removing his clothes, he folded them neatly and set them on a shelf in the closet. He grabbed a towel and wrapped it around his waist, keeping it in place with a tuck at his hips.

He wanted everything about tonight to be perfect for her. His pulse skittered in anticipation. What was taking her so long?

It seemed silly that they'd been engaged for so long, yet due to circumstances, he hadn't had an opportunity to court her in an old-fashioned southern way. Wine and dine, take her to nice restaurants or trips away for the weekend. When Katrina came, the aftermath required everyone to commit to meeting the basics of human needs. It was months before they graduated to a stabilized life. Anything other than rebuilding smacked of frivolity, and they hadn't had time for that.

He turned when the bathroom door's antique hardware clicked. Framed in the doorway, Camilla stood haloed by soft light. The pink filmy gown hid almost nothing from view. His erection hardened as his gaze traveled slowly up her body. She licked her lips. Their eyes locked.

"You are gorgeous." He was transfixed by the love he found in her eyes.

"You're gorgeous, too," she whispered. Her focus landed between his legs, and when she involuntarily licked her lips, he held himself in check as lust, tension, desire, and love swirled in a madding rush.

As he held out his hand, she glided to him. He led her to a couch by the window where moonlight streamed in and danced on the skin of her shoulders. She sat back, resting on the couch. She crossed her legs, offering him a view of their beauty. He nearly forgot to breathe.

When he found his brain and his voice, he asked, "Would you like champagne? We have strawberries and chocolate, too."

"You're offering to feed me?" She smiled playfully

and winked. "I remember something like this long ago, almost another lifetime. A picnic in the shade in Wyoming."

"Yes." He chuckled. "My first attempt at seduction with you."

He secured the champagne bottle. Popped the cork. A mist of carbonation floated out of the bottle. After pouring, he offered her a glass. "Take a slip."

On a table next to the chaise, he set the tray of fruits and sweets within reach and settled himself next to her. Plucking a strawberry, he held it between his teeth and offered it to her. Their lips met. She took a bite, then ate the red fruit and sipped from her glass.

"I could get used to this," she said. Then she turned on her side and faced him. Running her hand up his leg, she slid his towel upward. Reached his groin. Stroked his hardness. He couldn't hold back a moan.

"Chocolate?" he whispered hoarsely as she massaged his stiffness.

"If it was liquid, I would pour it over you and lick it." She playfully licked his lips.

"Oh baby, let me call room service and order melted chocolate."

"Not now." She pulled the ends of the towel open, exposing his nakedness. "I don't want any interruptions. I want it slow and steady all night."

"Don't tease me now," he cautioned.

She moved on top of him, her legs straddling his hips. Her hands massaged his chest. "You're tan and strong." She kneaded his arm muscles.

"We have Fleur de Lis to thank for that. All the work in the sun."

"My panties have a special secret," she whispered.

It was all the invitation he needed. His finger deftly explored. The slit in the fabric parted, giving him access to her wet sweetness.

"Oh," she moaned.

He reached for her breast, massaging and teasing, just as she was doing to him. When her back arched, he guided her to take him inside her. She rocked. He held her hips, the round smoothness exciting him more.

Slowing his pace, he witnessed the joy of Camilla losing her inhibitions. His heart expanded more. "We've got all night."

"Yes. And we'll do this over"—she ground herself on him—"and over again. Until we can't move."

Together they touched, stroked, rocked. Want grew to need. Urgency pressed them further. Soft puffs of moans escaped from her. The sexy sounds drove him crazy. He steadied her and pumped upward in quick thrusts.

"Jared! Yes!"

He closed his eyes. Bubbles appeared, floating upward, carrying his desire. The tiny bubbles burst, and it was as though a million white hot stars exploded in the night sky. Slowly they streaked back to Earth.

His rocking slowed.

Camilla collapsed on top of him. Moving her hair away from her face, he had to see her expression. Softness. Sweetness.

"I think my bones turned to putty," she whispered. "Lordy, man, you know how to satisfy me."

"I aim to please, ma'am," he drawled, Western-style.

"Excellent." She kissed him hard. "Hand me the champagne. Let me feed you a chocolate. Get your strength back—we're gonna do this again."

"As I said, I'm here to please."

Chapter 10

Four months later, sunshine lit her bedroom at Fleur de Lis. Camilla stretched. A lightness enveloped her. She grabbed the sheets to be sure she wasn't actually floating. "I'm getting married today," she sang. She hadn't seen Jared in several days, since Valentine's Day when they had their rehearsal dinner, complete with the Richardsons and the Dupis family—all of Jared's immediate family.

Camilla gazed at her beautiful white dress made of chiffon, tulle, and silk hanging from a clothing rack in the corner of her room. Behind it, bridesmaid dresses in lavender. The color of their dress represented the purple in Mardi Gras colors.

Soon, Branna and Biloxi would wheel the rack of dresses out onto the second floor landing. Yesterday, they'd hung sheets to make the entire area into a dressing room. She imagined the pitch of chatter now that Haley and Sophie had arrived at Fleur de Lis. It would fill the upstairs. Camilla's heart swelled with joy and flooded her completely.

Branna and Biloxi burst through the bedroom door. "Are you up?"

Startled, Camilla sat up.

Greta followed her sister and cousin inside the room with a tray. "Bacon and biscuits and fruit. Hot tea. Food for the bride." She set the food on the side table and shuffled from the room. "Got lots to do."

Biloxi kissed Camilla's cheek. "Cousin, I'm so happy for you." She tugged on the rack and began to pull it out of the bedroom. "I've a group of cackling little hens to organize out here."

"This is so exciting!" Branna plopped on the bed next to her. "Momma nor I could have planned a better wedding for you."

"The parade!" Camilla raced to the window. "They're already all lined up!" Decorated flatbed trailers hitched to large pickups lined the driveway for nearly a half mile. She'd insisted on decorations made from the local flora and fauna. Her throne was covered in green magnolia leaves—to represent the green of Mardi Gras.

She had created a list of who would ride where, designating a float for the Lind relatives from Louisiana, another for other cousins and family members, one for their parents, one for Jared and his groomsmen, the final one for her and her bridesmaids.

It wasn't a dream. She'd envisioned this wedding procession, but seeing it come to life—no better dream for any bride. Tingles of excitement burst like sparklers, and excitement raced through her. "It was so much work, but so much fun!"

"Yes, James, Nick, all the guys, and Daddy helped this morning," Branna said. "I'm surprised you slept through diesel engine noise. Jared's brother even came over and pitched in. His wife joked she wouldn't mind being here when it's time to deliver her baby."

"What about the marching band?"

"They're arriving now on school buses," Biloxi said, returning to the bedroom. "The caterers are feeding them out in the back garden. As soon as those buses leave, the ones bringing the dance team will arrive."

"Haley was so excited last night," Camilla said. "She's never been on a float, let alone ridden on one in a parade. She said riding a horse down the street or at the rodeo might be a close second."

"Sophie thinks we're crazy!" Biloxi said, returning to the room. "Oh, the florist just arrived. They're going to finish decorating the ballroom under Aunt Macy's supervision." She lowered her voice. "My brother did the sweetest thing. He bought Haley a wrist corsage."

Camilla eyed her curiously.

"I'm beginning to wonder about those two. Do you think there's something brewing?"

"Better not be," Camilla answered. "My Haley's going to finish college before…"

"Your Haley?" Branna and Biloxi asked in unison.

"Well, what can I say? I do feel maternal toward her."

"Knock, knock," Macy said. "May I come in?"

"Momma!" Camilla ran to her and hugged her tightly. "I can't believe this day is here."

"Darlin', I'm such a proud momma. I did want you to know, I heard from Mrs. Sterling. They send their regrets. They won't be attending. Seems Steven is taking them on a vacation—Mardi Gras in Brazil."

"Yeah," snorted Biloxi. "Maybe the man had some sense beat into him after all."

"It makes no matter to me," Camilla said. "Nothing will ruin this day for me."

"Eat up," her mother told her. "We have to get our bride dressed."

An hour later, after slipping into a robe to have her makeup done, butterflies in her stomach threatened to float her away. "Let's get you into your dress before we apply the lip gloss," the makeup artist said.

"Branna and Biloxi, please help Camilla. Honey, I'll be right back. There's something I forgot."

Camilla stood in front of the mirror while the makeup artist applied the final touches when her mother returned.

"Oh," her mother murmured. "You are a vision. So uniquely you." She kissed Camilla's cheek. "Girls, if you don't mind, as the mother of the bride, I would like a moment with my daughter."

A quiet fell over the room as everyone but her mother exited. Outside a few voices rose above the sounds of the marching band warming up. Her mother came to stand behind her. Together they gazed in the floor-length mirror. "You're my baby girl. I am so very proud of you." Her mother stepped to the side. "This is a bride's handkerchief. It's a present from your great-grandmother. She asked me to give this to you on your wedding day."

Camilla's eyes welled. "Momma, quick, a tissue. I don't want to ruin my makeup."

"You were gone for so long." Macy handed over a couple of tissues. "I worried so much about your safety."

Camilla's heart swelled. The Old Aunts would be with her in spirit. She fingered the handmade lace. Once before, she'd seen the delicate hankie when she was a child, impudent child that she was, digging through Great-Grandmother's dresser.

"The Old Aunts both loved you so."

"I loved them, too." Tears spilled, and she dabbed the corners of her eyes.

"Now, more than a year ago, you gave me these and told me to hold them for you." Her mother lifted up the string of perfectly matched ivory pearls with a dangling diamond pendant, her inheritance from her great-great-grandmother. "You said you wanted to truly be a virtuous Fleur de Lis woman before you ever donned this necklace. Today is the day."

"Oh, Momma," Camilla cried. "Do you mean it?"

"My darlin' girl, you have shown the true nature of your character since before coming home. Haley and her father's presence here at Fleur de Lis proves it." Macy dabbed her eyes. "Let me fasten this around your neck. These are a blessing. You risked your life to rescue these pearls before the storm hit."

For Camilla, it was as though she were being crowned queen. Queen of Fleur de Lis. She would never be Keeper, never be the matriarch, however, she would always honor her heritage.

"Thank you, Momma. And today, I'm going to marry the man of my dreams."

The clock ticked to eleven thirty a.m. and a whistle sounded outside. Carson shouted on a bullhorn, "We're about to roll. Once again, we're going to Bayou Petite, around the square. There Jared will disembark, as will his groomsmen, then the bridesmaids. My dad will walk the bride down the aisle to the gazebo. After the ceremony, we'll all trek back to Fleur de Lis. Band leader, got all that?"

"Yes, sir!"

"Dance team?"

"Yes!"

"Let's go, Camilla. Your Prince Charming is waiting."

Camilla descended the stairs with her mother as the marching band started down the drive. Her heart pinged with happiness. Even if she wanted to, she couldn't stop smiling. Joy floated her like a cloud in the beautiful morning sky.

The lead flatbed trailer hauled the country band. When their vehicle began to move, they played *Jambalaya* by Hank Williams.

People of Bayou Petite lined the streets as the wedding parade rolled. Family members and friends tossed throws of tiny plastic bottles of bubbles, whistles, and Mardi Gras beads.

As the marching band circled the roundabout in the main square downtown, the parade stopped. Jared's groomsmen, his brother as his best man, all dressed in black tuxedos, exited their float. Each man wore a boutonniere made from a single red rose. They walked the path to the gazebo. The crowd gathered closer to witness the nuptials and cheered.

Two friends rolled out a white runner over the sidewalk, creating a bridal aisle leading to the altar.

Charles stepped down from the parents' float and waited as Branna and Biloxi and all the bridesmaids descended. A hush fell over everyone when the string quartet played Pachelbel's *Canon in D* for the procession.

Camilla took her father's arm after all the wedding attendants were in their places. She carried a cascading bouquet of colorful roses. Forever, when she saw a red one, she would think only of Jared and remember the night at the bed-and-breakfast where they had made love all night.

When her father released her hand, Jared stepped next to her. The only thing preventing her from reaching for him was the bouquet she clutched in both hands. The officiating judge, dressed as a Renaissance king, complete with fur hat and a crown, began, "Dearly beloved, we are gathered here…"

Dazed, Camilla drank in the sight of Jared. He stood tall and handsome. The white of his shirt brought out the tan of his cheeks. His hair, she rarely saw it this way, was combed and styled neatly. She loved him to the moon and back.

Her heart pounded like the beat of a thousand drums. The sound pounded loud in her ears. For a second, she swayed.

"Bend your knees," Jared whispered. "Give your flowers to your sister."

She nodded, barely able to think.

"Miss Lind, you must speak aloud," the judge said. "Not just nod your head. Do you take Jared Richardson to be your lawfully wedded husband?"

"I. Do."

Jared slid a gold band on her finger. The ceremony continued.

A few minutes later, the judge said, "I pronounce you husband and wife."

Jared pulled her close. Kissed her tenderly. The crowd cheered. Whistles blew. When he broke the kiss, she blinked. At first, she thought she was floating like bubbles on the air. Love surged within her. Her heart sang with happiness.

Captain Jack appeared on the other side of the gazebo leading a horse pulling a carriage decorated with swags of flowers.

"What's this?" Camilla asked.

"Well," Jared said. "I know you planned the wedding down to the smallest detail, but we never discussed which of these"—he gestured to the parade of floats—"you intended for us to ride on to our reception at Fleur de Lis after the wedding ceremony."

"I didn't think the convertible would be quite suitable, given the size of the train of your dress," Biloxi said.

"And I didn't think it right for the bride and groom to be split up," Branna interjected.

"So, I called Captain Jack," Nick added.

"He's been kind enough to lend his carriage," Jared finished.

"You're a fabulous husband." Camilla lifted her chin. Jared's lips claimed hers. "I love you dearly, madly, and forever." She pressed her lips to his.

"Camilla," Jared said when they broke the kiss.

On cue, the marching band began to play, and the attendants filed back to their floats.

"Yes, Jared."

"Do you remember all those times you said I didn't know you?"

The heat of a blush warmed her cheeks. He brought that up now?

"Darlin'," he said, bending down. "I do know you." He scooped her in his arms and carried her to the carriage. "Happy wife. Happy life. I aim to please."

Their carriage took the lead in front of the marching band. Like a grand marshal, they led the parade all the way through Bayou Petite and up the driveway of Fleur de Lis.

"Jared," Camilla said.

"Yes, Camilla."

"You never told me where we're honeymooning."

Jared beamed. "Camilla, wife. I do know you. You're going to love where we're going. It's a surprise."

****

The next morning, Camilla's and Jared's families gathered on the front gallery of Fleur de Lis in robes and slippers. Sunlight slanted across the lawn dotted with streamers and shrinking balloons, telltale signs of yesterday's Mardi Gras party and wedding reception. Jared set down their suitcases and started making the rounds, saying his good-byes.

"Momma, don't cry," Camilla said, taking her mother aside.

"I can't help it," Macy said. "My girls are both married now. And, I'm a grandmother, too. I don't know if Carson will ever find a good girl. I'll rest easier when he's married."

Branna snorted. "A good girl would never have him."

"Well, maybe a reformed party girl will help tame his ways," Biloxi chimed in, winking at Camilla.

"Wife"—Jared came up behind Macy—"we need to leave for the airport now. We'll be back in two weeks."

Her father carried the suitcases to the limo.

Camilla reached for Jared's hand. "Are we going to Jackson? Shall we dance at the Lucky Seven where we met? Breakfast at Mountain View Diner?"

"Maybe," Jared said. "We *could* go visit our friends. But I think it will mostly be just you and I.

Alone."

"But where are we staying?" she asked.

"Well, you never got to see my house. It's been completely cleaned out for our arrival, except for a new bed. I'm taking you home. To our home in Wyoming."

She pulled him close. "Darlin', you do know me. You're truly the perfect husband for this reformed party girl."

She had returned to Fleur de Lis only to learn her true home was wherever he was.

A word about the author...

Linda Joyce is an Amazon bestselling author who writes about assertive females and the men who can't resist them in her Fleur de Lis series and Fleur de Lis Brides series. Linda's a big fan of jazz and blues. She attributes her love of those musical genres to her southern roots, which run deep in Louisiana. If you walk through several New Orleans cemeteries, you'll find many of her people buried there. She penned her first manuscript while living in Japan, the country where her mother was born and raised. Now she lives in Atlanta, Georgia, with her husband and four-legged boy—General Beauregard, who thinks she's his pet.

www.linda-joyce.com

~*~